...ing a pub and beautiful coun... ... ...otel.' She was also a media agent representing many celebrity chefs.

When she's not writing, Caroline likes to go wild water swimming or walk with Fred, her Westie.

If you would like to find out more about Caroline's books, please visit her website:

www.carolinejamesauthor.co.uk

Also by Caroline James

The Spa Break

THE CRUISE

CAROLINE JAMES

One More Chapter
a division of HarperCollins*Publishers* Ltd
1 London Bridge Street
London SE1 9GF
www.harpercollins.co.uk
HarperCollins*Publishers*
Macken House, 39/40 Mayor Street Upper,
Dublin 1, D01 C9W8

This paperback edition 2023
4
First published in Great Britain in ebook format
by HarperCollins*Publishers* 2023
Copyright © Caroline James 2023
Caroline James asserts the moral right to be identified
as the author of this work

A catalogue record of this book is available from the British Library

ISBN: 978-0-00-861176-7

Printed and bound in the UK using 100% Renewable Electricity
by CPI Group (UK) Ltd

This book is produced from independently certified FSC™
paper to ensure responsible forest management .
For more information visit: www.harpercollins.co.uk/green

For Vicky, who taught me that creativity comes from within and to write from the heart. Thank you, Sis, with my love.

Chapter One

On a damp December evening, the class of '74 from Garstang Grammar School for Girls Reunion was in full swing at the Dancing Bear, a stylish 16th-century coaching inn nestled in the heart of the Lancashire town. Women who hadn't seen each other for many years packed the lounge bar where a fire crackled in a wood-burning stove and wine flowed. Outside, driving rain pelted the steamy leaded glass windows, but the atmosphere inside the inn was jolly. Long-held memories of school reminded the chums of lighter days when youth was taken for granted and the future for the post-war baby boomers looked bright.

'Isn't that Sylvia Adams?' Jane Bellwood nudged her two companions. The three women turned to look around the packed room where a female held court at the adjoining table. Tall and willowy, she shook her perfectly styled hair, the sleek blonde locks falling on shapely shoulders. A glass of chardonnay nestled in one hand whilst the other made exaggerated movements to emphasise the joke she was making.

'Yes, it is,' Anne Amberley replied and stood to get a better view. 'Don't you remember we used to call her Snobby Sylvia at school?'

'I remember the nickname we gave her. She was always superior and looked down her nose at me.' Jane poured wine from a bottle she was sharing with Anne and stared. 'How on earth can anyone of our age look that good? I'd love to know her secret.'

'A rich husband and cosmetic surgery,' Anne said and toyed with the collar of her dress as she watched their former school acquaintance. No stranger to the enhancing effects of anti-ageing treatments, Anne ran her hands down the sides of her svelte body and pursed her pearly pink lips.

'She's a double-barrel now,' Kath Taylor said. Kath sat in the corner of the bar and scowled through heavily framed glasses as raucous laughter burst out from the crowd surrounding Sylvia.

'More than one double-barrel,' Anne added, 'she's doubled and tripled so many times I've lost count.'

Kath adjusted her glasses, picked up a list on their table, and then checked the reunion attendees. 'She's currently Mrs Adams-Anstruther.' Looking up, she stared at the mature version of the Sylvia Adams she'd known at school.

'Double A in her surname, she must have chosen her husband on purpose.' Jane gulped down her drink and ran fingers through her closely cropped hair. 'She always got A grades at school, and I loathed her.'

'You still do by the scowl on your face.' Anne giggled.

'Do you remember PE lessons?' Jane asked, 'Sylvia used to place a pencil under her boobs then let it fall to the floor, just to prove that her boobs were pert and upright.'

'I remember that.' Kath shook her head. 'It was torture and my pencil always got stuck.'

'You were lucky. Sylvia made me put a bulging case under mine.' Jane tugged on her bra straps to hoist her ample chest. 'My boobs drooped so badly the case never budged and Sylvia announced that I was officially saggy at sixteen.'

'I hear she's celebrating her latest divorce,' Anne said.

'Celebrating?' Jane shook her head. 'Crikey, how does she do it? I haven't got one wedding ring on my finger, unlike the jewellery shop she's flaunting.'

Jane tugged on Kath's cardigan-clad arm and pointed to the diamonds that sparkled on Sylvia's fingers. Shimmering droplets hung from her ears and matched a large heart-shaped pendant necklace.

'Why don't you ask her?' Kath said. She gripped her knees and clasped both hands around a cumbersome tote bag. 'Look, she's coming over...'

They watched as Sylvia slipped away from her group and, fixing her catlike green eyes on the three friends, headed in their direction. Kath shrank back, and Jane shuffled her cumbersome body. But Anne stood as tall as her sixty-three inches allowed and thrust out a hand. She gripped Sylvia's arm and stood on her toes to air-kiss both cheeks.

'Sylvia Adams, we were just saying how marvellous you look,' Anne exclaimed. 'What a gorgeous dress.'

'Harvey Nicks, Diane Von Furstenberg.'

'But you've added to the Adams with yet *another* surname.' Anne glanced at the list on the table. 'You're now Mrs Adams-Anstruther.'

'Double-A, for short, darlings,' Sylvia said as she towered over Anne. 'Goodness, I hardly recognised you all. It's Kath and Jane, isn't it?' Tilting her head, she fluttered false eyelashes, 'To think we were all at school together.' Sylvia studied Jane's shapeless tunic and wide, baggy trousers before treating Kath to the same critical gaze.

'Not in the same class,' Anne said, 'but you were an A-stream girl, like me.'

'Yes, I remember.' Sylvia looked at Anne. 'We A-streamers have certainly looked after ourselves.' Her bright red lips curved into a smile, and she nodded with approval as she studied Anne from the top of her neat side-swept updo to the tip of her animal-print kitten heels.

She turned to Kath. 'You were in the B stream and always won a prize on sports day for hockey. A goalie as I recall?'

Kath gripped her bag. Her lips were pursed as she listened to Sylvia.

'I remember your unflattering padded shirt, belted trousers and steel-capped boots. Not a glamorous outfit.' Sylvia grinned. 'Unlike Anne and me, who wore short,

4

pleated skirts and neat navy knickers as we sped around the pitch.' Sylvia turned to Jane, a puzzled expression barely cracking a line on her smooth forehead. 'Jane,' she began, 'you never progressed higher than the D stream, rarely played hockey and always came last in the sack race.'

Kath felt Jane shuffle forward. Her legs were planted wide, and her chair creaked. Tugging on Jane's tunic, Kath managed to stop her friend from rising to her feet. If Jane had a hockey stick in her hand, Sylvia would be on the receiving end of a forearm swing.

'So, tell me, ladies, what are you up to after all these years?' Sylvia looked from one to another.

'I've spent my career in aviation,' Anne said, 'I've travelled the world.'

'Ah, yes, I heard that you were a trolley-dolly,' Sylvia was dismissive, 'and recently divorced?'

'Er, Barry and I decided to part company after a long marriage.' Anne failed to admit that the errant husband she'd put up with for many years had recently disappeared with the Ladies Captain of Garstang Golf Club. The two-timing rat now propped up the bar on the nineteenth hole at La Manga Club, on the Costa Calida.

'Barry Amberley,' Sylvia pondered, 'very good looking.' She winked. 'I remember him well, he was something on a flight deck?'

'An airline captain.'

'Who has finally flown away.' Sylvia laughed.

Anne tensed and wondered if Sylvia had enjoyed a fling

with Barry. He'd slept with many women behind her back and most of the cabin crew working for the airline.

'Kath, of course, has had a highly successful career in banking,' Anne continued, 'and Jane is the darling of the celebrity culinary world, having worked with some of the finest chefs in the country.'

Kath's jaw dropped, and Jane, who'd finished her wine, was wide-eyed. But Anne was not to be outdone. 'But Sylvia, what did *you* do in all these years, to set the world on fire?' she asked, noting that Sylvia had taken a step back as three pairs of eyes swivelled towards her. Before Sylvia had time to reply, Anne, with an innocent expression, asked, 'Didn't you make husband-hunting your mission in life?'

'Well, I may have been married a couple of times.'

'At the last count it was four and I hear you're on the market for number five.' Anne stroked Sylvia's arm. 'What a shame that you never had a proper job. Still, for sixty-six, you must need a new funding source to pay for all the work you've had done.'

'Well, really!' Sylvia hissed and turned to make sure that they hadn't been overheard. 'I'm nowhere near the age of sixty-six...'

'Oh, my dear, your memory is going too.' Anne frowned. 'I remember my mother telling me you'd been abroad with your parents. When you enrolled at Garstang Grammar, you were three years behind with schooling.' Anne studied her French-polished nails. 'Mum told me not to say anything about your lack of education but to make you feel welcome as you took all those extra lessons to catch up.'

Jane crossed her arms. 'At least you can pick up your state pension.' She grinned. 'We're still waiting for ours as we haven't reached pension age yet.' Despite feeling every day of her sixty-three years, Jane felt smug that she was younger than Sylvia.

'Hopefully you've applied for your bus pass,' Kath added. 'You probably won't be driving much longer.'

Lost for words and spinning on her heels, Sylvia muttered that she must rejoin her friends.

'She didn't stay long.' Jane watched the school bully move away. 'Snobby Sylvia was always such a cow to me, but I had no idea she was older than us.'

Kath sipped her orange juice and narrowed her eyes. 'I'd love to know where she finds her husbands.'

'Cruising,' Anne said.

'Eh?'

'She's always on a cruise with her mate Beverly Barnett, who used to own a dress shop.' Anne shrugged. 'Sylvia sets sail until she digs her claws into a wealthy widower with a limited life expectancy and bingo!' Anne clicked her fingers. 'Mrs double or triple barrel, or whatever she becomes, is engaged again and soon sailing down the aisle, supporting another geriatric, before adding a new surname to her marriage certificate.'

'And not long after the wedding, when husband number five pops his clogs, she'll receive a large inheritance?' Jane guessed.

'Exactly,' Anne agreed.

'It all sounds sordid to me.' Kath sighed and flicked away a mop of fringe that had fallen over her forehead. Her hair was still as thick and wayward as it had been when she was a girl, only the colour had changed from a glorious chestnut brown to an ageing salt and pepper.

'On the contrary, look at us.' Anne motioned with her hand. 'We've worked our socks off all our lives, and none of us are getting any younger. Jane is single and recently sacked from a job she loved, Kath is widowed and worried about her future, and I'm divorced. Isn't it about time that we allowed ourselves the luxury of putting our cares to one side and having some fun?'

Jane bristled at Anne's words. The truth hurt. But she was thoughtful as she replied, 'A cruise might be fun, with buffets groaning with exotic food that I haven't prepared.' She looked from Anne to Kath. 'I've heard there are restaurants where delicious grub is served around the clock and there's a housekeeping team on standby to clear up all your mess.'

'But cruises cost a lot of money.' Kath shook her head and rearranged the bag on her knee, 'Jim wouldn't entertain the idea, and we never got further than Bournemouth.'

'Well, it's not as though you haven't got any money!' Anne laughed. 'I bet that bag is full of it.'

Kath rolled her eyes. 'As if I'd carry cash around with me.' She patted her bag. 'I keep everything I need for emergencies in here.'

'But we never go anywhere where there is likely to be an

emergency.' Anne raised both hands. 'Jim must have left you a tidy pile, with his sudden death prompting an insurance pay-out. You've no mortgage on the house and have a pension from the building society.'

She turned to Jane. 'You must have saved up a good amount too over the years?' Anne asked, 'and inheriting your mum and dad's property means you'll never be short.'

As Kath and Jane digested these words, Anne raised her head and looked to where Sylvia was now back in the thick of things and the centre of attention. Sylvia's arm linked with Beverley Barnett, and they shrieked with laughter over a tale of husband-hunting on the high seas. The group around her listened in awe.

'You're miles away,' Kath said, 'what's going through that head of yours?'

Anne sighed. 'Seeing Sylvia reminds me that she was probably on Barry's list of house calls. He was sleeping with so many women I lost count.' Tears began to trickle down her cheeks.

'Now, don't get upset.' Jane, tall and broad, grabbed the arms of her chair and hauled herself to her feet. She placed her arm around Anne's shoulders and held out a tissue. 'We're supposed to be having a pleasant evening catching up with school friends.'

'I always thought that we had a reasonable marriage, but you both know that he's left me high and dry,' Anne snuffled. Her eyes were still damp as she looked at her friends.

Kath and Jane were aware that there was little to show

from Anne's marriage. The heavily mortgaged house she'd shared with Barry was about to sell, leaving little for her to live out her days in comfort. Her airline pension was a help, but it wouldn't buy Anne a property.

'I've told you countless times that you can come and live with me.' Jane smiled. 'I rattle around in the cottage on my own.'

'Thank you,' Anne said and patted Jane's arm.

But Anne could still smell the expensive perfume that Sylvia had been wearing and thought of the designer bag and heels that matched her exquisite outfit. Anne knew she had difficult days ahead as everything she'd known dissolved, and her chest felt tight as she watched Sylvia's carefree performance.

But suddenly, Anne had a lightbulb moment. The solution to her problem was obvious! As Sylvia's voice drifted across the pub, Anne felt a giddiness in her stomach.

'Christmas is coming,' she announced, 'and instead of sitting at home watching the grey rooftops and drizzling rain, why don't we treat ourselves and book ourselves on a sunshine cruise?'

'What did you say?' Jane reached for the wine, but the bottle was empty.

'Are you serious?' Kath's jaw dropped.

'I am deadly serious.' Anne straightened her back and turned away from Sylvia. 'I'll get a round in and you two can whip out your phones and type in a Google search for Christmas Cruises.'

Kath and Jane stared as Anne sashayed across the room.

She suddenly had a spring in her step and stopped to chat with old school chums, occasionally nodding in her friends' direction.

'Damnation,' Kath swore, 'she's telling everyone that we're going on a cruise!' Kath looked down at the floor to hide her face. 'I haven't got over her telling Sylvia that I had a highly successful career in banking.'

'Well, you did.'

'Sitting behind the cashier desk at Garstang Building Society for forty-odd years doesn't quite cut it in the world of global finance.'

'Neither was playing second fiddle to all the movers and shakers I cooked for. I was invisible to everyone as long as my food preparation was perfect.'

'She wants to go husband-hunting, like Sylvia.' Kath peeped under her fringe to see Anne order more drinks at the bar.

'I can't say I blame her,' Jane said, 'she hasn't got much to look forward to.' Jane tilted her head. 'But I'd put money on the fact that Anne would be the life and soul of a cruise and attract a man before reaching the first port of call.'

'Well, I don't want to husband-hunt,' Kath said. 'Jim was the only man I really knew, and I was married to him for what feels like a lifetime. I don't want another husband.'

'I couldn't possibly look for a partner at my age. I didn't find one when I was younger so who on earth would find me attractive now?' Jane shook her white hair.

'We don't have to husband-hunt though, *do* we?' Kath

was thoughtful. 'And I can see Anne's point about treating ourselves.'

'I can't remember the last time I had a holiday, and it would be a wonderful break,' Jane said consideringly.

Kath looked across the room and saw Anne charming the young barman. 'Anne wants to find a new partner,' Kath said carefully, weighing her words, 'and she needs our support. She's not awfully good on her own.' Kath thought of Anne's distress as her marriage broke down. Together with Jane, she'd spent many hours comforting their troubled friend.

Jane had a far-off look. 'I can't remember the last time I went anywhere that wasn't connected to work.' She'd begun to visualise tropical beaches and a turquoise sea.

'Maybe we *could* accompany her,' Kath said. She sat up and, letting go of her bag, straightened her cardigan, and pushed up the sleeves. 'After all, it would be our duty to censor unsuitable suitors.'

'And make sure she doesn't fall into the Bad-Barry syndrome again.' Jane began to warm to the idea. It might have been the effect of the wine she'd consumed, but suddenly, she felt reckless. 'Do you know how to use Google?'

'Yes, of course.'

'Well, let's get cracking!'

A little while later, Anne appeared, carrying an ice bucket. 'I told the delightful lad behind the bar that we are celebrating singledom in our sixties and he said he wished his mum was more like me.' She deftly popped a cork from a bottle of prosecco and began to pour.

'That's timely.' Kath took a brimming glass and held it up. 'These bubbles are like little diamonds,' she said, 'and Jane has just found a wonderful cruise on a ship named the *Diamond Star*.'

'What?' Anne's blue eyes were wide. 'Are you both up for it?' She stared at her friends. 'I was expecting to put up a fight.'

'We're in!' Kath raised her glass.

Jane held her drink in one hand and phone in the other. She squinted at the screen as she began to narrate her Google search. '"The *Diamond Star* is a small ship that prides itself on luxury cruises for the over-fifties."'

'Perfect,' Anne said, 'but are there any spaces?'

'Yep, I've checked on the online booking system and reserved inner cabins, that's all they have left, and we only have twenty-four hours to confirm and pay in full.'

'Go on,' Kath instructed.

'"Once onboard the *Diamond Star*,"' Jane said, quoting from her phone, '"your Christmas cruise begins, and you can relax knowing that all your favourite traditions will be taken care of."' She took another slug of prosecco. '"With touches of luxury and sparkle, you'll enjoy delicious food, festive fizz and feel-good experiences."'

'Wow,' Anne said, 'bring it on.'

'And I won't have to peel a single sprout!' Kath thought of all the years she was glued to the kitchen, working over a hot stove, preparing the large family meal.

Jane lowered her phone. 'I've saved the details but as it's only a week or so away, can I suggest we meet at mine for coffee tomorrow and make plans to set sail?'

'I'll drink to that.' Anne beamed.

'Me too,' Kath agreed, and they chinked glasses.

'To the *Diamond Star*.' Jane grinned.

'And all the lovely fellas who sail on her.' Anne smiled. Her eyes were alight with anticipation as she joined her friends, and they toasted the exciting adventure ahead.

Chapter Two

Selwyn Alleyne sat in the living room of his home in Carlington Crescent in Lambeth and tapped his neatly manicured nails on the polished surface of a walnut table as music from a nearby stereo blasted one of his favourite tunes. It was a reggae beat played and sung by his hero, Bob Marley. Selwyn nodded when Bob rose with the rising sun, as three little birds pitched up on his doorstep, singing sweet songs. When Bob reached the chorus, Selwyn rose from his chair and began to dance.

'Don't worry, 'bout a thing,' Selwyn sang, his arms raised, eyes closed, 'every little thing gonna be all right.' The song played on, and Selwyn was lost in the moment, his face upturned, body swaying.

When the song ended, he reached across the table until his fingers connected with a glossy brochure. The cover portrayed a gleaming cruise ship channelling its way through a deep blue ocean. 'I'm going to enjoy some sunshine.' He smiled and stroked the embossed gold lettering: *Cruising on the* Diamond Star. Propping it against a vase of fading silk flowers, Selwyn walked over to a bevelled mirror that hung on a chain above a mantel. At six feet tall, Selwyn dipped his knee to catch his reflection as his fingers toyed with the knot on a bow tie that peeped between the collar of a cotton shirt, newly purchased and neatly pressed. Selwyn reached for braces that stretched across his chest and gave the scarlet elastic a tweak. Moving one hand to his full head of hair, greying at the sides, he flicked a heavy knot of dreadlocks between his shoulder blades, then turned his face to stroke the rich dark skin, which crinkled in laughter lines at the corners of his eyes.

A silver frame was perched on a shelf. It held a photograph of a couple in wedding outfits, young and smiling, their arms interlinked. Their expressions oozed happiness, and Selwyn studied the sepia image. He held a finger to his lips and, with a kiss, pressed it to the woman's face. 'Sweet dreams, Florence,' he whispered.

Outside, a horn tooted, and Selwyn hurried to the window. Lifting a net curtain, he looked out to see a taxi. Acknowledging the driver with a wave, Selwyn closed thick velvet drapes and looked around the room to ensure everything was in order. He picked up a jacket and placed a red Fedora on his head as he stepped into the hallway, where suitcases sat on the polished parquet floor. Selwyn patted his pockets and reassured himself that he had his passport, money, and tickets. Setting the alarm, he called out to the house, 'Stay safe while I'm away.' He rattled the door handle to ensure it was locked and, lifting the cases, handed the larger to the driver, who placed it in the cab.

'Heathrow?' the driver asked and began to pull away.

'Yes, please,' Selwyn replied.

'Are you going anywhere interesting?'

'The Caribbean, my friend, the beautiful islands.'

'First time?' the driver asked and eased his vehicle into a heavy traffic lane.

'First time on a cruise,' Selwyn replied.

As he sat back for the ride, leaving Lambeth behind, Selwyn looked out the window at the suburban houses and apartments that stretched through Battersea and Putney. The road headed west and wound its way over spaghetti-like flyovers and junctions, far from the streets of London where Selwyn had spent most of his life. As they travelled along the A4 through Hounslow and signs for the airport came into view, he thought of his daughters. Gloria was pleased that her father was having a holiday, but his eldest, Susan, had been aghast when she'd learnt that their father was heading off to spend time with a group of strangers. Susan could not come to terms with Selwyn travelling abroad so soon after their mother's death.

'It's not right,' she'd argued, 'you should show some respect – what will the community think at our church? It wouldn't be so bad if you were taking Mum home.'

By 'home', Susan meant Jamaica, the island where Selwyn and Florence's parents had grown up before settling in England.

Selwyn thought of the community at the Baptist church

in Lambeth, where he'd worshipped each Sunday throughout his married life. The kindly brothers and sisters had rallied around the newly widowed member. So generous were the ladies, with their offerings of food and nourishment, that Selwyn could feel the waistband on his well-cut trousers tightening almost daily. He hadn't told the congregation about his holiday but had mentioned it to Pastor Gregory after the previous Sunday service. The pastor appeared anxious when he learnt that Selwyn intended to overcome his grief by going on a cruise.

'It may be too early for you to follow this path,' Pastor Gregory said, frowning. 'I'd recommend a more religious retreat.'

But Selwyn had no intention of changing his mind. He knew that Florence, or Flo as he'd liked to call her, would be frowning from above, her bulky body braced, arms folded, lips pursed, and eyebrows raised beneath her Sunday-best bonnet. Silent in words but deadly in meaning.

'May the Lord go with you,' Pastor Gregory said when he realised that Selwyn was determined, 'and as you trust in Jesus in your hours of need, may the memory of your wife never dim, through your thoughts and actions, prayers and meditation.'

Sitting in the back of the cab as the driver turned off the motorway and headed to the airport, Selwyn tapped his fingers on the side of his hand luggage. Pastor Gregory had no need to worry about the memory of Flo ever dimming. Concealed in an old Typhoo Tea tin, Flo's ashes were packed securely in Selwyn's case and would accompany him on his journey.

Music played on the cab's radio, and Selwyn leaned forward to look out the window and watch flights overhead. 'Every little thing, gonna be all right,' The cheerful voice of Bob Marley sang out.

'Isn't that the truth.' Selwyn smiled and began to sing along too.

———

Dicky Delaney was running late. The train from Doncaster had been delayed and he had to race across London to ensure that he caught the flight he was booked on. Of medium height and slim build, he stood on the tube train headed to Heathrow Airport and gripped an overhead strap, bracing himself against the huddle of bodies crushed into the carriage. Dicky avoided eye contact with the nameless faces of travellers, loaded with rucksacks, cases and carry-ons. The mass exodus for Christmas had begun.

He couldn't afford to miss this gig. His future depended on the money he'd earn from the two-week cruise, and he would be handsomely paid to entertain the passengers. In addition, Dicky had several tricks up his sleeve to supplement his income. He'd earned the nickname Dastardly Dicky among fellow comedians on the circuit, and stints in holiday resorts, hotels, and nightclubs had created rumours about his out-of-hours shenanigans. Still, there was an unspoken code between fellow comedians and what happened on tour very firmly stayed on tour, as far as Dastardly Dicky was concerned.

Dicky's cheeks burned, and he felt his face flush with heat. The previous day he'd overdone the session timing on his wife's ancient tanning bed. But looking good was the name of the game to Dicky Delaney, and, in his mid-fifties, he knew that he still cut a dash with his bronzed skin, head of curly hair, and straight white teeth. He kept in shape and felt confident when it was time to strip off and lounge around the pool. To eliminate all signs of greying hair, a dark tint, in Dicky's opinion, took years off. As the tube reached the final stop, Dicky caught his reflection in the glass door panel and felt pleased that he'd gone to some trouble with his appearance.

'The next station will be Heathrow Airport, Terminal Three,' an automated voice rang out, and Dicky reached down to grab his cases. Walking slowly with the crowd, he joined the pack heading towards the terminal. At the check-in desk for his flight, no amount of flattery got him an upgrade, and with a sigh, Dicky took his boarding card and searched for the nearest bar. In years gone by, a couple of crisp notes in his passport and his engaging smile had moved him smoothly into business class, but those days were gone, and he'd have to put up with economy for the next nine hours. At least he'd be comfortable on the ship, he thought as he ordered a scotch and soda. The Diamond Star Cruise Line was notoriously generous when accommodating their entertainers, and Dicky knew that his cabin would be an outside berth with a porthole, at the very least.

His phone rang, and he reached into his pocket.

'All ship-shape and ready to board?' Clive, Dicky's agent, yelled.

'Yes, I've checked in,' Dicky replied, grimacing, and holding the phone away from his ear.

'Don't mess this up, I've put my reputation on the line to get you this gig,' Clive boomed.

Dicky visualised his agent in his dark office, just off Wardour Street in Soho. With his comb-over hair and feet propped on his desk to ease painful gout, cigar smoke clouded the airless room.

Taking a slug of his drink, Dicky replied, 'I know you have, Clive, and I'm grateful. I'll make sure that my show receives a glowing report from the Entertainment Director.'

'Sod the E.D. I want a call from the skipper, Captain Kennedy, at least,' Clive roared. 'Keep your hands in your pockets and your eyes on the job and stay away from women!'

Clive slammed the phone down.

Dicky sighed and nodded to the bar staff for a refill. He'd worked with Clive for as long as he could remember, and in his heyday, Clive had always ensured that Dicky got the best billing at whatever gig he sent him to. Clive certainly earned his agent's ten per cent and had never let Dicky down. But an incident with a theatre manager's wife had created a scandal when it hit the headlines in the seaside town where Dicky had a summer residency. The local paper had gone to town:

Comedy Couple Caught in the Act!

The headline screamed above a compromising photograph, and Dicky's contract was abruptly cut short. His marriage had barely survived, and Dicky fell on a lean time, struggling to pay his bills. When he heard through the grapevine that a comedy act had fallen ill and couldn't take up a cruise in the Caribbean, Dicky raced to London and stormed into Clive's office.

He demanded that he get the job.

'You owe me,' Clive had threatened, following his call to the cruise company. 'Peter, the Entertainment Director, is a close friend so don't mess it up!'

Dicky finished his drink and heard his flight being called. He had no intention of messing this job up and hurried to the departure gate. But he would take advantage of any opportunities. After all, he'd gotten away with it in the past and, with thousands of miles between himself and Clive, he was confident he could get away with it in the future.

'Good morning.' Dicky's charming smile was wide as he greeted the attendant who welcomed him onboard the flight. 'Any room for a little one in business class?'

Chapter Three

Anne, Kath, and Jane sat in a café at Manchester Airport and stared out of the windows, where lights from aircraft could be seen moving across the concourse. Icy rain ricocheted against the glass as the dawn sky changed from charcoal to soft grey.

'When I was flying, I always thought that dawn was like an invitation to a different day,' Anne reminisced as she sipped a cappuccino and stared out. 'An unopened gift. I never knew what was inside until the layers of light were peeled back and the aircraft flew into a new time zone, full of possibilities and hope.'

'Goodness, how can you be so poetic at this unearthly hour?' Kath muttered from behind her latte. A layer of milky foam formed a moustache on her top lip. 'I'm so tired I can barely string a sentence together.' She removed her glasses and began to polish them.

'It's a long time since we've been up so early.' Jane

glanced at her watch. She hadn't slept a wink and had been dressed and ready long before the taxi had arrived to take them to the airport.

'Oh, I do miss flying,' Anne sighed, 'I had such a wonderful life.'

'Before you fell to earth with a bump and Barry and a baby buggered things up.' Jane yawned.

Kath held up a trilby, turning it around as she studied the black fabric. 'Do you think we were impulsive buying these? Should we have gone for something more subtle?' She looked doubtful as she turned the hat in her hand.

'No, they're a bit of fun.' Anne wore her trilby at a jaunty angle. 'It makes us stand out.'

Kath pulled a face. 'Sixty-something singletons on tour,' she mumbled, 'there should be a slogan saying, "Kiss Me Quick." I feel like we are on a hen night in Blackpool.'

'Hardly.' Anne laughed. 'Barbados and the wonderful islands of the Caribbean beckon.' Gathering her hand luggage, she stood. 'Come on, our gate number has just been announced.'

With Jane and Kath trailing behind, Anne raced across the terminal, caught up in the swell of holidaymakers. But in her haste, she tripped and accidentally bumped into a man making his way through the crowd.

Captain Mike Allen reached out a hand to steady the person who'd almost knocked his flight bag out of his hand. 'It can't be?' Mike said as he gazed at the blonde gripping his uniform sleeve. 'Is it Anne?' he asked as frown lines fell in grooves across his leathery forehead, and his eyes lit up in recognition.

'Mike!' Anne exclaimed, 'I thought you'd retired years ago?'

'I'm a training captain now, only a few months to go before I hang up my wings,' Mike replied, 'but what about you?'

Anne explained that she'd flown for as long as the company allowed and then taken severance pay. She was on her way to Barbados with friends to join a cruise.

Coincidentally, Mike was on the flight deck. To their amazement, he upgraded the three friends into business class, and they boarded a little while later.

Anne, Jane, and Kath could barely believe their luck.

'Oh, my Lord,' Kath whispered as she settled into a deep leather seat, 'I had no idea that planes were as nice as this.' She looked around the cabin. 'It's better than a trip to Bournemouth and a stay at the Sunnyside Hotel.'

'It's not first class but it's a big improvement from our seats in economy.' Anne beamed. 'And all the drinks and meals are free.'

Jane was wearing a thick wool poncho, which she regretted as she tucked swathes of fabric into the sides of her seat. *Please, please don't make me wear a seatbelt extension,* she silently pleaded when an immaculate attendant in a neatly tailored suit approached.

'You may be more comfortable with this.' the attendant smiled and handed Jane the extension.

'Take your poncho off,' Anne whispered.

Humiliated, Jane didn't want to take her poncho off. Knowing that it would be hot in Barbados, she'd chosen a thin, short-sleeved top to wear underneath and preferred to leave sight of her batwing arms and chunky chest to the very last moment. With a sigh, she clipped the extension into place and settled the curves of her tummy around it.

The attendant held out a tray, and the friends eagerly took a glass of champagne.

'So, this is what you did for a living?' Kath looked at Anne. 'Spent all your time in a fancy get-up flying around the world.' She was in awe as she watched the crew prepare for take-off.

'It's not as glamorous as you think,' Anne replied. 'Although in my early days, the job was easier, and we wore gorgeous uniforms of kilts and matching jackets with beautiful starched white blouses.' Anne smiled, her eyes dreamy. 'We used to get long stays down-route and generous expenses.'

'And cosy nights away with Captain Mike,' Kath added. 'He hadn't forgotten you, despite the years.'

The plane was ready for take-off and taxied down the runway before roaring into the sky. Kath gripped her seat and began to pray and Jane, wriggling uncomfortably, adjusted her safety belt. Anne smiled and remembered bygone days when her time as a flight attendant was enviable. Her working hours consisted of being in one exotic location after another with crazy crew parties that lasted all night. A ten-day stint in Rio de Janeiro with Mike had been memorable, filled with sun-drenched days and passionate nights.

But the bubble had burst when their homeward flight took him back to his wife.

Anne's role as a number one gave her the privileged position of working first-class, administering to the needs of well-heeled passengers. But when the company was taken over, everything changed. Stop-overs were minimal, expenses non-existent, and even her new uniform seemed shoddy. Like many cabin crew, Anne's ambition was to marry a pilot. When an overnight in Ibiza allowed her to encourage Captain Barry Amberley into bed, he'd put up little resistance. Within weeks she knew she was pregnant and punched the air with happiness. *Result!* Anne told herself before breaking the news to Barry.

'Penny for your thoughts?' Jane asked as the plane began to cruise at high altitude, and Kath stopped praying.

'I was remembering when Barry and I got married,' Anne said.

'Oh, it was such a lovely wedding,' Kath sighed, 'it was the talk of the town, Garstang had never seen anything like it,' she reminisced. 'Jane and I looked so pretty as bridesmaids.'

Jane winced. The matching dress Anne had insisted they wear was buried deep in a box labelled 'The Worst Day of My Life'. She'd felt like a giant meringue moving down the aisle, breathless in a corset where pink satin and lace bows bounced on every bulge. Anne, meanwhile, sailed ahead, stunning in a silky designer gown. Kath had caught Anne's bouquet, and as Jim, a groomsman, winked at her, the rest, as they say, was history for Kath.

'Do you remember your wedding cake?' Jane asked, 'You insisted on six tiers, and I made every one of them.' She shook her head. 'It took weeks of work, but you were able to use the top tier for Belinda's christening not long after.'

'How is Belinda?' Kath peered over the pages of an inflight magazine.

'She's very happy,' Anne replied and thought of her daughter, who lived Down Under with surfer-boy and their four kids. Her daughter had fallen in love during a gap year in Australia and never returned. 'She thinks our cruise is brilliant.' Anne smiled as she remembered their recent phone call.

'I wish my two were on the other side of the world,' Kath grumbled. 'They still want me to sign the house over to them and both are convinced I'm losing my marbles since Jim died.'

'Grief shows its form in different ways. It's no wonder you forget things, Jim's death was so unexpected.' Jane reached out and patted Kath's arm.

'Maybe, but I'm not ready for an old folks' home with a recliner and a plastic bib.'

'Pah!' Jane snorted. 'I should think not.'

'Hugh and Harry can be very persuasive boys.'

'They're not boys,' Jane insisted, 'they are men, with families, and quite capable of making their own way in life without grabbing your money while you still have time to spend and enjoy it.'

Jane remembered Hugh and Harry from many get-togethers over the years. She had no time for either and thought they took after their father, treating Kath as a skivvy and expecting her to wait on them hand and foot. Even now, Jane knew that Kath's evenings were taken with babysitting duties. Daytimes were spent cleaning and cooking for her daughters-in-law, who never reciprocated with kind words or a grateful bunch of flowers.

The seatbelt sign had been turned off, and Anne stood and stretched her arms. 'Can I suggest that we leave our current lives behind,' she said and stepped into the aisle. 'For the next two weeks, we will have the holiday of a lifetime and to start things off, let's have champagne in the bar.' She began to walk through the cabin until she reached a stairway.

'She can't go up there,' Jane whispered, 'it's for first-class passengers.' Together with Kath, she watched wide-eyed as Anne's jewelled sandals disappeared up the stairs. 'Sod it, we can only get thrown out,' Jane said, unbuckling her belt.

Poking Kath, she encouraged her friend to her feet. Like two furtive schoolgirls sneaking out of a dorm at night, the pair waited until the coast was clear of cabin crew, then hurried after Anne.

'I feel like one of the Blues Brothers,' Jane said as she gripped the arms of Kath and Anne and placed one unsteady foot in front of the other. Wearing their new Trilbys, sunglasses and smiles, the trio staggered down the steps of the aircraft and strolled towards the customs hall at Grantley Adams International Airport. The tarmac burned underfoot as a glorious sun beat down on the new arrivals.

'Can we be locked up for arriving blotto in Barbados?' Kath tripped on the hanging strap of her voluminous bag.

'Shu...shush,' Anne said, 'look sober and straight ahead.'

Jane tilted her hat over her eyes. 'Well, we did spend most of the flight in the bar,' she said.

'Nonsense,' Anne replied, 'you both ate lunch followed by afternoon tea and were asleep and snoring in between.'

'Gosh, it's hot,' Kath gasped and fanned her face with her hand.

'I feel like we've stepped into a roasting oven,' Jane said as she adjusted her poncho and mopped her brow.

'*Diamond Star* passengers!' a voice called out, and the women turned to see a man, head and shoulders above the crowd, holding a clipboard. 'This way.' He smiled as he checked names and gathered guests. 'Go through the separate customs channel and straight outside to coach A. Your luggage has gone on ahead.'

Kath squinted to read the name badge pinned to the man's uniform, but Jane tugged Kath's cardigan and pulled her back.

'Peter Hammond, Entertainment Director, Diamond Star Line,' he said, 'pleased to meet you.'

In no time, the friends cleared customs and found themselves sitting on the front seats of a luxurious air-conditioned coach. Having collected all his guests, Peter boarded the coach.

'Good afternoon, everyone,' he said, using a PA system, 'and welcome to what is the beginning of a memorable holiday.' Several travellers applauded. 'The time has changed, and you've gained four hours, so please adjust your watches.' He pointed to his wrist. 'We are a small company and personal service is something the company prides itself on. Myself or one of my team are on hand, and you are now officially members of the *Diamond Star* family so feel free to come and talk to us with any queries you may have.'

As the guests stared out, he commented on the sights coming into view. 'The city of Bridgetown is the capital of Barbados,' Peter explained. 'As well as being recognised for being a UNESCO World Heritage Site, it is well known for its British colonial architecture and the famous parliament buildings.'

The three friends were fascinated as the coach travelled along the busy highway adjacent to the island's south coast. Kath nudged Jane as they caught glimpses of the sea beyond the roofs of houses and colourful little shacks lining the road.

'Oh, look!' Kath exclaimed and pointed to a man standing next to a stall stacked high with green coconuts.

He wore jeans hanging low from a belt, and his torso was naked. Sweat glistened on a muscled body that held a machete in one hand. Swinging the knife wide to decapitate a coconut, he handed the coconut to a woman wearing a bonnet and brightly patterned dress, and she drank the contents thirstily.

The coach slowed as a group of children waited to cross the road, and Jane smiled as she watched the hand-holding line of immaculately dressed little ones, neat in shirts and shorts. The girls wore lacy white ankle socks with colourful beads and ribbons threaded through their hair and they waved at the passengers on the coach.

As the driver negotiated the busy streets of Bridgetown, Peter explained that they were passing an area known as the Garrison Savanna. Guests gazed at a collection of military buildings. They learnt that they were built in 1790 as barracks for soldiers when Barbados was used as a base for the British Regiment. Peter pointed out that the savanna was a natural environment for horse racing since the colonial days and home to the famous Barbados Gold Cup. 'As you can see,' he said, 'the area attracts other activities such as kite flying, jogging, or simply sitting and watching the world go by.'

Kath gazed at the swaying palm trees lining the route and shaded her eyes as a shimmering heat haze sparkled over the turquoise sea. 'I'd give anything to dive in there,' she muttered, 'I've never seen a sea so inviting.'

Jane looked wistfully at the alluring water and longed to cool her body. But she shuddered at the thought of stripping off and exposing her flesh. She prayed there would be a private place on the ship to sunbathe, away from toxic stares. Jane thought about her lovely mum, who'd been unaware that she'd created Jane's addiction by giving her daughter food as a treat. Unlike invisible addictions, Jane's was too obvious to miss.

The driver turned off the highway towards the port, and Bridgetown Cruise Terminal came into view. Anne pointed excitedly. 'Look,' she said, 'there's our ship.'

The *Diamond Star* rose from the teal-coloured water, its bow painted navy with a regal gold stripe. A magnificent floating sanctuary with deep, gleaming decks. Everyone climbed off the coach and strode towards the ship, where a steel band played Christmas calypso music as more vehicles arrived and passengers crowded the concourse. Dancers in colourful carnival outfits, many wearing Santa hats, moved through the crowd in welcome. They cavorted alongside characters, some stilted, wearing traditional 17th-century costumes as a smiling uniformed crew offered glasses of rum punch and soft drinks.

'We've been upgraded again!' Anne exclaimed as staff checked them in. 'They've run short of inner cabins, and we've been moved to a suite. It's called Hibiscus.'

'Crikey, how wonderful,' Jane said as she removed her heavy poncho and, taking Kath's arm, followed Anne into a lift that sped them to an upper deck.

The trio wandered down a long corridor, searching for their accommodation. They checked doorways that bore brass plaques with the names of Caribbean flowers.

'Orchid, Bougainvillaea, Jasmine, Lily ... oh look,' Anne said as she studied the plaques, 'here's Hibiscus.' She held the key card to the door, and they tumbled over the threshold, their eyes alight.

'We've got a balcony!' Kath exclaimed as she hurried into Hibiscus. Her mouth fell open as she slid the door back to reveal an outdoor seating area.

In the large lounge-like bedroom Jane flung her poncho onto one of the beds and picked up a towel folded into the shape of a swan. 'Oh my,' she whispered and stroked the soft fabric. Beside the swan lay a Christmas cracker containing complimentary toiletries.

'There's a bar,' Anne called out and crouched down to wrench open a fridge door stacked high with miniature bottles of spirits and wine.

'It's so Christmassy,' Kath said as she gazed at a pretty tree in one corner, 'just look at these decorations.' Gold and silver ornaments twinkled in the sunlight.

'Our cases have arrived ahead of us.' Jane pointed to a luggage rack where their bags were neatly stacked. 'Everything is so efficiently organised.'

The three women each claimed a bed and, throwing themselves on the thick quilted counterpanes, stretched out their arms and stared up at the ceiling, sighing with happiness.

'Ah, air-conditioning.' Jane sighed. She closed her eyes and snuggled onto the comfortable mattress.

'I can't believe I'm here –' Kath closed her eyes and lay

her hands across her breastbone '– but I'm exhausted, and I think I've got a hangover.'

'Don't get too comfortable,' Anne said. 'If you sleep now, you'll never sleep later, and there is so much to see.'

'This is bliss,' Jane said. She was enjoying the cool air that caressed her tired and sticky body.

Anne unbuttoned her shirt. 'Why don't we get changed and find our way around the ship before dinner?'

'Good idea.' Kath carefully swung her legs over the side of the bed.

'I'm up for that.' Jane wriggled to a sitting position and tugged on her tunic top to pull it over her head.

Anne waved her blouse and tossed it into the air, 'Ladies,' she announced, 'our Christmas cruise has begun!'

Chapter Four

It hadn't taken Selwyn long to unpack, and his clothes hung neatly in the inner cabin he'd been allocated. Standing in front of a long mirror that fronted the wardrobe, he straightened the lapels of his linen suit. Pulling at the sleeves of his jacket to show a glimpse of the colourful shirt cuff, the smoothed gold links enamelled in the red, green, and yellow of the Jamaican flag, Selwyn turned and picked up his red Fedora. Tempted to place it on his head, he decided it was best to leave the hat perched on the dressing table beside a battered Typhoo Tea tin.

The vintage tin was worn, and Selwyn remembered Flo's long fingers reaching to lift it from their kitchen cupboard, her hand an automated machine. The task of making cups of tea for the many sisters and brothers from the Baptist church in Lambeth was endless. Much to Selwyn's frustration, worshippers had regularly assembled in his home. They chose to read passages from the bible and sing gospel songs when Selwyn wanted to listen to Bob Marley, whose sweet vocals were biblical to Selwyn and the only form of religion he wanted to practise.

'Sleep soundly, Flo,' he whispered, his fingers positioning the tin.

Selwyn sang as he stepped into the hallway and followed signs to guide him through the ship, stopping every now and again to familiarise himself with the surroundings. Taking the stairs to the main deck, he wandered through a lounge area where an elderly gentleman sat at one end of a bar. He wore deck shoes, shorts and a captain's hat decorated with gold braid. His T-shirt bore the slogan *Living Life One Cruise At A Time.*

'Good afternoon, Captain,' Selwyn said as he walked past.

The captain looked up. 'Greetings!' He raised a glass of whisky, wrapping knobbly, arthritic fingers tightly around the base. 'Care to join me?' Rheumy eyes focused on Selwyn. 'You look like a man who's travelled many a high sea.' Wrinkled skin, as dry as parchment, trembled on the older man's throat and reminded Selwyn of a turkey.

'Maybe later, my friend.' Selwyn affected a salute and moved away.

Passengers mingled in different areas of the ship as Selwyn strode through, smiling as he made his way. In the duty-free shop, he decided to buy something to read. Conscious of his single status, a book might be a valuable item to bury himself in should the need arise. As he browsed shelves filled with novels, Selwyn overheard a man talking to a female crew member who stood next to a point-of-sale area.

'My book needs to be placed in a prominent position,' the man instructed and reached into a box. 'Passengers will queue up for these once they've seen my shows. It needs to be at the front of the shop.'

Intrigued, Selwyn turned to watch the man as he moved a display of Christmas shortbreads and began to stack a pile of books on the counter.

'Mr Delaney...' the woman began.

'Call me Dicky, darlin', let's not be formal.'

Selwyn noticed the woman wince. She tucked a wayward strand of sleek blonde hair behind her ear. 'My name is Diane, not "Darlin",' she said. 'Diane Johns, to be precise and I am the manager of the shop.'

'Diane, Darlin', it's all the same to me, I'm just being friendly.' Dicky beamed.

'I will place your merchandise where I deem suitable,' Diane replied and pursed her lips, 'and your commission will be paid on sales, at the end of the cruise.' Ignoring the books, she rotated her slim body to block Dicky and examine goods on a shelf.

Dicky saw that Selwyn was watching. *'Stuck up madam,'* Dicky whispered and rolled his eyes. 'You all right there?' he called out. 'Don't forget to come to my show tomorrow night, in the Neptune Lounge, after dinner.'

Selwyn nodded and watched the man walk away. He glanced at the book on top of the pile and read the title, *Dicky Delaney – My Life in Show Business*. The man was obviously an entertainer, and Selwyn studied the smiling face on the cover. 'A comedian,' he said out loud.

Diane swung around and stared at Selwyn. 'Some people call him that.' She cleared her throat and picked up a book. Narrowing her eyes, she paused as though considering where to place it.

'I'll take one of those,' Selwyn said, reaching into his pocket.

'I hope you enjoy it.' Diane was polite as she took Selwyn's payment. 'You'll see quite a lot of Dicky Delaney over the next two weeks.'

'I'm looking forward to his show.'

Diane nodded and completed the purchase. 'Enjoy your evening,' she said.

Selwyn tucked the book under his arm and strolled out of the shop. As he continued to explore, he came to a foyer where a curved reception desk lined a long wall. Smiling staff assisted guests who queried dining times and shore excursions. Selwyn stepped forward, and a pretty girl looked up.

'How may I help you?' she asked. A badge pinned to her white blouse told Selwyn her name and that she was a customer service agent.

'Good evening, Diwa,' he began, 'please direct me to the Terrace Restaurant. I'm dining there.' Diwa gave clear instructions and explained to Selwyn that pre-dinner drinks were being served in the main hall.

Following her directions, he set off and soon found himself at the correct location. A server appeared and

Selwyn accepted a colourful cocktail and took a sip. He licked his lips at the delicious flavour of rum and syrup combined with a hint of nutmeg. 'Oh, that's good.' He sighed with pleasure and began to study the vestibule, where a giant Christmas tree dominated a central staircase. It was trimmed with bows of tartan ribbon and embellished with baubles and hundreds of twinkling lights.

'Flo,' Selwyn whispered as he observed the magnificent sight and looked heavenward. 'This tree puts your Santa to shame.' Selwyn remembered the tired old battery-operated Santa that stood on the mantel in their living room. His wife's favourite festive adornment had been in the family since their children were small. As Selwyn stared at the tree, he knew that the raggedy dancing Santa wouldn't see the light of day again.

A steel band began to play, and Selwyn's face lit up as he recognised the tune.

Selwyn tapped his foot and swayed his hips as he stood under the glittering lights and watched with delight as guests assembled. Like him, they took note of the assorted gathering of passengers who would be their shipmates for the next two weeks. Taking another rum punch, Selwyn began to chat with a couple standing alongside. They introduced themselves as Harold and Nancy from Yorkshire and Selwyn replied without hesitation when Harold asked if he was looking forward to the cruise.

'This is a holiday of a lifetime and I'm going to make the most of every moment.' Selwyn's smile came from deep inside like the petals of an unfolding flower, and he held up his glass. 'Cheers,' he said, 'and happy holiday.'

In the Terrace Restaurant, a pianist sat at a grand piano and played popular tunes as guests were guided to their tables. The impressively dressed maître d' greeted Anne, Kath, and Jane. His tailed suit was pristine, and with a voice as smooth as silk, he oozed charm. 'My name is Nathaniel,' he said. 'Welcome to The Terrace and allow me to show you to your table.'

Checking the name Hibiscus on his seating plan, Nathaniel indicated that they follow him as he glided across the room.

'It looks like we'll be sharing,' Jane said and eased herself onto a seat, grateful that there were no arm rests. The table was laid for six, and Jane felt uneasy. 'Keep together, don't leave me on my own.' Most people only saw her size and often treated her as contagious.

'You'll be fine,' Anne replied, sitting down on the opposite side. She waited while Nathaniel skilfully unfolded a napkin and placed it on her knee. 'We're sure to have interesting dinner companions.' Licking her peach-coloured lips, she looked hopefully around the room.

But Jane was uncomfortable. Terrified that her seat wouldn't support her weight, she felt her dress pull tight. She'd manipulated herself into a body-sculpting Lycra slip which threatened to split at any moment.

'I'll keep you company,' Kath said and sat next to Jane. She nodded thanks as a server poured iced water into sparkling crystal glasses.

Jane fiddled with her napkin and watched the assembly of well-heeled guests as tables filled and introductions were made. She noted that the women wore stylish outfits that must have cost a fortune. Their jewels glistened in the subtle light as her spirits plummeted. If only she'd bothered to go shopping for more comfortable clothes and accessories.

It wasn't that Jane couldn't afford to be on the cruise. On the contrary, she pondered, she'd worked hard and saved all her life and as an only child, inheriting her parents' home, she didn't have to worry about money.

When her contract was abruptly terminated with the television company she'd worked with for years, she settled mortgage-free into life in Garstang. But without routine, her days dragged. Cookery shows filled her time as she checked out the names of her successors. Jane knew that she'd been dropped because of her advancing years. An ageing, overweight home economist no longer fitted the bill with young, ambitious, upwardly mobile executives at the trendy production team. Jane put familiar faces to the names when the credits rolled on the shows she'd worked on, and despaired that none were over the age of thirty.

'You're very quiet.' Kath nudged Jane. 'What are you thinking?'

'That I'm feeling my age and this cruise was a mistake.' Jane tugged on her dress, willing the fabric to lie comfortably. 'I don't think I'm going to be able to get on with strangers.'

'Does it matter?' Kath asked. 'You have us as companions, and Anne will ensure we have a good time.' She looked across the table where Nathaniel assisted an elderly gentleman to his seat. Anne greeted the new dinner guest and made a fuss to ensure he was comfortable beside her.

'She can smell money.' Jane smiled as she watched the performance and noted that the new arrival wore a navy blazer with shiny brass buttons and a nautical captain's hat perched on his head.

'Do you think he got his hat in a fancy-dress shop?' Kath whispered.

'It's impressing Anne,' Jane said, 'she's called him "Captain".'

'Husband-hunting has begun.'

'I'm not sure that I can bear to watch.'

'Just relax,' Kath said, she touched Jane's arm with affection. 'Don't ever think you're not as good as anyone else.'

'I feel so out of place.' Jane looked around the room. 'Everyone is glamorous, and I feel so big and awkward.'

'I'm not exactly the belle of the ball.' Kath touched her greying hair and straightened the front of a dress that had seen much better days. 'But let's make the most of things.'

Jane sighed and took a sip of her water. She twirled the ice in her glass and then picked up a menu from the centre of the table to study the various courses they'd soon be tucking into.

It was Jane's habit to analyse each dish whenever she ate out. She imagined the ingredients and method of cooking and, having supported many talented chefs over the years, wondered what their take would be on the food that would soon arrive. Her skilled fingers had spent hours of preparation, attending to the finest detail before the cameras rolled, enabling the chef to be the show's star. Deep in thought, Jane didn't notice that the chair beside her had been pulled back, and a smartly dressed man sat down. Like an electric shock, his leg touched her own and Jane recoiled. To her horror, water spilt from her glass, drenching the menu, and pooling on the table.

'Oh, goodness, I'm so sorry,' Jane said, a flush creeping over her face.

The man reached out and dabbed at the table with his napkin. 'No harm done,' he replied.

Nathaniel appeared and instantly remedied the upset. As he replaced the menu in Jane's hand, her heart sank. She was in the agonising position of having to converse with a stranger and glared across the table as Anne made introductions.

'Hello, I'm Anne,' she said, 'may I introduce the Captain, on my right, and these two ladies are my friends, Kath and Jane.'

'Delighted to meet you all,' the man replied with a smile, 'my name is Selwyn.'

'Any room for a little one?' A woman pulled out a chair

and sat between Kath and the Captain. She clutched a sequinned bag and placed it on the table. It matched her beaded dress. 'Bridgette Haworth,' she announced. Smoothing a heavy dark bob with petite fingers, she laughed, 'My friends call me Bossy Bridgette, but I can assure you I'm not. I'm on the cruise as a guest speaker.'

'Good evening,' the group replied.

Conversation struck up, and details of their journeys were disclosed as dinner commenced and wine poured. Everyone bar Jane began to relax.

Selwyn explained that he'd travelled from London. His flight from Heathrow had been most enjoyable, and despite the time difference creating tiredness, he felt relaxed already.

Guests learnt from Bridgette that the Captain had the penthouse suite and spent his time travelling around the world.

'Imagine how much money it takes to spend all that time on a ship,' Kath whispered as she studied the Captain. 'He must be loaded but looks a bit vague to me.'

'He probably forgets to disembark after each cruise,' Jane replied.

They watched as asparagus soup trickled down the side of the Captain's mouth. He peered under his hat, and his eyes were vague as he stared at the guests, as if questioning how he'd travelled through so many decades to arrive at this table.

'Let me help you,' Bridgette said. She explained that she knew the Captain from previous cruises and over the years they'd become friends. Leaning in, she dabbed at his mouth with a napkin, then gently removed the hat and placed it to one side. The worry lines on his wrinkled face softened.

'Thank you, my dear.' The Captain smiled.

'Do you think he has the early stages of dementia?' Jane whispered to Kath.

'If he has, I'll get on well with him.' Kath had finished her soup and, puzzled, touched her fingers to her ear lobes. 'I thought I was wearing earrings – and where are my glasses?'

'There was a pair of earrings beside the bathroom sink and your glasses are on your head.'

'Ah, of course.' Kath sighed.

'Your earrings will be there when we go back to the suite, no harm done,' Jane said.

'Bridgette tells me that she's a gardener.' Selwyn turned to speak to Jane, and her heart sank. 'An excellent gardener who has won many awards.'

'That's nice.'

'She'll be hosting talks that include *From Your Garden to Show Garden*.' Selwyn took a sip of wine. 'Do you like gardening?'

'Not really, my cottage is mostly lawn,' Jane said.

'I'm more of a pot man myself.'

Selwyn coughed, and his leg touched Jane's thigh again. Flinching, she gripped her knees and shuffled her feet away. Jane noted Selwyn's dreadlocks and beautiful smooth skin. It was the colour of ebony and shone with good health. 'Do you mean that you like marijuana?' Jane asked, 'Oh, I'm sorry, I shouldn't have said that.'

'Well, yes, I like that too.'

Selwyn's voice was rich, his gaze hypnotic, and Jane's jaw dropped as she stared into deep brown eyes, as indulgent and inviting as chocolate.

Bridgette interrupted, 'I've won lots of awards, including gold at Hampton Court and the Chelsea Flower Show.'

'You must be very talented,' Jane said but she wasn't paying attention. Something about Selwyn was unsettling, and Jane yearned for the dinner to be over. Ignoring Bridgette, she turned to Kath. 'Please, will you talk to me,' Jane hissed.

'You seem to be doing very nicely on your own.' Kath nodded as she tucked into her main course. 'But eat up, this sea bass is delicious, although I'm not sure what else is on the plate.' She poked at the carefully arranged food with her fork.

'Fried basil leaves, curried cauliflower and caper vinaigrette,' Jane replied robotically.

'I wonder if there are seconds?' Kath munched happily.

'There will be mountains of food over the next two weeks. I'll have to be airlifted off.' But as Jane stared at her dinner, she realised that suddenly, she had no appetite, and there was an unfamiliar thud in her chest.

'Are you all right?' Kath asked, 'you haven't touched your dinner.'

'I'm fine,' Jane snapped, terrified that others on the table might notice. Was she having a panic attack or something more serious? Pushing back her chair, she struggled to her feet. 'I'm terribly sorry,' she began, 'but I feel exhausted and I'm going to have an early night.'

'It must be the long journey,' Kath said and eyed Jane's unfinished meal.

'Off you go, run along, it's far better to catch your sleep than spoil your holiday,' Bridgette insisted. Everyone exchanged glances. It was easy to see how Bridgette had earned her nickname of 'bossy'.

'May I walk you back to your cabin?' Selwyn was concerned and placed his napkin on the table.

'Goodness, no!' Jane was flustered, and before Selwyn could rise to his feet, she picked up her bag and lumbered away.

'I knew I shouldn't have come on this cruise,' she announced to Nathaniel as she squeezed past the diners.

Nathaniel, fearing that something she'd eaten had been upsetting, showed concern. 'Is there anything I can do?' he asked.

'Put me on a diet and send me to confidence classes.' Jane sniffed, and as tears pricked at the corners of her eyes, she hurried from the room.

Chapter Five

The following morning Kath woke early. It took her a few moments to remember that she wasn't waking up on one side of the sagging mattress she'd shared with Jim for many years. This bed was comfortable. It hugged in all the right places, and Kath realised that she'd just experienced the best night's sleep she'd had in a very long time.

The room was dark as she pulled the duvet aside and inched her legs over the side of the bed until her toes touched the soft carpet. Kath sat still, enjoying the quiet. It was peaceful in Hibiscus, with only the gentle hum of air-conditioning.

A ray of sunshine peeked out from behind heavy drapes, giving enough light for Kath to see Jane in the next bed, a rhythmic mound, slumbering soundly. Anne, also asleep, lay on top of her covers, a shortie nightie covering her hips

– arms and legs akimbo. Kath stretched out and rotated her head. Despite the comfort, she ached after all the travelling. She missed her daily walk, and her body told her she needed to move. Stiffness in her joints was progressing with every year that passed but Kath's regular exercise of walking at least five miles a day helped keep her upright and robust. Her mind might be playing tricks, but her body behaved itself.

Easing from the bed, Kath tiptoed across the room to the balcony. The *Diamond Star* was still in port and wouldn't leave until early evening and they had a whole day in Barbados. Kath remembered that Anne had suggested that they disembark after breakfast and, if possible, experience an island tour.

Kath stared out at the Caribbean. The black starry night had melted into the horizon, and sunshine washed over the sea. The light was as pure as she'd ever seen, and the endless sky all blue and bright, with puffs of drifting cloud. She held the rail and tilted her face to the sun.

What would Jim think of her now? He'd be turning in his grave if he could see her standing in her pyjamas on the balcony of a cruise ship in the Caribbean. Imagine his horror at the expense. Barbados replacing Bournemouth.

It was eight months since her husband had died, and Kath had spent her days clearing necessary paperwork, sorting bills and accounts, and sending a mountain of Jim's clothes to charity shops. She opened her eyes, stared out, and remembered that it was also a sunny day when Jim had left their house and suddenly fallen on the steps down from the front door. As his feet, encased in soft leather brogues, scrambled to grip the weathered undulations of stone, he catapulted through the air. Both hands responded too late and his body, a dead weight, dropped alarmingly face-down on the pathway. Kath had raced to his unconscious side and kneeling, grabbed Jim's wrist, to feel for a pulse.

Their postman appeared at the gate. He was ashen-faced as he phoned for assistance. Jim's breathing had slowed, his skin cooled, and Kath had swallowed rapidly as she stared at the man with whom she'd spent all her adult life. Blood pooled around a cut on his head, and she'd held her fingers to the gash with a shaking hand, feeling the warm sticky fluid. The minutes dragged as Kath tried to make sense of what had happened. She'd looked around in confusion, 'But … he….' She spoke in fragments, her voice shaky.

Kath recalled the sound of a distant siren and the postman touching her arm. 'Help is here,' he'd said. Then, all hell broke loose as a rapid responder appeared at the scene, followed by paramedics in an ambulance. Anxious neighbours gathered by the gate and what followed was a blur. In the house, Kath's fingers, still sticky, left a brownish-red print on the embroidered cloth on the kitchen table. She sipped a mug of sweet tea, and a paramedic gently told her they were sorry, but her husband had passed away. Then the local police arrived to query the nature of Jim's death.

Now, rubbing her eyes and swaying as she gripped the rail, Kath vaguely remembered them speaking to the postman before offering sympathy.

'Don't blame yourself,' the postman had said, 'I told the

police that the steps to your house are steep, and I often have a wobble myself as I push mail through the door. Your old man came a right cropper when he tripped, it was no one's fault.'

Tears dripped down Kath's face, and she brushed them away. She turned as the door slid back and Anne stepped onto the balcony.

'You're an early bird,' Anne said and yawned. She raised a hand to shield her eyes from the sun and stared at Kath. 'Are you okay? You look like you've been crying.'

'I was remembering Jim's accident and feeling guilty about this holiday. Jim will never have a holiday again.'

'But you mustn't,' Anne said. Her voice was soft, and she reached out to put an arm around her friend. 'His fall wasn't your fault; accidents happen all the time.'

Kath sighed. She reached into a pocket and dabbed at her eyes with a tissue. 'I suppose I'm still suffering from shock,' she said, 'it was all so unexpected and now, as you know, the boys want me to go and live with one of them and sell the house.'

'But why? You're happy there, it's been your home for a lifetime.' Anne eased herself onto a chair.

'I've already given them a comfortable sum.' Kath sniffed. 'But I think they are hoping I'm developing dementia and if I sign the house over to them, they can sell it and put me in a nursing home.'

'Oh, *please…*'

'Maybe I should.'

'Let's not discuss this subject again while we're on holiday.' Anne sighed. 'There is absolutely nothing wrong with your mind, other than the normal signs of ageing.'

'That's what my doctor said. Do you remember the memory test I did, at Hugh and Harry's insistence?'

'The doctor said your memory was better than his!' Anne smiled. 'So you'll remember that last night we agreed we will do a tour of the island today.'

'Yes, and I'm looking forward to it.' Kath felt brighter. 'Should we arrange something through the concierge?'

'No, they'll take a percentage of the cost, and we'll only get to see all the touristy things.' Anne crossed her legs and wiggled her toes, tilting her head to admire the glittery nail polish. 'We'll head into Bridgetown and find a taxi with a local driver, that's the best way to get around.'

'Are you sure?' Kath, unused to foreign travel, had visions of being kidnapped, but, on reflection, she guessed that they were probably perfectly safe at their age.

'Yes, it will be fun. Now let's stir Jane and have a decent breakfast before we get going.'

'Jane hardly touched her food last night,' Kath said.

'She was overtired and uncomfortable which was why she went to bed. We are going to have to do something about her wardrobe. Jane needs clothes that will help her to relax in the heat.'

'I could do with a few new dresses too.' Kath smiled and imagined spending money on clothes. She could almost hear the grind of the rusty lock on Jim's wallet. Well, what the hell? It was her time now, and she was going to make the most of it. Kath flung back the drapes and opened the doors wide. 'Wake up, Jane!' she called out, 'we're off on a jaunt!'

Chapter Six

The friends didn't have to trudge far to find their driver for the day. With enormous relief, Jane flung her hot and perspiring body onto the rear seat of a taxi that waited for customers beyond the Port Authority gates. She tugged at cotton trousers that bunched uncomfortably and pulled at a T-shirt that clung to her skin.

Anne negotiated a rate with Errol, their host for the day, and he assured her he would give the ladies a tour they would never forget.

'Are you sure he's trustworthy?' Kath whispered to Anne. She wore a sleeveless top and knee-length cotton shorts and placed her heavy bag on the floor as she climbed into the car and slid alongside Jane.

'What could go wrong?' Anne said as Errol secured the door and ran around the vehicle to the driver's side. 'There are CCTV cameras by the port that have captured us getting into the taxi. We're quite safe.' She looked through the window and smiled.

Jane raised her eyebrows, and Kath shrugged.

Errol explained that he was a knowledgeable guide, born and raised in Barbados. He knew all the hidden treasures found by veering off the beaten track. 'Safe man, safe,' he muttered as he pulled away from the port, and they began their excursion.

Jane frowned. She struggled to understand Errol. His accent was thick and opening her phone googled *Bajan Words Explained* – a complete glossary of colloquial expressions. Satisfied that she would get through the day with a perfect understanding of the local conversation, Jane settled back for the ride, silently thanking Errol for the air-conditioning in the car. After feeling so unexpectedly out of sorts the previous evening, she was determined to enjoy the day.

Errol left the highway and headed across the centre of the island. He explained that eleven parishes made up the island's geography. The friends clung on tightly as he manoeuvred his vehicle down another tricky incline or hairpin bend in the road. It was with relief that they emerged at a hamlet in the parish of St Joseph, nestling precariously on the side of a hill.

'Refreshments!' Errol announced as they tumbled out.

Kath stared out at the view ahead. It was stunning. Colossal mahogany trees lined the road, and Jane, studying a tourist guide on her phone, suggested that the area had once been part of a sugar plantation. Beyond the trees and high above sea level, they could see the land swept down dramatically. Massive waves rolled in the distant ocean, making their way with force to the shore, and Errol told her that she was looking at the Atlantic on the island's east coast.

'Goodness, it's stunning,' Kath said, 'not at all like the sea where the ship is anchored.'

'This is different,' Errol said. 'Unlike the Atlantic here, the west coast is blessed with the calm Caribbean Sea along its coast.'

'Time for a drink. I'm parched,' Anne called out, and Kath and Jane turned to see her heading into a shack made entirely of wooden pallets painted in vivid red and orange. 'Do they serve alcohol here?' she asked.

Errol smiled, 'Twenty-four-seven,' he said. 'You can buy a quart of Cockspur here at any time of day.'

'This must be a rum shop.' Jane consulted her glossary. 'Apparently, there are hundreds dotted around the island, and they provide everything from groceries and provisions to alcohol and a game of dominoes.'

They stepped into the shack, where a large woman in tight Bermuda shorts and a tiny vest sat on a stool by the bar. Cornrows of shiny black hair circled her head, and she nodded in greeting. The room was open to the elements in one corner and a group of men sat on wooden pallets, slapping dominoes onto a table.

Jane's nostrils twitched. Something was cooking and it smelt delicious.

'What's the local drink?' Anne asked Errol. Wearing

denim shorts with pretty embroidery on the pockets, Anne had knotted a gingham blouse under her breasts, revealing her tanned tummy.

'It says here, "suck-a-bubbi" is a drink you buy in a rum shop,' Jane said, reading from her phone.

The men in the corner looked up.

'I think you might get more than you bargained for if you ask for one of those.' Anne glanced nervously at the men, then turned to Errol. 'What would you recommend?'

'Try coconut water and rum,' he replied, taking note of Anne's shapely legs as she perched on a stool.

'Three of those.' Anne reached into her purse. They'd pooled money together for spending, and Anne was in charge.

Outside they sat on a bench and stared at the view. The drink was refreshing, and Jane, who was hot and thirsty, supped up and asked for another round of the same.

Errol pointed out a plantation house in the distance and explained that it was one of the first historic sites in Barbados. Today, it was a wedding venue with a distillery producing the finest rum for global export.

'If this is the same rum that we're drinking, it certainly is fine,' Jane said. 'It's one of the nicest tipples I've ever tasted.' She licked her lips and took another swig.

'Here, you can have mine,' Kath said and handed her rum to Jane. She wasn't used to alcohol, and the drink made her lightheaded.

'I'll fetch a soda,' Errol said and disappeared into the

shack. He returned and handed Kath the soft drink, then, holding out a bowl, offered her a snack.

'What is it?' Kath asked, taking a strip of deep-fried batter, and placing it in her mouth.

'Chicken gizzards, a delicacy.'

Kath began to gag and hastily dug into her bag to find a tissue. Gizzards weren't the five-star food experience she'd expected.

'Ah, that's what I could smell, how delicious,' Jane said and, grabbing a handful, began to munch.

'I think I'll pass,' Anne said and patted her flat stomach, 'but I see your appetite has returned?'

'Hmm, I felt quite off last night,' Jane replied, taking a second helping. 'I thought I had a heart palpitation at one point.'

'You'll have a heart attack if you keep eating those types of snacks,' Anne reasoned as she thought of the calories in the batter Jane was crunching.

Jane licked her greasy fingers and rubbed them on her trousers. She took another swig and found the rum comforting. It gave her an inner glow, and, feeling very relaxed, she was pleased that, at that moment, she didn't care about her size and uncomfortable clothing. She picked up her phone and swiped until the glossary reappeared on the screen, 'Did you know that "pick-pick" is the penis?' she asked and began to laugh, 'I'm learning so much today.'

'Time to get her out of here.' Anne rolled her eyes. She hoped that the men playing dominoes hadn't overheard

Jane's remark, and with Kath, they took an arm each and guided Jane back to the taxi.

'Safe man, safe,' Jane giggled.

Errol cranked the engine and set off again. He drove to a pier where the sea lapped against several small fishing vessels. White egrets, wings flapping, swooped over the water, and cried out overhead. Instructing his passengers to follow, Errol led them into a large shed. 'Meet Carnetta,' he said and raised a hand to acknowledge a woman working at the far end.

Carnetta, in white overalls, held a knife and was busy cleaning and gutting fish. Her fingers were bloody as she waved a sizeable beefy forearm. 'Yo, big man! Yu want flying fish?' she called out.

'Flying fish?' Kath asked, her brow furrowed.

'Another local delicacy,' Errol replied. He pointed to a counter where layers of pre-cooked fish sat on slabs of ice. 'You must try it.'

Jane was intrigued. She'd attempted to prepare this delicacy for a West Indian chef on lunchtime TV. But as she tasted the pure white flesh marinated in fresh herbs and spices, she knew she'd been way off the mark with the recipe. Nothing could replicate the real thing.

Carletta explained that the herring-like fish could glide through the air and spread its fins, so it appeared to be flying to escape from predators. She motioned with her bloody fingers. 'It sure stops the big fish bitin'.' She beamed.

Errol headed east for their next stop. The coast featured

rugged stone formations with panoramic views and was a perfect journey for the sightseers, with undulating landscapes and rustic scenery. He parked under overhanging trees beside a secluded cove where a natural pool lay ahead, enclosed by low-lying cliffs.

They stared out at the calm blue waters.

'You want to swim?' Errol asked as they piled out.

'I'm first in,' Anne called out and stepped out of her shorts. She untied her blouse and revealed a pink bikini.

'I've got a swimsuit in here somewhere.' Kath rooted about in her bag and beamed when she found one. Once aqua blue, the garment was faded and worn, but Kath didn't care as she reached for a towel.

Jane puffed out her cheeks. She longed to dip in the water, but she hadn't swum for ages and could hardly swim fully clothed as she hadn't anything suitable to swim in.

'Did you bring a spare T-shirt?' Kath asked, sensing Jane's discomfort.

'Yes.'

'Well, slip it on,' Kath encouraged, 'there's no one here to watch us change.'

Jane looked around the deserted beach. Errol had disappeared into the folds of a hammock slung between two trees, and circles of grey and white smoke drifted above his prone body as the hammock gently swayed.

'Oh, sod it,' Jane said as she stood on the pink and white sand. 'Why not?' she exclaimed and, in moments, had flung off her clothing and slipped the T-shirt over her head.

'You only live once!' Anne shouted as she splashed

about in the waves, encouraging her friends to join her. 'Dive in, it's gorgeous.'

Holding hands, Kath and Jane strode across the beach. They gasped as they waded into the water, but like children, they were splashing about in no time.

'This is heaven,' Kath said as she lay on her back and stared at the sky, swishing the smooth sea with her fingers.

'It's what holidays are made of.' Anne laughed.

'Look at me,' Jane giggled, and as Kath and Anne watched, she gripped the edge of her T-shirt and pulled it over her head.

'Bloody hell…' Kath gasped.

'Well, I never!' Anne laughed.

'Seize the day!' Jane cried as her bare breasts bounced and her broad buttocks dipped beneath a wave. She emerged triumphant and punched the air. The sun smiled from the heavens, and their sing-song words echoed around the little cove.

'What happens on the island, stays on the island!'

Chapter Seven

Selwyn had begun his day with a satisfying breakfast in the Deck Café. Sitting at a table under a canopy, shaded from the bright sunshine, he'd enjoyed a pleasant conversation with Harold and Nancy, the couple from Yorkshire he'd met the previous day, who told him they were celebrating their ruby wedding anniversary. Coincidentally, they had booked the same excursion as Selwyn. They were looking forward to leaving the ship to board a coach to take them to Harrison's Caves, located in the middle of the island. Harold explained that Nancy suffered from motion sickness, and outings such as swimming with turtles or a catamaran trip weren't suitable. Selwyn wondered why Nancy had chosen a holiday on a ship for their big celebration but decided to keep his thoughts to himself.

Diwa assured Selwyn that he'd enjoy Harrison's Caves. As he sat in a comfortable seat on an electric tram, which navigated the maze of tunnels in the enchanting caverns, he admired the natural formations of stalactites and stalagmites. Selwyn was spellbound as the guide explained that these wonders had been forming for hundreds of years. He heard Nancy gasp as they rode alongside underground waterfalls, while at the same time, Harold, clutching hold of a handrail, stated that he felt he was on a magical Disney ride.

Back in his cabin, Selwyn remembered the beauty of the aquamarine pools and smiled as his fingers reached into a pocket and took out a small, zippered plastic pouch. 'Did you enjoy your day out?' he asked and lay the empty bag alongside the Typhoo Tea tin on his dressing table. He wondered what Flo had made of the cool silky water as he'd scattered a handful of her ashes into the pool. Flo had never been a swimmer and was probably cursing Selwyn for her unexpected dip.

Later in the afternoon, Selwyn enjoyed a relaxing couple of hours by the ship's pool. Now, he was changed and ready for the evening ahead. Dinner would be in the Terrace Restaurant again, and he had to admit that he was looking forward to it. He'd certainly worked up an appetite.

Smoothing his loose hair, Selwyn felt the thick dreadlocks fall freely across his shoulders and wondered if his dinner companions would be the same as the previous evening. Bridgette was eager to share her extensive horticultural knowledge, and he'd enjoyed talking to her. They'd also spoken confidentially about the merits of growing marijuana. Bridgette explained that she'd been experimenting at her home in Lancashire, a manor house with a magnificent garden that she opened to the public. She'd retained a series of old iron pipes in her Victorian greenhouse, fuelled by an original stove. The heat provided ideal growing conditions in a sheltered spot. Sophisticated lighting ran twenty-four hours a day from a combination of solar panels and electricity generated for the manor by a wind turbine. Selwyn was impressed. The herb was for her private use and she told him it had been most beneficial for her grief and mood swings since she'd lost her beloved husband, Hugo, almost a year ago. A heavy cold had turned into pneumonia, she'd explained, and Hugo's demise was swift.

Though sympathetic to Bridgette's loss, Selwyn chuckled as he dabbed aftershave and admired his reflection. He doubted Bridgette would share that little nugget of helpful 'pot' plant information in her talks.

Satisfied with his appearance, Selwyn set off to enjoy his evening entertainment of a cocktail in the bar, followed by a fine dinner. A cabaret in the Neptune Lounge would feature a female vocalist, and the night would be completed with entertainment by Dicky Delaney.

Earlier, by the pool, he'd read the opening chapters of *Dicky Delaney – My Life in Show Business* and was keen to see the comedian perform his comedy routine. Selwyn wondered how much of the book was real or if the author's life was as fanciful as the words suggested. Dicky had written about well-known venues he'd appeared at over the years and name-dropped celebrities he'd worked with.

Seeing the comedian come to life would be interesting, and he hoped the show would be entertaining.

Approaching the bar, Selwyn noticed The Captain sitting at one end. The old boy raised a glass and invited Selwyn to join him. 'Put it on my tab,' The Captain said as Selwyn ordered a drink.

'Have you ventured far today?' Selwyn asked.

'Eh?' the Captain looked puzzled. His eyes were hazy as he stared at the newcomer.

'Been off the ship?' Selwyn walked his fingers on the bar top.

'Ah … no, my friend, I've been too busy on the bridge with the chief engineer, in preparation for sail away.'

Selwyn noted the Captain's T-shirt. Today, the logo read *Travelling the World, One Cruise At A Time.* He wondered how long the Captain had been at sea. Perhaps it was true that the elderly gentleman spent his later years sailing around the globe from one ship to another, fantasising about captaining the vessel.

'What time is the midnight buffet?' the Captain asked. He glanced at his watch and drained his glass.

Selwyn smiled. 'Plenty of time yet,' he replied and asked the server for refills.

'Don't want to miss it.' The Captain rubbed his stomach. 'It's been a busy day.'

Selwyn charged their drinks to his account and patted The Captain on the shoulder. He thanked him for his company and said he would see him later. Minutes later, he was one of the first to arrive at the Terrace Restaurant, where Nathaniel showed him to his seat.

'You can change tables, if you prefer.' Nathaniel explained that guests didn't have to sit with the same dinner companions each evening.

'I'm happy here,' Selwyn replied and leaned back in his chair to watch the arrivals suddenly filling the room. After a day ashore, many had sun-reddened faces and elated expressions. He wondered if the three ladies who'd dined at his table the previous evening would be joining and hoped they would. Anne, the pretty blonde, had mentioned an island tour, and he looked forward to hearing about their adventure.

'Cooee!' A voice called out, and Selwyn saw Bridgette approaching. 'I could eat my hat, I'm so hungry,' she said as he pulled out a chair, towering over the petite woman. Dressed in a floor-length gown patterned with leaves and foliage, Selwyn thought Bridgette resembled one of the many plants she spoke about so knowledgeably.

'I've been up on the crew deck all day, practising my talks,' she said as she slid in beside him. 'Hotter than hell up there, no shade, but I've topped up my all-over tan.'

Pouring water for them both, Selwyn did a double-take, 'All over?' he asked.

'God, yes, good to be at one with nature,' she replied. Ignoring the water, she reached for a bottle of wine. 'I told the purser that I must have my own private corner, away from prying eyes.'

Selwyn nodded, confident that the purser wouldn't refuse this bossy little woman.

'There's plenty of room up there, if ever you care to join me.'

'Er, thank you, I'll remember your kind invitation.'

Selwyn reached for the wine too. The image of a fully exposed Bridgette required something more robust than water. He visualised her strutting about in the sunshine as she rehearsed her lines.

'I took to naturism whilst staying at a spa, it's so freeing,' Bridgette explained.

And as Selwyn sipped his sauvignon, he wondered what the next revelation would be.

Kath, Jane, and Anne entered the restaurant and greeted Nathaniel like old friends. 'How beautiful you ladies look,' the maître d' said as he guided them. 'The sunshine suits you.'

Kath gave Anne a knowing look. Earlier, they'd given Jane a pep talk, encouraging her to be more outgoing and friendly with the other guests. As they sat down, they left Jane no choice but to sit beside Selwyn. Unable to manoeuvre away, Jane bit her lip and acknowledged Selwyn and Bridgette, forcing a trace of a smile.

'My word,' Bridgette exclaimed, 'you've brought sunshine into the room.' She was wide-eyed at the transformation of Jane and Kath, who wore gowns in a kaleidoscope of colour. 'I take it that you discovered the west coast boutiques on your day trip?' Bridgette smiled her approval. 'My favourite designers are at the Lime Grove mall.' Bridgette touched her waist and stroked the gold H of her Hermes belt.

'We had a wonderful shopping trip,' Kath interjected. She was reluctant to explain that Errol, acting on their request for a shopping spree, had taken them to a tiny back-street shop way off the tourist route in a salubrious area of Bridgetown, a million miles from the expensive designer stores that Bridgette mentioned. 'Our driver took us to a very exclusive shop specialising in bespoke garments,' Kath assured Bridgette.

Kath wove a tale about their exclusive shopping experience. But as she smoothed the skirt of the new dress, she remembered the purchase of the outfits.

Following their beach exploit, they'd climbed back into the taxi, which Kath had nicknamed the weed wagon. 'Errol likes his whacky baccy,' she'd whispered, wafting her hand to ward off the fug as Jane eased a window open.

Focusing on the road, Errol puffed on the remains of a spliff he'd begun whilst relaxing in the beach hammock. Anne, sitting forward, closed her eyes and inhaled deeply, 'It takes me back to being down-route in Lagos.' She grinned. 'Wonderful stuff, I lost three whole days...'

'And you in charge of a first-class cabin.' Kath tutted.

Kath listened now as Anne, joining in with the duplicity, explained to Bridgette that their driver had taken them to an exclusive boutique. She failed to describe the dark, poky room that Errol had led them to at the back of a derelict building. Jane was about to bolt, but Kath and Anne, both nervous too, frogmarched her into the room, stacked high with bales of cloth, where an old Singer sewing machine stood in one corner.

'Er, we need something bright and comfortable for our friend,' Kath stammered as a colossal woman came forward. She towered over Jane in both girth and height, her eyes like satellites as she stared at the trio.

'Whatcha bought me?' the terrifying figure spoke to Errol.

'Auntie, these ladies need your help, I come back soon,' he replied and disappeared into another room.

With beefy hands on her generous hips, Auntie circled Jane. She pursed her full lips and nodded, 'As yuh land, yuh come ashore...' she said, eyeing Jane as though mentally measuring her size.

'What did she say?' Jane asked and crossed her arms across her chest to form a barrier between herself and the female, who circled a finger intimately around Jane's middle.

'I think she means she's going to utilise whatever resources she has,' Kath replied. In truth, she hadn't a clue what Errol's auntie meant, but, with any luck, she'd sort Jane out.

Auntie disappeared. Within moments, she returned with a length of grey fabric in her hands and indicated that Jane take off her T-shirt and trousers. Encouraged by Kath and

Anne, who pulled at her clothing, Jane soon stood in the middle of the room in her bra and knickers.

Auntie knelt and manipulated the fabric into place. Her lips gripped pins snatched at with nimble fingers as she moulded a garment around Jane. Looking around the room, Auntie stood and selected a bale of fabric. Sharp scissors tore a neat length, and, unpinning her pattern from Jane's body, she sat at the sewing machine and began to work.

'How long will this take?' Jane wailed. 'Can't we go and find Errol and head back?' She hated all the attention and dreaded what was coming. There was little chance that this local woman could create anything to enhance Jane's appearance.

'Give her a chance.' Kath spoke firmly. She was fascinated by the seamstress at work.

Time seemed to drag as the machine pedal squeaked beneath Auntie's slipper-encased feet. Kath wandered over to a clothes rail and, lifting a hanger, unfolded a garment. 'Can I try this?' she asked and looked hopefully at Auntie.

'Sure t'ing, lady.'

Eventually, Auntie triumphantly held up a dress. She marched across the room and, turning the garment to the right side, slipped it over Jane's shoulders and watched it fall softly into place.

'G… gosh!' Jane stammered. Her mouth fell open as she felt the soft, colourful fabric melt over her body.

Auntie produced a full-length mirror that had once been part of a wardrobe. Rusty hinges hung loosely on one side. She laughed as Jane twirled and swung the skirt of the dress. Her silhouette appeared slimmer, and the cut of the dress made Jane appear pounds lighter.

'Oh, Auntie!' Jane exclaimed. 'You're a miracle worker and I absolutely love it!'

'If greedy wait, hot will cool.' Auntie smiled, her expression now soft and warm.

Kath looked bemused. 'I take it that patience is rewarded,' she said and nodded her approval.

'You look fabulous!' Anne beamed as she watched Jane hold out her arms and hug Errol's auntie.

Jane's eyes were bright as Errol strolled into the room. 'Lookin' good,' he said, 'how many dresses do you want?'

'Can Auntie make more?'

'As many as you like, and I'll deliver to the ship before you sail tonight.'

'Whatever she can produce in lots of different colours.' Jane agreed to a price with Errol.

'I'll take three of these too,' Kath said and held out the garment that had fitted her perfectly.

As Kath began to eat her dinner, she glanced at Jane. Her friend spoke to The Captain, who'd arrived late, gripping his walking aid. Jane's shoulders were relaxed, and the tension she usually wore around strangers appeared to have lifted. The colourful dress suited her. It softened her skin tone, unlike the harsh, ageing blacks and browns she customarily favoured.

With any luck, Kath thought as she tucked into a delicious chunk of salmon fillet, Jane's new wardrobe would help her to enjoy the days ahead.

Chapter Eight

Dicky Delaney sat backstage in the Neptune Lounge and stared at his face in the illuminated mirror. Tinted and tanned, he smiled his approval. 'Not bad, not bad at all,' he said.

The room was small and littered with female garments draped over an adjacent chair. Lipsticks, mascara, and eyeshadows covered the dressing table. Reaching out, Dicky grabbed a tube of bronze makeup and smoothed a layer onto his skin. He shared a dressing room with Melissa Montana, the ship's leading vocalist, who was the untidiest woman he'd ever known. But Dicky saw no reason not to use her cosmetics. Gone were the days when he had a private area. Regardless of gender, artistes now had to bunk up and divvy the facilities.

Eyeing Melissa's concealer pen, he dabbed the tip onto the shadows under his eyes. Dicky considered brushing translucent powder onto his cheekbones. 'Best not.' He grinned and gave his reflection a cheeky wink. 'I don't want to leave evidence on anyone's pillow.'

He thought of the passengers he'd met as he wandered around the ship. As usual, women outnumbered men, and there was a good percentage of singles. Mostly retired, widowed and wealthy, they needed entertainment and Dicky's stomping ground would prove fruitful during the cruise. His victims never spoke of their illicit relationships. They were too embarrassed to admit being sexually active and deceived out of money, and Dicky had enjoyed scores of deceptions over the years. Only once had he narrowly missed being pursued by an angry husband. But the ship had docked, enabling Dicky to disembark and speed away.

Dicky removed the towel he'd placed in the collar of his crisp white shirt to protect the fabric from makeup. Pushing his chair back, he stood and fastened his cuffs, then, taking a deep breath, rolled his shoulders and slowly circled his head.

A knock on the door alerted Dicky, and a voice announced, 'Ten minutes to showtime, Mr Delaney.'

'On my way,' Dicky replied and reached out to remove his jacket from a wooden hanger. The jacket had sparkling lapels, which matched a similar strip on the side seam of his trousers. As he tied the laces on his shoes, Dicky saw his face in gleaming black patent. He picked up a bottle of spicy lemon aftershave and, closing his eyes, sprayed generously.

'Five minutes, Mr Delaney!'

Dicky straightened up. He took one last look in the mirror and then patted his pockets for his notes. Not that he'd need any prompts, he'd performed this routine a hundred times to similar audiences and knew that they would be eating out of his hands.

Opening the door, Dicky stepped out.

At the side of the stage in the Neptune Lounge, he peeped out of the curtains. It was a first-night full house. The audience erupted as Melissa Montana hit the high note of her closing song to cheers and whistles.

'Beat that!' Melissa smiled as she stepped off the stage and bumped into Dicky.

'I'll have them standing on their seats, begging for more and clawing to get at me,' Dicky flashed a smile.

'Not with that stink you're wearing…' Melissa wrinkled her cute little nose.

'Watch me…'

'Is that my concealer on your eye bags?' Melissa jerked her head to study Dicky's face. But Peter was announcing Dicky's act, and as the band struck up an introduction, Dicky escaped. He blew Melissa a kiss and stepped out into the lights.

'Ladies and gentlemen, let's hear a big round of applause for our number one cruise ship entertainer. Here's Dicky Delaney!'

After dinner, guests were invited onto the decks as the *Diamond Star* gently eased out of the dock, and they gazed out at the inky star-studded sky. On the quayside, a steel band began to play a medley of festive songs to serenade the ship away from Bridgetown.

'I thought that the calypso Christmas songs were lovely,' Anne said as they headed to the Neptune Lounge for the evening's cabaret and settled on a banquette at the front of the auditorium. 'I'd almost forgotten that Christmas is only six days away.' She wore a pretty peach-coloured dress that sat just above her knees, and crossed her legs as she looked around to see if she had any admirers.

'What a relief not to be decorating the house with all my old Christmas decorations,' Kath said. 'Jim would never let me buy anything new, and I lived in fear of the ancient fairy lights fusing the whole house on Christmas morning.' She shook her head. 'Nor am I stuck in the kitchen for days cooking and baking; this is the first Christmas since my childhood where I'll be waited on.'

'Do the family always come to you for Christmas?' Anne asked.

'Always. Hugo, Henry, their wives, and offspring. Plus Jim's ancient relatives.'

'I'm surprised that you never put your foot down and refused to cater each year.'

'I couldn't argue with Jim, it was easier to just get on with things.'

They ordered drinks and noticed that the lounge had filled with guests who, like the three friends, were also looking forward to the entertainment.

'The swim this afternoon was so good,' Anne said. 'It

was such a beautiful little bay that Errol took us to, we'd never have found it ourselves.'

'We only had to ask for Shark's Hole Bay.' Jane folded her arms. 'Thank goodness Errol didn't tell us what it was called until we were back in the car. I would never have entered the water.'

'At least there were no sharks while we were swimming.' Kath said with a frown.

'But fancy,' Jane said, 'Bridgette is a naturist!'

'How do you know that?' Anne and Kath were wide-eyed.

'Selwyn told me over dinner. Apparently she has her own private area on the top deck where she sunbathes.'

'Crikey, tomorrow is a day at sea and I'm going to listen to her talk. I wonder if she'll mention it?' Anne raised her eyebrows. 'Or invite us to join her?'

'No chance,' Jane said, 'I'm not stripping off.'

'And I'm not stepping out of my swimsuit for anyone.' Kath touched her ear lobes and frowned. She'd forgotten to put her earrings on again. 'But, tomorrow, we have the whole day at sea.' She brightened. 'I loved the sail-away; the steel band was wonderful and the perfect way to leave Barbados.' She stretched out her legs and admired a pair of yellow leather sandals. Bought for her eldest son's marriage ceremony, little knowing they'd get their next airing onboard a luxury cruise ship.

'I like those sandals,' Anne commented. Their drinks arrived, and she sipped a coconut-flavoured liqueur.

'Jim hated them,' Kath replied, 'he made me change into

sensible flats on Hugh's wedding day, saying the sandals were too modern for the mother of the groom.'

'What a misery, I hope you told him where to go,' Anne said.

'I never stood up to him, he always dictated my wardrobe, and I always wore boring pumps. I felt like an old maid as the years progressed.'

Anne and Jane exchanged glances. They'd discussed the stages of grief following Jim's death, and it seemed that Kath was going through anger, but they'd never heard her disparage or criticise her husband. On this holiday, however, it was as though she was letting go.

'Just look at you now.' Jane grinned. 'We are like two colourful peacocks in our new dresses.'

'I need to do something with my hair.' Kath raked her heavy fringe to one side. 'I had an appointment at the hairdressers in Garstang before we came away. But I forgot to go.' Her eyebrows pulled together, the crease deep. 'My memory let me down again.'

'I've never been to a hairdresser,' Jane said, 'I've always cut my own hair.'

'Maybe treat yourself?' Ann reasoned. 'Your short cut is quite masculine, and white hair can be ageing.'

Jane peered at Anne over the rim of her Irish whiskey cream liqueur. She rattled the ice in the glass, then pulled a face and poked out her tongue.

Anne ignored Jane's grimace. 'There's a beauty salon on board, why don't we see if we can get appointments while we're at sea?'

'I'd be up for that; I seem to be embracing change.' Kath stroked her new dress and sipped her coconut liqueur.

'Not on your life.' Jane shook her head. 'You can dream on if you think I'm going to be tweaked and permed. My hair has got me this far just as it is. I'm sure it won't make one bit of difference to keep the same style to see out my days.'

'You shouldn't be afraid to come out of your comfort zone,' Anne said. 'You've made a start by buying brighter clothes and look how much happier you feel.'

'My hair is fine.' Jane was adamant. 'The cabaret is about to start, so let's sit back and enjoy it.'

Jane wriggled into a comfortable position and glanced around the auditorium. She could see that Bridgette was sitting next to Selwyn, a few rows away. As she stared, Selwyn looked up. His large eyes fixed on Jane, and his face broke into a smile. They'd spoken briefly during dinner, and there was something about the man that unsettled her, but she couldn't work out what it was. She wasn't good at engaging with members of the opposite sex. Most people considered Jane sexless and described her as a spinster.

As the cabaret began, Jane knew that Selwyn was still watching her and, embarrassed, she turned away.

The *Diamond Star* Dancing Troupe performed a dazzling routine for the next fifteen minutes and was joined on stage by a female vocalist. Melissa Montana had a powerful voice as she sang a repertoire of cover songs familiar to the audience, many of whom joined in. As Melissa left the stage, Peter appeared and introduced the final act of the evening.

'This comedian should be good.' Anne nudged Kath and clapped enthusiastically. 'I've seen his book in the duty-free shop.'

'Ladies and gentlemen, let's hear a big round of applause for our number one cruise ship entertainer. Here's Dicky Delaney!'

Dicky stepped onto the stage. Already, he was buzzing from the audience's warm response. The band struck up, and, taking the microphone from Peter, he launched into song.

Oh, the weather outside is frightful.
But the fire is so delightful.
Since we've no place to go
Let it snow, let it snow, let it snow.

'That fooled you!' he called out, searching the faces before him, 'you thought you were on the wrong cruise.' There was a titter of laughter as Dicky studied the audience. Confident that they were all of a 'certain age', he began his routine.

'Your pension doesn't go far on a cruise, does it?' He paused. 'Barbados, Bermuda, Aruba...' The audience began to laugh. 'The housekeeper was hoovering the floor by my cabin today, and I heard the boss say, "Can you hoover the carpet in the lift?" Dicky placed his free hand on his hip, '"What?" the housekeeper replied. "On every floor?"'

His jokes continued.

'I've had my hair cut today...'

'Which one?' Harold called out.

Dicky held his hand up and smiled. 'I've had it cut for a film, ladies and gentlemen.' He paused again. 'I'm watching a movie tomorrow.'

Relaxed at the end of a busy day and sipping drinks from the tempting cocktail list, the audience enjoyed Dicky's dated jokes. By the time he broke into his final song to end his act, Dicky had made eye contact with the most attractive woman in the room and gave her a wink as he left the stage. He'd always preferred blondes and intended to seek out the pretty woman in the peach-coloured dress, with deliciously tanned legs, who'd sat on the front row and smiled throughout his act.

As he high-fived Peter backstage, he thought, 'So far, so good.'

Chapter Nine

The Deck Café was busy as Kath, Jane, and Anne wandered amongst the early risers until they found a table under the shade of a large umbrella. The sea was calm, and overnight the soft, steady hum of the ship's engines had soon lulled them to sleep. Feeling refreshed after a good night's rest, they looked forward to the day as the *Diamond Star* made its way to Grenada.

'A whole day at sea – what are we going to do today?' Kath asked. She'd selected fresh fruit salad from the breakfast buffet and, peeling the lid from a pineapple yoghurt, spooned it into a bowl.

'I'm going to buy a book and sit by the pool,' Anne said as she nibbled on a croissant. 'My tan needs topping up.'

'Just add another layer of St Tropez mousse, it's far healthier than exposing yourself to the harsh Caribbean sun,' Jane said as she poured honey over a bowl of mango and began to tuck in. She hated sunbathing and avoided exposing her flesh to the sun.

'I always wear lots of sunscreen and I'll wear a hat, and lather factor fifty on my face,' Anne replied.

'I've never really been a fan of sunbathing,' Kath mused. 'Jim wasn't one to sit on a beach.'

'But you always looked tanned in the summer months,' Anne commented, remembering how healthy Kath looked when she sat behind the counter at the Garstang Building Society.

'Oh, that was from gardening. I spent all my spare time working on the vegetable plot – Jim liked to have everything fresh with his meals – and of course, there are the lawns and borders to take care of too.' Kath licked the creamy yoghurt. 'Jim was always busy at the office and tired when he got home. He liked the garden as an area of relaxation, and said it was an extension of the house and should always look pristine.'

Anne gave Jane a sideways look and rolled her eyes. They knew that Kath's husband had been too mean to employ a gardener. As well as running the home and working full-time, their friend had been expected to transform into Monty Don whenever she had a spare moment.

'But he spent a lot of time on the golf course,' Jane said, 'and you were a golf widow several times a year when he went away.'

'That was business. He always said the golf course was the best place to meet clients.'

'Hmm, and lovers in Barry's case,' Anne added. She sighed as she reminded them of the endless rounds of golf her husband put in with the Lady Captain.

'I didn't mind,' Kath continued, 'a garden is a very peaceful place. Nature is clever. New shoots spring up and become something purposeful.' She sighed. 'But I've made my mind up to get some help. It's too much for me these days, and I prefer to potter about and not worry about the hard labour.'

Anne reached for a slice of toast. As she spread a thin layer of apricot preserve across the crisp granary bread, she noticed that Bridgette had finished her breakfast and was hurrying from the café. 'You should go and listen to Bridgette this morning,' she said, holding up a copy of the *Diamond Star Daily* to read the activities. 'It says in the programme that Bridgette is hosting a talk entitled *How Does Your Garden Grow – On a Cruise Ship*.' Anne looked at Kath and smiled. 'You'd find it interesting.'

'I'll come with you if you like.' Jane forked bacon into her mouth.

'I hadn't really thought about all the plants onboard,' Kath said, 'but I suppose there are hundreds to attend to.' She looked around, suddenly aware of the small bowl of cacti on their table and troughs of lush greenery at the edge of the deck.

Anne continued to read from the programme. 'There's lots of things to do, from a creative writing class to a cookery demonstration, and tonight, there's a group playing in the Mermaid Theatre, they're called the Marley Men.'

'Sounds like a reggae group, I can't bear that sort of music.' Jane dabbed at her mouth with a napkin and took a slurp of coffee.

'It will be fun, something different,' Anne urged, 'we might be able to have a dance too.'

Jane groaned. She would be happy to relax in their suite. There was a gorgeous shop that sold handmade chocolates and Jane intended to treat herself.

'Well, whatever you decide.' Anne glanced at her watch. 'If you are going to Bridgette's talk, you'd better get a move on if you want a good seat, it's bound to be busy.'

'You're almost as bossy as Bridgette,' Kath said and pushed back her chair, 'but I'd like to hear what she has to say. Are you ready, Jane?'

'If I must.' Jane grabbed an iced pastry and wrapped it in a napkin. 'One for the road,' she said and tucking it into her pocket, followed her friend.

In a quiet corner of the library, a group had gathered for the creative writing class. Selwyn sat by a window, his pen poised over the blank page of a notebook. The tutor had set a ten-minute task whereby students would write a letter to a loved one, which, he said, would stimulate their creative flow.

Selwyn's creative flow was stimulated by staring out at

the distant horizon, where the sun shone rays like golden highways on an infinite blue. He wasn't in the mood to write a letter, and as his mind drifted, Selwyn was fascinated by the sea. The ebb and flow of cresting waves reminded him of the elaborate coiffured hairdo that Flo styled on special occasions.

Flo had been a great letter writer. She refused to engage with the internet, claiming it to be the devil's work, spreading folk's secrets globally. The World Wide Web would create a worldwide war, in her spirited opinion. Selwyn remembered how Flo regularly wrote to friends and distant relatives in Jamaica and across the globe. But now, since her passing, Selwyn's short emails announcing Flo's death replaced the blue airmail envelopes that bulged with updates of the Alleyne clan. All that had ceased, for Selwyn had no intention of continuing with correspondence.

He turned away from the window. His page remained blank, unlike Flo's. She spent hours sitting alone at their walnut table with a pot of tea to hand, her meaty fingers wrapped around a ballpoint pen, spewing out news to extended family, second-generation cousins, and anyone she'd met on holiday. Her round-robins at Christmas were legendary, and Selwyn often wondered if anyone bothered to read the monologue of their life in Lambeth.

Suddenly, Selwyn felt that he needed to get out of the room. Memories were too powerful and were upsetting his mood. Taking a plastic pouch from his pocket, he glanced around. No one paid him any attention, and heads were lowered over notepads. Selwyn reached out and scattered a handful of Flo's ashes into the soil of a nearby plant. 'Write to your heart's content, my dear,' he whispered.

He stood and, apologising to the tutor, hurriedly left the library.

As Selwyn walked through the lounge, he saw that Kath and Jane were approaching. Dressed in bright clothes, they were impossible to miss.

'Hello, Selwyn.' Kath stopped. 'We're off to Bridgette's talk, would you like to join us?'

'I would be delighted,' he said, indicating that they each take his arm.

Oh hell! Jane thought. She reluctantly linked with Selwyn, who wore a cream short-sleeved shirt with tropical flowers in sunny shades. His warm skin gave her goosebumps. Jane wasn't used to being so close to the opposite sex, and she felt a rush of heat colour her face as she tried to relax alongside Selwyn's rolling gait.

Kath, in contrast, gripped Selwyn. She was delighted they had a man to accompany them and chattered about plants and her love of gardening as they made their way. 'Look,' she called out as they entered the Neptune Lounge, 'there's the Captain.' She pointed to the front row. The old boy sat upright, poised with a walking stick held firmly in his hands. His T-shirt announced, *I Don't Need Assistance – I Need A Cruise.*

'That's debatable,' Jane said as they stared. 'Shouldn't he have an able-bodied companion accompanying him?'

'He may be borderline,' Kath replied, 'but the rules are

most likely bent for such a frequent traveller and Bridgette seems to spend time with him.'

'Let's go and join him.' Selwyn moved forward.

Jane found herself sandwiched between the Captain and Selwyn and hoped neither would attempt to talk to her. She felt exposed sitting at the front of a large audience and wished they'd sat nearer the back.

The room was packed, and conversation ceased as Peter walked onto the stage. 'We have a special treat for you all this morning. I am pleased to introduce a lady who has won more gold medals for her gardening skills than an Olympic team.'

He turned and held out an arm to sweep the stage, and Bridgette appeared behind the curtain. 'Let's put our hands together as we enjoy finding out, *How Does Your Garden Grow – On a Cruise Ship*. Please give a warm *Diamond Star* Welcome to Bridgette Howarth!'

Bridgette stepped out. She wore a shorter version of the dress patterned with leaves and foliage, and her neat bob was enhanced by a velvet band trimmed with ivy fronds. Jane stared at the speaker's feet, expecting to see muddy wellingtons, but Bridgette's size threes moved gracefully in a pair of nude-coloured court shoes.

Polite applause greeted Bridgette as she took her place behind the rostrum. By way of introduction, she spoke of her qualifications as a trained horticulturist. She showed images on a screen of the estate at Flaxby Manor, her palatial home, and explained that the gardens were open to the public. As Bridgette's Victorian greenhouse came into view, Selwyn was disappointed that the camera didn't delve inside to see rows of healthy marijuana plants.

Bridgette amused the audience with anecdotes that embellished her talk. Selwyn found himself smiling when she interacted with the audience by asking what they would suggest to add colour to all the green plants on the ship.

'Garden gnomes!' Harold called out, and everyone giggled.

Gritting her teeth, Bridgette ignored the heckler and described the care required to maintain the trees and shrubs on the rooftop garden.

The Captain had fallen asleep, his hat at a crooked angle and head bowed. As his snores rivalled Bridgette's voice, Jane wondered if she should nudge him awake. Bridgette appeared uncomfortable as she glared from under her page-boy fringe at the dozing dodderer, willing him to be quiet. Suddenly, one of the Captain's snores reached a crescendo and jolted him from his slumber.

'Man overboard!' The Captain cried out and began waving his stick.

'Steady on,' Selwyn said, calming the old man with a reassuring pat on his shoulder. The Captain looked confused but soon settled and, in moments, fell asleep again, his snores a gentle rumble.

Bridgette battled on. She described the care of the luscious trees and plants on the *Diamond Star* that enabled guests to enjoy a carefree aesthetic, especially bordering the pool, where they would find potted Sago palm trees.

'I'd sooner watch paint dry than stare at plants all day,'

Jane mumbled and dug into her bag to find the *Diamond Star Daily*.

'I thought that was excellent,' Kath said, enthusiastic in her applause when the talk ended, 'especially when Bridgette told us why we have holly and mistletoe at Christmas. I fancy a coffee, and we could go and find Anne and tell her all about it.'

'I'm sure she'll be riveted,' Jane replied, stifling a yawn as she read through the list of activities scheduled for the day. She brightened when she remembered the cookery demonstration. 'I shall be browsing the shops then going to watch the ship's head chef.'

'Will you be going to the show in the Mermaid Theatre tonight?' Selwyn asked.

Jane glanced at the *Diamond Star Daily* again and searched the page for the evening's entertainment. 'Hmm, that would be for the Marley Men?' she asked.

'It will be one of the highlights of my holiday.' Selwyn smiled.

'I'm sure we'll be there,' Kath said. 'We'll catch you later, enjoy your day.' She could see that Jane was scowling, and not wanting to upset Selwyn, Kath took her friend's arm and led her away.

As the women left, Selwyn saw Bridgette sitting at a table beside the stage, signing copies of her books. A banner displayed the titles *Harvesting Herbs* and *A Horticultural Hobby*. Intrigued, Selwyn wondered what herbs the gardener was prepared to harvest with her readers and, leaving the Captain to slumber on, went to chat with Bridgette and purchase a book.

Diane, the shop manager, sat beside Bridgette, taking payments. She looked up when she saw Selwyn. 'Are you a gardener?' she asked.

'I have an interest in certain plants,' Selwyn replied. He picked up a copy of *Harvesting Herbs* and gave Diane his charge card.

'Is it a gift or for yourself?' Bridgette asked.

'It's for me,' Selwyn replied.

Bridgette dedicated the book to Selwyn and signed her name with a flourish. She leaned back and, tucking a stray frond of ivy into her hairband, stared into Selwyn's eyes. 'I thought you might have stopped the Captain taking centre stage with his snores. I noticed you were sitting next to him.'

'I'm not his custodian.'

'Fair play.' Bridgette handed the book to Selwyn. 'I hope you enjoy it.'

'I shall treasure it.'

'If you fancy a bit of relaxation this afternoon, I'll be on the top deck,' Bridgette called out. 'Behind the Sago palm trees.'

Selwyn gave a thumbs-up. But he had no intention of taking Bridgette up on her offer. His afternoon's relaxation would be spent with a book by the pool. 'Fully clothed,' he whispered, and he smiled as he walked away.

Chapter Ten

O n the lido deck of the *Diamond Star*, steamer-style sunbeds curved in lines around an oval-shaped swimming pool where bodies of all shapes and sizes were sunning themselves. Any unoccupied bed was reserved, covered with a blue and white towel from a nearby stack. For those attending activities, sun hats, books, and beach bags marked their territory too, assuring a prime spot on their return.

At one end of the pool, a hot tub simmered. A well-rounded woman wearing a baseball cap and skirted tankini clung tightly to a rail before tentatively dipping her toes and sliding slowly into the water. The top of the tankini ballooned in the warm bubbles, doubling in size as she steadied herself and lay back. 'Eh, that's lovely.' She laughed and called out to her husband, 'Harold! Get yourself in here, it will do your lumbago the world of good.'

Harold stood by the edge of the hot tub with his hands

on his hips as he watched his wife splashing about. His torso was lean, the skin pale, and the fabric of his brief trunks clung where it had no right to cling. 'Steady on, Nancy,' he said, 'you don't want to set your motion sickness off.'

Lying on a bed, screened from prying eyes by a row of mini–Sago palm trees, Anne peered out from under a wide-brimmed hat and watched as Harold joined his wife. Harold's exposed skin appeared blotchy under the fierce Caribbean sun. Anne hoped he'd covered his body with a high factor cream before spending the morning by the pool. The sun's powerful rays would reach parts he'd forgotten he'd got if he didn't cover up soon.

Accepting that third-degree burns weren't her problem, Anne lay back. She'd been enjoying reading about the life of the comedian they'd seen the evening before. *Dicky Delaney – My Life in Showbusiness* was as amusing as his routine. She'd picked the book up earlier and asked the shop manager if she'd recommend it.

'The book is selling well. Passengers enjoyed Dicky Delaney's performance last night,' Diane commented. 'You'll find him wandering around the ship, if you want your copy signed.' Diane charged Anne's card before adding, 'He's quite a character. I have a feeling he'll find you quite soon.'

Anne considered this an odd comment and wanted to question Diane further, but the manager had turned away and was busy with other customers. Now relaxed and comfortable in the shade, Anne watched as an agile young female dressed in skimpy shorts and a *Diamond Star* vest appeared.

'Come on, cruisers,' she called out, 'it's time for aqua aerobics with Armani!'

Nancy and Harold heaved themselves out of the hot tub. 'On our way, Armani,' Harold replied and helped his wife into the pool.

'Armani?' Anne raised her eyebrows and wondered if Armani had sisters named Dolce and Gabbana.

Guests were crowded together as the fitness instructor began to jog on the spot, encouraging the swimmers to do the same. Several ladies in the deep end began to cough and splutter as the water rolled up their necks.

'Crikey, it's like a tsunami,' Anne giggled as bodies of all shapes and sizes bounced up and down and water spilt over the side. With no desire to plunge in and risk drowning, Anne adjusted the straps of her pretty pink bikini and reached for her tanning lotion, smoothing coconut cream over her skin. Anne enjoyed having a tan but was determined not to burn. She endeavoured to keep her face out of the sun and spent ages massaging anti-ageing potions over faint wrinkles that might tell her age.

Thank goodness for Botox, she thought, and picked up her book, placing the lotion to one side. As she began to turn a page, she was distracted. It was hard not to think about Barry and the woman that had stolen her husband. The Lady Captain had been the darling of the club with a low golfing handicap. Anne prayed that Barry would leave his new lover in as much mess as he'd left Anne. In truth,

Anne still loved Barry, if only for the man he once was and not the man he became. But why had she been such a fool? Their finances had rapidly decreased, and Anne had been unaware of his reckless spending on other women.

She watched the huddle of mature bodies bouncing about in the pool. They all looked happy and carefree, with no worries spoiling their day. Despite being determined to enjoy the cruise, Anne knew it was stretching her resources, almost to breaking point. Her wonderful friends were chipping in to help, but Kath and Jane had no idea how bad things were for Anne. The house she'd shared with Barry for most of their married life would soon be sold, his debts repaid, and if she didn't take up Jane's kind offer, Anne would have nowhere to live. She thought of how far she'd fallen and slumped onto her sunbed with a heavy sigh.

'Why is a beautiful girl like you hiding behind these palms?'

Anne turned her head. A man's voice was close. Frowning, she tilted her hat and peered over her sunglasses.

'You should be in the water, having fun.'

A shadow darkened Anne's corner, and she raised her hand to shield her eyes and see who was talking to her.

'Dicky's the name,' he said, 'but you might already know.' He pointed a finger. 'You're reading my book.'

'Oh, goodness.' Anne sat up and, moving the book to one side, sucked her stomach in. She arranged her legs in a position she'd practised many times over the years, ensuring a flattering pose. 'Er, yes, I saw you last night,'

Anne stammered, 'in the N... Neptune Lounge, you were terrific.'

'And let me tell you that I saw you too.' He crouched down, his eyes level with Anne's. 'You were wearing a peach-coloured dress and I remember thinking how beautiful you looked.'

Anne was startled. One minute she was pining for the only man she'd really loved, and the next moment she was being propositioned by a well-known entertainer. Feeling nervous, she took a deep breath and reached into her bag for a lipstick.

'May I join you?' Dicky didn't wait for an answer, and as he rose to his feet to move to the adjacent sunbed, Anne hurriedly smoothed gloss over her lips.

'Er, I think someone is already sitting there.' Anne nodded towards a towel held in place by two plastic parrot-shaped pegs. She pursed her lips in what she considered a sexy pout and held her pose despite the pain of a possible dislocated hip.

'Oh, these little birdies have flown,' Dicky replied, unclipping the pegs, and placing them some distance away. He reached for the towel draped over his shoulder and, laying it out, sat down. 'Now, what about a drink?' Dicky held up his hand and summoned a server. 'Two Double D specials,' he ordered.

'What's a Double D?' Anne asked.

'It's a Dicky Delaney cocktail, made to my own recipe. The bar crew know what I like, and you'll like it too.' He picked up Anne's tanning lotion and began to smooth it over his body.

Fascinated, Anne stared, drinking Dicky in.

The evening before, when Anne was in bed, she'd commented to Kath and Jane that she thought Dicky Delaney was lovely. He'd put on an excellent show. But now, she could hardly believe her eyes. Had Anne rubbed Aladdin's lamp? Had the Christmas fairy granted her wish? For Dicky was handsome, of slim build and the perfect height. He wore fetching shorts in a tropical print, and she noted that he looked good in swimwear, unlike many passengers. With a show business career, the entertainer was sure to be financially secure, and with no wedding ring on his finger, he ticked all of Anne's husband-hunting boxes.

As he turned to hand back the lotion, Dicky ran fingers through his thick curly hair and smiled. His teeth, a perfect white, gleamed. Cosmetic dentistry must have cost him a fortune, Anne thought and resisted a sudden urge to sit up and kiss him.

Their drinks arrived, and Dicky handed Anne a creamy cocktail decorated with mango and pineapple. 'Here's to you,' he said, biting into a chunk of ripe fruit, 'now tell me all about yourself.'

Anne took a sip of her drink, and the delicious ice-cold nectar slithered welcomingly down her throat. *'Eat your heart out, Sylvia Adams-Anstruther.'* Anne thought of her school chum and smiled. *'You can keep your double-barrels, and your tottering old men!'*

In the celebrity chef theatre, Jane was in her element. First to arrive, she plopped her bottom on a front-row centre seat and, folding her arms, waited patiently. The 'theatre' was a mobile kitchen, cleverly assembled to provide a long counter with cooking and prepping facilities. An overhead mirror enhanced the view for the audience, enabling them to watch the chef chop and stir. Jane had worked in countless similar set-ups, always behind the scenes as she carefully prepared every ingredient required for the demonstrating celebrity. She felt at home in this environment and couldn't wait to see what the ship's head chef would be cooking for them that afternoon.

Despite enjoying a buffet lunch with Kath in the Deck Café, Jane was still hungry. She reached into her bag until her fingers touched the silky ribbon tied to a box of chocolates. While digging into the handmade selection, Jane hardly noticed someone sitting beside her.

'Thought I'd join you,' Selwyn said. He crossed his legs and placed a book on his lap.

Jane was mortified. Surprised by Selwyn's sudden appearance, she'd gripped a chocolate and squashed it. Now the sticky mess was melting all over her fingers.

Selwyn was unaware of Jane's discomfort as he tapped his nails on his book and looked around at the gradually filling auditorium. 'I was going to sit by the pool after lunch and read,' he began, 'but there were no seats. Your friend Anne was there, enjoying herself,' he added.

Jane wondered what Anne was up to. She hadn't turned up for lunch, and Jane and Kath had assumed she'd wanted to stay by the pool. 'Was Anne all right?' Jane asked.

'Very much so – she was being entertained by the ship's comedian. It seems that Dicky Delaney enjoys appearances on and off the stage.' Selwyn smiled. He liked people to be happy, and it warmed his heart to see Anne and Dicky laughing and joking as a server kept them supplied with cocktails.

But Jane wasn't listening. She felt a flush creep up her neck as she wondered what to do with her horribly sticky fingers. She couldn't keep her hand in her bag throughout the session and knew that the oozing chocolate was making a terrible mess.

Sod it! Jane closed her eyes and slowly withdrew her hand. Opening her mouth, she placed her chocolate-covered fingers on her tongue and began to lick them clean. When she opened her eyes, Selwyn was staring at her.

'Good?' he asked.

'Very.'

'Care to share?'

'Why not.'

Jane pulled out the box of chocolates and offered them to Selwyn. He pondered for a moment, then chose a square-shaped fondant.

'Delicious,' he murmured and reached for another as the lights dimmed in the auditorium and a spotlight highlighted the stage.

Peter appeared and welcomed the audience, then

introduced the man they'd all come to see. 'Ladies and gentlemen, it gives me pleasure to welcome someone who makes your cruise worthwhile,' he said as a spotlight shone on the back of the stage. 'This chef has travelled the world and trained in some of the finest culinary establishments to bring you the global cuisine served on the ship.'

Jane was wide-eyed as she popped another chocolate into her mouth.

'Please give a very warm *Diamond Star* welcome to our head chef.' Peter raised his arm. 'Jaden Bird!'

The chef stepped out to enthusiastic applause, led by Jane, who clapped the loudest. Jaden Bird epitomised professionalism by wearing neatly pressed chef's whites, a colourful bandana and a starched apron tied at his waist. He smiled at the audience and thanked Peter for his kind introduction.

'The chef is from Trinidad,' Selwyn whispered. A fact Jaden confirmed as he detailed two of the dishes he was about to prepare. A tasty roti and Buljol on a coconut bake, using fresh ingredients from the island that was his home.

Jane's mouth watered as she watched the chef grate fresh coconut. The aroma of saltfish frying gently with tomato, onion and peppers was tantalising. As Jane shared her treats with Selwyn, she felt a surge of happiness. A working chef, cooking and chocolate. Jane had stepped back into her world.

Jaden explained that everyone could try these dishes at home to remind them of their holiday, and recipe sheets would be handed out at the end of the demonstration. Jane thought of the many chefs she'd worked with over the years. Not all were as handsome or talented as this olive-skinned expert, and she longed to wander into the kitchens and watch his teams at work.

But soon, the session was over, and Jane stuffed the empty box of chocolates into her bag. Selwyn was talking to Diane, who was distributing recipes. As Jane watched his tall figure stand confidently, body language in tune with Diane's, the rapport they'd shared during the demo dissolved. The companionable cosiness whilst jointly munching on Jane's chocolates had gone. Selwyn unnerved her, and she wasn't sure why. Over lunch, Kath had asked Jane why she didn't talk to him. Receiving a grunt in response, Kath had surmised that Jane was uncomfortable with any man who wasn't part of her previous working environment. It was as though she pushed them away.

As Jane crept out of the auditorium, she thought Kath was probably right. At work, Jane had hidden her size behind aprons and concentrated on doing what she did best. She was respected by chefs because she was a perfectionist, and the only weight that mattered was the weight of ingredients and perfectly prepared portions of mouth-watering food. But away from work, Jane's size had been her downfall. The monkey on her shoulder had been with her since her teens. It nagged that she wasn't good enough and whispered that no one wanted a plain fat woman as a companion or lover. No matter how many diets Jane tried, she always grew heavier than when she began. It was a burden that she carried, accepting her ever-increasing size, knowing that singledom was her lot in life. Men like Selwyn were merely being kind, and she didn't need sympathy in the guise of polite conversation.

Jane breathed a sigh of relief as she escaped and headed through the ship. She knew Kath had gone to lie down and was probably still asleep. Kath had misplaced her bag before lunch, and all hell had let loose. They'd found it in the Neptune Lounge. The Captain, still napping, had hooked the handle of his walking stick around the bag. 'Pirates!' he'd shouted as Kath woke him and gently eased her possession away.

As Jane walked along an open deck, she wondered if Anne was still by the pool. She'd look like a fried tomato if she'd been sitting out all day. Had Anne really been entertained by Dicky, as Selwyn mentioned? Or was it just two people passing pleasantries whilst enjoying the sunshine? Jane smiled. Knowing Anne as she did, it would be far more than that. Her friend's husband-hunting had begun.

Chapter Eleven

The Mermaid Theatre, at the stern of the *Diamond Star*, differed from the tiered banquette seating of the Neptune Lounge. Instead, guests could sit at circular tables grouped around the stage. The room was large, with two generous platformed areas and a well-stocked bar. At night, blinds were drawn over windows that offered stunning views during the day. The theatre's theme blended with the ship's colour palette, and both bright and bold blues reflected the sea and sky. Tiny ceiling lights twinkled, and two decorated Christmas trees stood on either side of the stage.

'Isn't this lovely,' Kath said as they took their seats at a table facing the stage. Her eyes were wide as she studied the room. 'I feel like I'm in a festive grotto and Santa is going to pop out at any moment.'

'You have to be a good girl if you want a visit from Santa.' Anne reached across the table to study the wine list.

'That removes you from his Christmas list,' Jane commented as she selected a chair without arms. Easing herself down, she wished she hadn't had a second helping of dessert. 'I heard that you were cavorting with a comedian for most of the day?'

'You've been listening to idle gossip,' Anne said and avoided Jane's penetrating stare. 'I had a relaxing day by the pool, chatting to other passengers.'

'Like hell, you were knocking back cocktails with Dicky Delaney all afternoon.'

'That's for me to know and you to find out.' Anne grinned. 'I fancy some prosecco, will you both join me?'

Jane waited for Anne to place their order and then asked, 'What's Dicky like?'

'Charming, funny, kind...'

'He's singing tonight before the main act,' Kath said. 'That's what it says in the *Diamond Star Daily*.' She'd remembered to wear her earrings and fiddled with two sparkly silver Christmas trees.

'Anne will know Dicky's timetable off by heart,' Jane added.

Not to be outdone, Anne gave as good as she got. 'I think it just goes to show that I still have the power to pull,' she said, stretching out her hand to admire her perfectly polished nails. 'Dicky is the most fanciable man on the ship, and we're meeting later to go to the casino.'

'Oh, Lord...' Kath and Jane groaned, exchanging anxious glances.

'It will be fun to have a flutter on the tables, and you never know, we might enjoy a winning streak.'

'Do be careful; it's not as though you are in a position to squander money,' Kath implored. Her voice was low as she leaned in and touched Anne's arm.

Jane was about to issue her own warning, but a man approached the table and, pulling out a chair, asked if he could join them. Tall and lean, he was smartly dressed in a neat shirt and linen trousers.

'Of course,' Kath said and shuffled her chair to make room.

He winced as he sat down, with a sharp intake of breath.

'It's Harold, isn't it?' Anne asked, 'I saw you with your wife at the pool today.'

'Aye, lass, it is, but Nancy won't be joining me tonight.'

'Oh dear, I hope she isn't ill?'

'She's suffering from her motion sickness, after all that jogging about in the aqua aerobics class, and is lying down.'

Kath and Anne made sympathetic responses.

'But you enjoyed yourself, and I can see that you've caught the sun.' Anne stared at Harold's face, which was the colour of beetroot.

'Aye, it reached parts I didn't know I had.' Harold moved uncomfortably. 'I've been to the infirmary for some lotion.' With a grimace, he pulled on the fabric of his trousers.

The curtains drew back on the stage, and a band began to play. The *Diamond Star* Dance Troupe, vibrant in Eighties costumes, began to perform an Abba medley. They stomped their platform heels and dipped padded shoulders, then circled into the audience to encourage everyone to clap and sing along with their favourite songs.

'You are the dancing queen...' Anne chanted, 'Young and sweet, only....'

'Sixty-three!' Kath and Jane sang out and laughed as Anne waved her hands to silence them. She looked anxiously over her shoulder to make sure Harold hadn't heard.

'Oh, come on, surely you're not trying to knock years off your age?' Jane said as their drinks arrived.

'Dicky thinks I am in my fifties. I couldn't help but say, "Just like me," when he told me he was fifty-five, it slipped out.'

'I shouldn't worry, it's only a holiday flirtation, he doesn't need to know your true age.' Kath stared at the bubbles in her prosecco and took a sip.

'He's probably knocked a decade off his own age too.' Jane slugged back her drink.

The dancers were coming to the end of their routine, and guests joined in with the finale song. 'Gimme! Gimme! Gimme! A man after midnight....'

Anne was singing at the top of her voice, face beaming. She wore a sleeveless white dress that had ridden up her thighs as she raised her arms and clapped.

Jane watched Harold, mesmerised by Anne's shapely legs, any pain from his sunburn now forgotten.

'I hope I haven't missed anything?' Everyone looked up to see Selwyn. He stood by the table and eased an empty

chair beside Jane. 'I want to see the Marley Men,' he said and sat down without waiting to be asked. He ordered a drink and another round for everyone. 'Cheers!' he said when the drinks arrived.

'I like your shirt, it's very appropriate,' Kath said and nudged Jane. 'Don't you think so?'

'Er, yes, it's lovely.' Jane glanced at Selwyn, her eyes averted from his face. His shirt was vibrant in red, yellow, and green stripes, and Jane realised that it mirrored the colours of her own dress. *Bugger!* She cursed herself for not giving a second thought to her outfit choice when she was getting ready. Auntie, in her wisdom, had made Jane a dress that reflected the colours of reggae music.

'We're like twins.' Selwyn laughed.

'Hardly…' Jane shook her head. She felt three times the width of Selwyn and half as tall.

'Oh, look!' Anne clapped her hands together. 'Dicky is coming on stage.'

The band played an intro as Dicky walked over to a microphone stand and gripped it in one hand. 'Good evening, everyone,' Dicky began, 'are you all having a great time?'

The audience was responsive.

'I hope you've seen my book in the shop. Don't forget to come and see me if you'd like it personally signed.' He held a copy of *Dicky Delaney – My Life in Show Business*.

'How much?' Harold called out.

'Ah, the Yorkshire war cry!' Dicky paced around the stage, pausing when the audience laughed. His timing was impeccable as he delivered his jokes. 'Women think I'm a sex god,' he said, 'they go, *sex? God...*' Unbuttoning the jacket of his suit, he continued, 'I once made love for an hour and five minutes, it was the night the clocks went forward.'

Anne giggled, and Dicky stopped at their table to smile at her, then turned to guests sitting to the left of the stage. 'Do you know that look women get when they want sex?' he asked, 'No, neither do I.'

Dicky's act continued, ending with a medley of popular songs that concluded with a song by Queen. The audience clapped along, some swaying to the tune, and as Dicky hit the chorus, he spun around to face Anne. 'Crazy little thing called love...' he crooned, ending his routine with a wink towards her smiling face.

'Eh, that was grand.' Harold applauded as Dicky left the stage.

'The main act is next,' Selwyn said and watched as technicians set up equipment and instruments. 'Now we're really going to enjoy ourselves.'

Jane didn't like reggae music and wondered if she could slip away. In his excitement, Selwyn was giving off enough body heat to light a furnace, and she'd be on fire if she stayed any longer. But she knew Kath would kick up a fuss if she escaped. Her folding fan was in her bag, and, waving it across her flushed skin, she picked up her glass, determining to make the most of things.

There was a brief intermission before Peter appeared,

and the audience fell silent as he began his introduction to the final act of the evening.

'Some of you will know that reggae music originated in Jamaica in the late 1960s and is influenced by ska, rocksteady, jazz and calypso. Its powerful music inspires people and is most appropriate as we sail around the Caribbean.' Heads turned as musicians stood at the side of the stage. 'I hope you will all feel uplifted after this evening's performance. It gives me great pleasure to introduce the Marley Men!'

Unaware of how uplifted the guests were about to be, Peter backed away as five musicians walked out, their hands raised in greeting. Dressed in vibrant tank tops, knitted headwear and deep layers of beads and bangles, they took up their instruments.

'Good evening,' the lead singer said, 'my name is Toots.' His eyes scanned the audience as he flicked long dreadlocks over his shoulder and adjusted the guitar strapped to his body. 'We'd like to start with a little song that many of you might know. Do join in.'

Jane felt Selwyn swaying beside her. She could see that his eyes were closed, and his face, upturned, wore an expression of pure joy as he sang along. Toots encouraged everyone, and as Jane continued to fan her face, she could see that Kath, Anne, and Harold had joined in too. When the song ended, Selwyn leapt to his feet, applauding wildly. He placed his fingers on his lips and whistled so loudly that Jane covered her ears.

The Marley Men had the audience in the palms of their

hands as they worked their way through their act. They played reggae and cover songs in a calypso style, and soon, most of the audience was on the dance floor. Selwyn held his hands to Jane, willing her to dance, but she shook her head and turned away. She found it difficult to watch him wind and grind. His hips had a life of their own, and his spine created snake-like movements. Surely a man of his years couldn't be so lithe and supple? As the music got louder and the audience more animated, Jane felt hypnotised as she peered around the edge of her fan.

'We're jammin'!' the Marley Men chanted as the last song was ending.

'And we hope you like jammin' too!' the audience responded. Mature arms were raised, rickety hips rocked, and chins wobbled as everyone danced.

Jane's mouth fell open when she saw Kath on her feet. She had removed her glasses and, with eyes closed, swayed her hips in time to Harold's while Dicky gyrated with Anne. But as the final chorus reached a climax, the dancers parted, and the Captain appeared in a wheelchair. Bridgette held the handles and pushed with all her might. He wore a tie-dyed T-shirt with a smiley face that read *Don't Worry – Be Happy!* Bridgette had a Jamaican flag knotted at her neck and sides, and it billowed as they zig-zagged across the dance floor.

'Good grief,' Jane muttered, 'Bridgette is naked beneath that flag!'

Peter, standing by the side of the stage, began to panic. Things were getting out of hand, and he reached out to grab a glass of dark-coloured spirits from the hand of a bemused observer. He closed his eyes, knocked it back, and, with a shudder, hurtled to intervene as the Captain and Bridgette, picking up speed, led a lively line of over-stimulated guests in a long conga. Grabbing the hips of the person ahead, the guests, singing loudly, pounded around the Mermaid Theatre, careering into everything that got in their way.

Jane rose to her feet and moved swiftly. When she reached the exit, she saw crew reinforcements hurrying to help Peter and recognised Diane, the manager of the shop.

'They'll be halfway around the ship in no time,' Jane said. 'Good luck.'

Diane stiffened her shoulders and, with a high-five, acknowledged Jane. 'Looks like we'll need it,' she called out as she followed her colleagues, 'this lot will wake up to regret their antics, and the infirmary is going to be busy tomorrow.'

Chapter Twelve

The following morning, after a good night's sleep, Jane sat in the Deck Café and studied the *Diamond Star Daily*. Her eyes wandered over the listings that detailed activities. It would be a quiet day on the ship, now berthed in Grenada. Passengers who could move about after their antics the previous evening were excited to disembark to enjoy the island and return later when the ship would sail eastwards to St Vincent.

As Jane tucked into an omelette, she made plans.

Having breakfast in her room, Kath told Jane that she'd decided to lie in following all her exertions on the dance floor. Anne was taking a leisurely bath after returning to Hibiscus in the early hours, high on her evening spent at the tables in the casino with Dicky. They'd all agreed to meet and head off to St George's, the tiny island's capital. Jane remembered that Diwa had told them about a sightseeing train outside the terminal. She explained that passengers could hop on and off, and it was a perfect way to discover the landmarks of the quaint and charming city.

'Just the job,' Jane mumbled as she buttered a slice of toast. 'I won't have to walk everywhere and get all hot and bothered.'

The café began filling with early risers eager to explore the island. As Jane munched on her toast and looked around the room, she saw Selwyn carrying a tray and heading her way. Jane dipped her head and prayed he hadn't seen her, but it was too late. He was by her side and pulled out a chair in an instant.

'Good morning,' Selwyn said, 'may I join you?'

Jane nodded. Her mouth was full, and she wiped at crumbs that had fallen onto her chest.

'You didn't join in with the dancing last night?' he asked.

Jane shook her head.

'I enjoyed myself. The entertainment reminded me that I have life in my bones, even though my bones don't thank me for it today.'

'I don't like dancing.'

'Perhaps, if you don't mind me suggesting, if you listened to reggae, the music would reach into your soul and encourage your body to move to the rhythm.'

Jane didn't want anything reaching any part of her body that involved movement. She was happy to plod along as she was.

'But you have taken the Caribbean spirit to your

wardrobe,' Selwyn added as he sat down. 'Your outfit is delightful.'

Jane swallowed and dabbed at her mouth with a napkin. Her palms were sweaty, and she wondered why she felt anxious when talking to Selwyn. 'Thank you,' she replied, 'I got it in Bridgetown.'

'Ah, yes, on your shopping trip.'

Jane was surprised that Selwyn had remembered the dinner table conversation when Bridgette had also admired her new clothes. What a bonus that trip had been. Auntie, as promised, sent Errol to the ship that evening to deliver a fabulous range of outfits that fitted Jane perfectly, including the loose and flowing trousers and matching top she was wearing today.

She sipped her tea and, peering over her cup, studied Selwyn as he drank a coffee and ate muesli topped with fresh fruit. Jane thought he was a very dapper dresser. Dark dreadlocks tumbled across the shoulders of his pale blue Oxford shirt and he wore bright red braces. He looked good in jeans that Jane suspected had a designer label. Selwyn smelt of spices, as inviting as the taste of an exotic dish, and Jane felt the now familiar twinge of unease that always unsettled her when he was near. Glancing at his dreadlocks again, she raked her fingers through her short crop and wondered what it would feel like to have hair as long and heavy as Selwyn's.

Noticing a small badge pinned to his lapel, Jane squinted as she studied it.

'You're wondering why I have the Jamaican flag on my

lapel?' Selwyn pushed his bowl to one side and reached for a croissant.

'Well, not really … er … yes?' Jane stammered and gulped her tea. She was cross with herself for being caught out and felt her cheeks burn.

Selwyn smiled. 'You're very pretty when you blush.'

Jane was mortified. She wanted the floor to open and swallow her up, away from this man who completely unnerved her. Battling to stay calm and not appear rude by leaving the table, she decided to ask him about the badge.

'It represents my heritage,' he replied, pausing between bites of fluffy pastry. 'My parents came from Jamaica, arriving on the *Empire Windrush*, in 1948. They arrived at Tilbury docks and settled in Lambeth.'

Jane forgot her discomfort. She'd heard about the passage of West Indian people who bravely left their homes to find a new life in Britain and was keen to learn more. 'Were you born in Lambeth?' she asked.

'Yes, in the 1950s, along with my siblings. We grew up in a very cramped two-up and two-down terraced house, but despite the lack of space, it was a very happy family.'

'What did your father do?' Jane shuffled in her seat and sat forward.

'He managed to find work as a bus driver and my mother trained to be a nurse.'

'You must be proud of them. It was a very courageous move to come to a strange and perhaps, at that time, a not so welcoming country.'

'My father had been a gunner in the RAF during the

war, he thought Britain would be the promised land.'
Selwyn nodded his head.

'And was it?'

'In many ways it gave them a better life than they might
have had in Jamaica, but they never strayed far from the
community that had settled in Lambeth.'

'Is that where you live?'

'Yes, born and bred.' Selwyn laughed. 'I married young
and worked for London Transport, eventually becoming a
tube train driver.'

'That's a good job.' Jane sat back and placed her hands
on her lap. The remains of her toast lay uneaten.

'Not really, under the ground in dark tunnels all day
isn't the best place to be.'

'I didn't think of that, but I'm sure you're a very capable
driver.'

'I was. I'm retired now. My parents wanted better for
me, but our first daughter was on the way, and I needed to
provide for my family. The years somehow seemed to slip
away without me realising that life was also passing me by.'
Selwyn ate the last of his croissant and wiped a finger
across his lips.

'Did your wife have a job?'

'Yes, Flo worked for the council, she was a domestic
operative.'

Jane saw Selwyn smile again. He had a twinkle in
his eye.

'That's a cleaner to you and me.' Selwyn sighed. 'She
liked her job, but the church was her life. She died a few

months ago.'

'Oh, I'm so sorry, I didn't mean to pry or upset you.'

Selwyn turned and looked directly at Jane. 'You haven't,' he said.

Jane wondered what Flo was like and surmised that they must have been together for an eternity if they had married when they were young. What sort of woman would Selwyn have spent his life with? She was keen to hear more, but before they could further their conversation, Kath and Anne appeared and stood by their table.

Neat and cool in white shorts and a shirt with the sleeves rolled back, Anne said, 'Good morning, Selwyn, we're here to steal Jane away, and are off to discover St George's.'

'Would you like to join us?' Kath asked. She was dressed in her yellow sandals, trousers and a pretty lemon-coloured blouse and gripped her bag close to her body. 'You'd be very welcome,' she added.

'No, thank you, that's very kind, but I would like to have a day by myself.'

Kath and Anne turned away, and Jane eased out of her chair. Her anxiety was returning, but she felt she couldn't leave without saying something to Selwyn. 'I've enjoyed talking to you,' she stumbled. 'Th … thank you for sitting with me.'

'The pleasure, my dear, is all mine.' Selwyn reached out and stroked Jane's arm. 'You go and enjoy yourself.'

Jane straightened her back and tried to walk gracefully away from the table. She had the strangest feeling that a butterfly was bouncing about in her belly. With his compliments and soft touch, Selwyn made her feel special, and somehow Jane knew that his eyes were watching her departure. As she followed Kath and Anne through the Deck Café, Jane stopped by the door and turned.

Selwyn was staring at her.

The butterfly began to dance, and her hand rose automatically. Jane was perplexed and pondered on the new-found feeling, 'It must be something I ate,' she thought and waved goodbye to Selwyn.

In cabin 1101 on the lower deck of the *Diamond Star*, Dicky lay on his bed, counting a thick pile of dollars. His fingers tingled as his skin caressed the crisp new notes, and Dicky relished the feeling. Tingling fingers were a sign of better times to come. No need for lucky horseshoes or a four-leaf clover, Dicky Delaney was on a roll.

He placed his stash on the bedside table and reached for a glass which had a measure of last night's brandy. Despite the hour, the rich amber liquid tasted good. It was soothing and lulled Dicky into a sleepy stupor. Nestling into a pillow, he closed his eyes and thought about his trip. Only a couple of days into the cruise, all was going to plan. His shows, as he'd expected, were a success. The audience lapped up his dated jokes and song and dance routines, which reminded the passengers of days gone by when life was for living and old age was for the decades to come. But the decades soon passed, and Dicky recalled Cat Stevens' song that every generation had its day. He liked to think that however many days the mature passengers had left, he would ensure that all, including himself, had a good time.

For happy punters were perfect prey.

Dicky sighed with pleasure as he thought of the money accumulating in the safe at the back of his wardrobe. Private sales of his book and DVD were profitable. He enjoyed wandering amongst the guests during his free time, letting them know they had no need to purchase his merchandise from the ship's shop, where they'd pay over the odds. He had a supply of goods he could drop off at their cabin for a discounted price. He also provided a discreet service, far more interesting than reading material. Dicky had identified a handful of wealthy widows who might seek out his 'extras', and he was willing to cater to their 'special needs.' It was far more lucrative than any fee he earned from his *Diamond Star* contract, and the tips for such services could be generous. The previous day a divorcee had purchased a Tag Heuer sports watch from the onboard jeweller. She insisted that the gift be the only thing Dicky wore when satisfying her lustful desires.

It was a drowsy Dicky who thought of Anne. She was as peachy as the dress she'd worn to his first night's show, and he remembered her pretty face staring up at him as he strode across the stage. Anne was the icing on his cake. He would indulge her and enjoy her company, for she seemed to bring him luck. Last night's winnings were proof, and he'd listened as she'd told him what numbers to play on the roulette wheel. Flushed with success, they'd danced in the disco until the early hours, and for once, Dicky enjoyed the company of a lovely woman. All thoughts of life at home in Doncaster were far from his mind.

Dicky had been chivalrous and walked Anne back to her suite. He hadn't taken advantage of her and decided that he would save that treat. Maybe he wouldn't even need the help of his little blue pills when the occasion arose, and he would rise unaided. In the meantime, he would enjoy her company and make the most of slyly charging his drinks to her account. Generous tips to the bar servers enabled this con, and she'd never know until she came to settle her bill, by which time Dicky would be long gone. Whatever trick he pulled, he felt safe knowing that acute embarrassment would prevent women from outing him. Their Dicky Delaney escapade would be put down to a holiday jape or an unfortunate mistake.

Dicky opened his eyes and glanced at his shiny new watch, then heaved himself upright and, with a yawn, stretched out his arms. After a rehearsal in the Neptune Lounge for the evening's show, the day was his own. Most of the passengers would have disembarked to discover the delights of Grenada, and there would be an abundance of empty beds by the pool. Dicky could top up his tan undisturbed. He might even treat himself to a facial with the pretty beautician in the *Diamond Star* Marine & Wellness Spa, who'd told him to drop by when the passengers were ashore.

Crumpled clothes lay discarded where he'd fallen into

bed a few hours earlier. Stepping over them, Dicky could hear his wife nagging him not to be so untidy. Still, as he cast a soiled shirt to one side, he was safe in the knowledge that the *Diamond Star* provided attentive housekeeping. Everything would be sent off to the laundry and delivered back before nightfall, clean and pressed.

Striding into the bathroom, he reached for a towel and turned the shower to full power. Dicky stared at his reflection in the mirror and thought of his spoils so far, 'Dicky,' he said and removed the expensive watch on his wrist, 'you're on your way and will soon be back in business!'

Chapter Thirteen

It was mid-morning when Selwyn decided to leave the ship. With a few late risers, he negotiated the ship's security and customs procedures and, draping a jacket over his shoulders, walked along the long pier leading to the heart of St George's. A tourist information kiosk offered leaflets detailing shops and duty-free stores. The smiling staff assured him that dazzling Colombian emeralds or beautiful Milano glass made excellent souvenirs.

Selwyn soon found himself on the historic St George's main street, where he ignored the sightseeing train that slowed beside him. He dismissed offers of a water taxi to take him to Grande Anse Beach, which he'd heard was one of the most beautiful in the Caribbean. Ahead, there was a market selling produce. He wandered through the bustling stalls piled high with fresh fruit and colourful vegetables and was reminded of the street market in Brixton, just a seven-minute tube ride away from his home.

West Indian voices encouraged Selwyn to buy.

'Yuh try my lead pipe!' a vendor called out, and Selwyn gave in, parting with two dollars for a cake made with freshly grated coconut, sugar, and flour. The sweet treat was delicious and prompted a memory of his mother's cramped but warm and aromatic kitchen, where she produced spicy meals and tasty treats.

Heading out of the market, Selwyn wandered into a side street. Shops displayed groceries, and household items were piled high and spread over pavements. Selwyn ducked his head to dip beneath a rickety ladder as he side-stepped brushes and tins of paint and saucepans of every size, which tumbled from boxes and crates. The buzz of the street was vibrant and bonded the locals, who milled about or sat in cafés, some passing the time of day with idle conversation, others playing dominoes, slapping the tiles face down on a table. Selwyn thought of home in Lambeth, with its sizeable and buzzing Afro-Caribbean community, but in St George the pace seemed slower, and Selwyn moved at leisure, enjoying his stroll.

He came to a gallery that appeared strangely out of place amongst other businesses on the street. Peering through the window, Selwyn saw vivid paintings, and a series of portraits captured in unguarded moments caught his eye. Two lovers kissed, hands caressing each other's faces. A jogger stretched, his face showing anguish as he held his leg at a right angle on a tumbled-down wall. An unkempt old lady sat beside a pile of rags, her eyes dull, staring vacantly at a single-stem flower held in her hand.

Selwyn was fascinated by the artist's ability to capture the subjects, perfectly representing their moment in time. His eyes turned to a canvas at the back of the room, which, though small, stood out. It depicted the shape of a woman who appeared to be dancing. The stout figure, curved, overweight, and alone, was a splash of vibrant colour. Hypnotised, Selwyn was sure he could hear the woman singing as she danced. The artist had given her movement and freedom as though unlocking the staid reality of her life.

Before he knew what he was doing, Selwyn opened the door and stepped into the gallery.

'Happy Christmas to you,' a voice called out, and a man came forward. Tall, dark, and smiling, he greeted Selwyn with a respectful fist bump. 'What can I help you with?' he asked.

'I'm unsure,' Selwyn said, staring at the painting of the dancing woman. 'I just knew I had to come in.' The image stopped him in his tracks. 'Who is she?' he asked.

'I don't know, she came to me in a dream.'

'But you must know the subject?'

'Who would you like her to be?'

Selwyn didn't reply. He was fascinated.

'Some people think it is crude, a poor representation of a female.'

'I love it.'

'Maybe it's the woman of *your* dreams?'

'I'll take it.'

'Don't you want to know the price?'

'Not really, I don't want the price to influence me.'

'I think you will cherish this work more than I.'

Selwyn handed the artist his credit card. 'Please wrap her carefully,' he said and tapped his pin number into the card machine without looking at the amount.

'Look after her,' the artist said, and they bumped fists again.

'I will,' Selwyn assured the man.

He walked back to the ship with the package tucked under his arm. Selwyn wondered what on earth he'd just spent but didn't care. He knew Flo would have hated the extravagance. A substantial amount of her wages went to the church, with a percentage of Selwyn's salary. Flo had insisted on it, and Selwyn was convinced that his wife's wish had been to pave her path to eternity with her generosity and ensure a comfortable afterlife.

What would Pastor Gregory have to say about Selwyn's indulgence? He remembered that the Pastor had been against Selwyn holidaying on the cruise and had recommended a more religious retreat. So far, the only religion Selwyn had encountered during his 'retreat' was wining, dining, and dancing, and now a frivolous expenditure.

As Selwyn reached the pier, he dipped his hand into a pocket and took out his plastic pouch. Opening it slowly, he shook it and watched a handful of ashes fall to the sea's surface. 'Here's to many more impulsive acquisitions, my dear Flo,' Selwyn whispered.

Feeling jaunty, Selwyn decided to search for a water taxi.

He'd head over to Grande Anse Beach. After all, there was bound to be a bar and maybe a restaurant serving local fare. Setting off again, Selwyn looked forward to finding a relaxing setting where he could think about his painting and dream away the rest of the day.

Anne, Kath, and Jane sat on the upper deck of the *Diamond Star* underneath a canopy that offered plenty of shade. Adjacent to the poolside bar, the seating area was comfortable, with large sofas and generous reclining chairs. As passengers returned from their day in Grenada, many found seats alongside the three friends. They began to relax, recounting tales of their experiences whilst touring the island.

Jane sipped a glass of iced water and cooled her perspiring face with her fan. Her feet had swollen, and she'd slipped out of her trainers. 'My toes are like trotters,' she said as she wiggled her puffy digits. 'Thank goodness we took the sightseeing train and didn't climb all those steps to Fort George.'

'It was well worth a visit,' Kath said. 'I thought it was so interesting with all the old cannons and plaques pointing out important landmarks.'

'There was a wonderful view of the town and harbour,' Anne chipped in.

'I liked the House of Chocolate the best,' Jane said. She reached into her bag to retrieve a chocolate bar and popped a square into her mouth, 'Organic chocolate is divine. Help yourselves.' Jane placed the bar on a low table and closed her eyes. She smiled as rich, smooth chocolate melted on her tongue.

'Wasn't it a lovely place, a sort of mini-museum and café.' Kath took a square of chocolate and nibbled thoughtfully. 'The chocolate and peanut butter brownie shake was delicious.'

'Chocolate for some is like water to a plant,' Anne said and helped herself to the chocolate.

'It's good for you.' Jane opened her eyes. 'Chocolate contains high levels of antioxidants and can lower cholesterol. Some say it can even prevent memory decline.' She took another piece. 'Kath, eat up.'

'You're very knowledgeable about food,' Kath replied.

'I had to be, it was my job, but I eat too much.' Jane patted her belly.

'Let's not worry about our waistlines while we're on holiday.' Anne touched the slim belt looping through her shorts.

'Remind me where my waist is?' Jane finished her chocolate and scrunched the wrapper into a ball.

Anne smiled. 'Don't worry about it, you look great and we'll send out a search party when the cruise is over.'

'I hope the Captain and Bridgette are okay,' Kath spoke up. 'They certainly ended the Marley Men's performance with a bang.'

'I'd hardly call the Captain's wheelchair colliding into

Harold a "bang",' Jane said, 'they almost crippled him. He's lucky he doesn't need surgery.'

'It's my understanding that Harold suffers with his back,' Kath replied.

'He'll certainly be suffering today. I thought Peter was going to have a fit when Harold managed to stumble back to his feet and lead the conga line out of the Neptune Lounge and into the bar.'

'Especially when passengers having a nightcap all joined in.' Anne giggled.

Kath turned to Jane. 'Have you seen Bridgette or the Captain today?'

'No, but the Captain rarely gets off the ship and Bridgette has probably been privately promenading in the buff, up on the top deck all day. He's probably with her. They seem to be good friends.'

'Bridgette knows the Captain from previous cruises.' Kath smiled. 'Good luck to them, but more importantly, I want to know what happened with Dicky last night.' She turned to Anne. 'You haven't told us where you went, after Jane and I went to bed.'

Anne was sipping tea and reached out to top up her cup. 'I had a wonderful time,' she said.

'Well, what happened?' Kath sat forward.

'We went to the casino, and I told Dicky what to do with his chips.'

'Add plenty of salt and vinegar.' Jane giggled.

'I gave him my lucky numbers.'

'That was risky.' Kath shook her head.

'On the contrary, he won on every single one.'

'Goodness, I hope he shared his winnings with you?'

'I couldn't ask him to do that.' Anne frowned. 'He used his own money as stakes.'

Jane rolled her eyes, and Kath shook her head.

'Did you stay in the casino?' Jane asked.

'No, we went to the disco and danced until the last song played.' Anne had a dreamy expression as she remembered moving around the dance floor. It was years since she'd had so much fun.

'I hope Dicky didn't make any improper moves on you?' Kath lowered her voice. 'Men like Dicky can have quite a reputation.'

'Oh, really, you read too many silly novels,' Anne said. 'Dicky was the perfect gentleman and walked me back to Hibiscus.'

'Only a matter of time.' Jane grinned. 'He'll soon be asking if you'd like to do the dance with no pants in his cabin.'

'For someone who is determined to stay celibate all her life, you have a very racy imagination.'

'I'm a realist. Dicky Delaney spells danger to me.' Jane tugged on her top, settling the fabric over her stomach. 'It's not that I don't want you to have a great time and husband-hunt to your heart's content, but I have a feeling that he might give you grief, that's all.'

'Well, it's up to Anne what she does.' Kath gripped her bag and stood up. 'If neither of you mind, I'm going to go to

Hibiscus to have a bath before dinner. My feet are aching, and a soak would be lovely.'

'I think I'm going to have a glass of wine,' Anne said as she watched Kath walk away. 'Fancy joining me?' She turned to Jane, who, having placed a stool under her feet, had eased back into her chair.

'That would be marvellous,' Jane replied, closing her eyes. 'I'm getting used to being on holiday.'

Anne ordered and, while she waited, sighed happily and watched the sun slowly descend into a flame-coloured sky. The horizon seemed endless, dark, and inviting as the ship sailed through the infinite blue sea. 'Me too,' Anne whispered.

Chapter Fourteen

K ath lay in the tub in their bathroom and swished at scented bubbles that rose to the edge, almost spilling onto the tiled floor. She'd never known such luxury. The dated family bathroom in Garstang seemed light-years away, as did the avocado-coloured ensuite in the Bournemouth hotel where she'd spent many holidays with Jim. On the *Diamond Star*, no spiders crawled into a cracked cornice, nor was there blackened grouting and the paper-thin towels that had, over the years, seen service to countless visitors at the Sunnyside Hotel.

She wondered why she hadn't insisted that they holiday somewhere more up-market but knew that any reasoning with Jim had been pointless. Much of their money had gone when Hugh and Harry both married. Their savings were swallowed up when they'd generously given their sons sizeable deposits to enable them to take out small mortgages. Kath had insisted that they should have the best start to married life, and, to her surprise, Jim had agreed.

But that was several years ago, and Jim's meanness became his obsession as time passed. He said they couldn't afford luxuries or fancy holidays. It was the accountant in him, Kath reminded herself as she idly toyed with the bubbles in her bath. Anyone would have thought they were as poor as church mice, when in fact, as she'd recently discovered, quite the opposite was true.

Kath's salary had been paid into her own account, and she'd been responsible for the housekeeping and utility bills that took every penny she earned. Jim paid the mortgage from his account. After Jim's death, Kath discovered that the mortgage had been paid off years ago, and his savings had accumulated considerably. She liked to think that Jim had been saving to take her on a world cruise for their ruby wedding anniversary or, she fantasised, a month in the Maldives. They might have stayed in a luxurious wooden bungalow beside a tropical beach. Still, Kath knew that would never have happened.

A leopard doesn't change his spots.

But Jim hadn't known that he would pop his clogs before his time, and his accidental death was an unexpected shock to everyone. Especially Mr Clarke, Jim's golfing companion, of Clarke & Co. Family Solicitors of Garstang, who couldn't understand why Jim hadn't updated his will. Not that Kath gave a hoot. With no instructions, Jim's estate had all come to her, including unexpected life insurance. Now, she had more money than she could ever imagine.

Hugh and Harry had naturally contested the will, and Kath parted with an amount to stave off their persistent demands. She told them she'd review things when she returned from her holiday, but in truth, she had no intention of financing or being bullied into signing the house over to her money-grabbing sons.

'What the hell, it's my time now,' Kath said, splashing bubbles into the air. 'I'm going to spend the money,' she called out to the ghost of her husband. 'All those years of frugality and counting every penny are over.'

Adding more water to the bath, Kath thought about the cruise. It would have been unimaginable months ago to contemplate such indulgence. Hugh and Harry would be goggle-eyed at the display of newly purchased potions and creams on Kath's side of the bathroom shelf.

Kath had never heard of the La Prairie brand and always bought her face cream from Aldi. She thought a prairie was a grassland area in the Rocky Mountains where cowboys and buffalos roamed. But she'd discovered skin caviar in the duty-free shop when the fancy packaging had caught her eye. The sales assistant, alert to a substantial sale, explained that the cream would restore the harmony of Kath's youth by 'strengthening and re-densifying her skin's vertical pillars'. At a cost that made her eyes water, Kath fully expected her pillars to be time-warped back to her youth within minutes of application. She intended to liberally apply the cream as soon as she eased herself out of this beautiful bath.

Kath stretched out her toes to the gold-coloured tap. She

reached for the Jo Malone bath oil that the assistant had assured her would soften and nourish tired skin, and the scent of sweet almond, jojoba seed, and avocado was intoxicating. Yawning, Kath stared at the ceiling, where soft lighting gave a flattering glow and made her feel years younger. She caressed her arms, noting only faint age spots on the delicate skin.

There were no fading bruises to cover with cardigans and no aching muscles recovering from punches. Blows that had been dealt out for the slightest wrong. Jim had been a large man. Though fleshy in parts, he was solid and able.

Able to abuse his wife.

Kath thought of all those fearful years keeping their life hidden behind closed doors and the pretence in front of her children and friends. The hidden bruises. The broken wrist she explained away as a 'gardening fall'. Her false smile at the golf club garden party and Jim's Christmas office event. Wearing long-sleeved dresses with high collars and flowing hems to cover her injuries, Kath would hand out Christmas gifts to his staff, all bought with her own money.

The smokescreen for a life well lived.

Hugh and Harry hadn't a clue. They'd been financed through university and gap years and, taking after their father, both worked at large accountancy firms. Kath wondered if they took after their father in other ways too.

With a sigh, she felt the water cooling and sat up. She could hear voices. Anne and Jane had returned.

'Anyone home?' Anne called out and opened the bathroom door.

Jane stepped in and reached for a fluffy towel. 'She'll be a wrinkled prune after all this time,' and went to help Kath heave herself up.

'Not for much longer,' Kath replied and picked up a pot of caviar cream. 'You can both keep your paws off, this is my treat.'

'You deserve it.' Anne studied her face in the mirror. 'Doesn't she, Jane?'

'Absolutely, it's good to see Kath enjoy a bit of luxury.'

Kath picked up her glasses, stared at her reflection, and then smoothed the cream over her pale skin. There was a fortune on her face. She dipped her fingers into the pot and slathered more onto her neck. She could almost hear Jim's protestations and see his arm raise, about to strike.

But the cowering Kath was gone.

Standing tall and defiant, she silently thanked her pig of a husband for his untimely death. Wherever he was, she hoped that he was watching her now.

Chapter Fifteen

The following morning the *Diamond Star* made its way to Saint Vincent, the largest of the Grenadines and the gateway for visitors to the chain of small islands which lay one hundred miles west of Barbados. As the sun came up those who'd risen early to witness the arrival were greeted by long stretches of beach under a fire-red sky.

'The sky is the colour of rhubarb,' Kath said as she stood on deck and gazed in awe as pinks and golds melted into soft molten rays. 'It reminds me of my vegetable patch at home.'

'I'm not sure that Kath Taylor's rhubarb triangle compares to a Caribbean sunrise.' Jane smiled. 'Although your crumble is the best I've ever tasted.'

Leaning on the railings, they watched with interest as the ship was guided by the harbour master's boat. Crew members below busied themselves in preparation for docking at the southern end of Kingstown, the island's capital.

'I noticed that the sand was very black as we approached. Do you think it's like that on all the beaches?' Jane asked as Kingstown came into view.

'Last night, I overheard Peter telling passengers that Saint Vincent has a volcano and it erupted in April, the first time in over forty years,' Kath replied. 'Volcanic ash blanketed everywhere and caused a national crisis. It spoiled a lot of the crops.'

They stared out at the clear ocean and sunny sky. Further inland shrubs were a myriad of greens, but patches of darkened earth and skeletal-like trees, destroyed by boiling lava, could be seen amongst the lush vegetation.

'The fallout from the ash was felt as far away as Barbados, where everything was covered too,' Kath said.

'Goodness, you'd never think that happened only eight months ago.'

'Apparently, there was support from all over the world, and the United Nations stepped in.' Kath imagined the chaos on this little island, thousands of miles away from her home. She wondered why she hadn't heard about the disaster, for she avidly listened to the news. But Kath realised that it would have coincided with Jim's demise, and at that time she had her own problems to deal with.

'What a massive thing to cope with; these poor folk probably lost much of their livelihood.' Jane shook her head.

'But Mother Nature has bounced back, and things must

be getting back to normal, or we wouldn't be stopping here.' Kath straightened up and touched her earlobes, where smooth pearl studs were safely fastened. 'I'm going to take a tour to the botanical gardens. Apparently they're one of the oldest in the world.'

'If there's anything left of it,' Jane said. 'Perhaps the volcano ruined it too.'

'I don't think so. Bridgette is the *Diamond Star* guide on the tour, and she said that it will be well worth a visit if you like gardening.'

'Oh well, good luck, I'll swerve that trip, probably too much walking for me.'

'Anne is going to a beach with Dicky,' Kath said as she watched the busy crew below ensure that the ship was secure. The gangway was in place, and several vehicles arrived laden with fresh supplies.

'She must be tired. I'm sure that she didn't come to bed until the early hours. Still, at least she returned to our suite and not Dicky's cabin.'

'I believe they were in the casino again,' Kath said, remembering Anne falling happily into bed. As Jane slumbered soundly, her steady snores a soft hum, Anne had whispered to Kath that Dicky had another winning streak on the roulette table. They'd drunk champagne in the disco to celebrate. 'They are going to Wallilabou Bay,' Kath added, 'there's a tour that leaves from the port after breakfast.'

'Where is Walli ... labou bay?' Jane struggled with the pronunciation.

'It's on the west coast and was the location for the

filming of *Pirates of the Caribbean*. Dicky told Anne that the set used on the film has been preserved and there's a museum that's got lots of photos of the cast.'

'Hmm, I've never seen any of those films so that wouldn't mean much to me.'

'So, what are you going to do all day?' Kath asked and reached into her bag for her sunglasses.

'I think I'll have a stroll into the town, I've read that there's an interesting market in the centre and I'd like to have a look and maybe try some of the local dishes.'

'Well, be careful, I'm not sure if it's safe for you to be wandering around the streets on your own.'

'I hardly think anyone will kidnap me; I'd squash them to death.'

'Don't be silly, you could be robbed.'

'Not a chance, I've no expensive jewellery and my money will be secured in my fanny pack.'

'I hate that word; can't you call it a bum bag?'

'I don't wear it on my bum.'

Kath sighed. Her friend could be impossible, and she wished she would come on Bridgette's tour. But Jane was more interested in sampling local delicacies, and who could blame her? Cooking had been Jane's life. It was her passion. Kath secretly thought it must be wonderful to feel so strongly about something. Although she enjoyed gardening, Kath couldn't honestly say it was her passion.

Jane turned away from the activity on the quayside and, checking her watch, announced, 'Let's go and get some breakfast. We can wake Anne up and hear all about Dicky.'

'Good idea,' Kath smiled and, taking Jane's arm, strolled back to Hibiscus.

―――――――――

Jane took her time after breakfast and wasn't in any hurry to leave. She'd helped Kath get ready for her tour of the botanical gardens by making a checklist of the contents of Kath's bag. This included her glasses – two pairs, insect repellent, a personal alarm, glucose sweets, sticking plasters, deodorant and a spare pair of socks and knickers. As Kath added a large bottle of water and a notebook, Jane wondered at her strength in carrying the bag around. But as she sat on her bed, she was diverted by Anne preparing for her day too. For some reason, Anne was taking for ever to decide what to wear for her date with Dicky.

'You'll miss the coach if you don't pull your finger out,' Jane said as she watched Anne discard another dress on her bed.

'I want to wear something I'm comfortable in, and we're bound to go swimming.' Anne picked up a bikini and packed it into a beach bag with a towel and sunscreen.

'A pair of pirate's breeches and a waistcoat would do. I'm sure Kath has an eye patch in the depths of her bag,' Jane commented, 'and I've got a scarf you can tie around your neck.'

'You are going to the setting of a film,' Kath said as she rummaged amongst her sweets and socks, 'you could be an extra.'

'Very funny. It isn't a fancy-dress outing, I don't have to look like a pirate,' Anne snapped, 'and the set hasn't been used for years.'

'Why not? Dicky would look good as Jack Sparrow, he's certainly cunning enough to play the part.'

'I don't know what you have against Dicky,' Anne said as she tried yet another outfit. 'He's a very decent person.'

'He's an entertainer and spends his life on the road. I don't want you to be hurt when he suddenly sails off into the sunset.' Jane wanted to add that Dicky had all the qualities that Barry possessed, from flirting and being fanciful to carelessness with money. Jane had never trusted anyone who spent time in a casino. She'd seen too many chefs gamble away their income over the years. 'He's not really husband material, is he?' she added.

'Well, I'm enjoying myself and he's good company.' Anne pressed her lips together, refusing to be drawn further. She smoothed her hands over the fabric of a cotton sundress that skimmed her hips, then slipped her feet into her jewelled sandals.

Comfortable in an armchair, Kath dug deeper into her bag. 'I *have* got an eye patch,' she called out, triumphant as she held up a small fabric circle. 'There's one in my medical kit.'

'Oh, for heaven's sake!' Anne was exasperated. 'You two are as bad as each other.'

Jane looked at her watch. 'You're both going to be late. Come on, I'll walk to the quay with you.'

They left Hibiscus and disembarked, and Anne beamed

when she saw that Dicky was waiting for her by the gangway.

'This way, darlin',' Dicky called out and waved his hand. Smartly dressed in checked shorts and a white T-shirt, he wore Ray-Bans and a Panama hat.

'Ahoy there, matey!' Jane called out and winced when Anne punched her arm.

Kath studied the crowds and smiled when she saw Bridgette standing beside a coach, ticking names off a list. 'That's me,' she said, 'see you both later.' Hauling her bag over her arm, Kath set off.

Jane stood alone. Already the sun felt hot. She flipped her fan and began to wave it across her face, then wondered which direction to take for the market. She was about to ask a crew member when someone touched her shoulder. Spinning around, she jerked her head back and did a double-take.

Selwyn, wearing a red Fedora, bright cotton shirt and linen trousers, stood to attention before her. He was accompanied by Toots from the Marley Men. 'Kath told me that you were heading into Kingstown by yourself,' Selwyn said. 'She asked me to accompany you.'

'Oh … whatever for?' Jane silently cursed Kath. She was perfectly capable of organising her day out and didn't need any assistance from Kath. Jane wasn't used to going anywhere with a man, and making conversation made her nervous.

'Your friend thought you would feel safer if you had someone with you.'

'I really don't think—'

But Selwyn interrupted. 'I would personally feel happier knowing that you weren't on your own. It's not unheard of for passengers to experience problems in environments they're not used to.'

Jane wondered why Selwyn didn't just say that a plain, overweight woman on her own was perfect prey for any pickpocket or hustler. She gritted her teeth and wondered how on earth she could wangle her way out of a day spent in his company. There was something about Selwyn that unsettled her, and his presence had a peculiar effect on her tummy. The butterflies were back and fluttering uncontrollably. Surely, she couldn't have feelings for Selwyn. Jane had long forgotten what 'feelings' were. It was years since she'd been on a date, which had been so disastrous she'd vowed never to put herself in such a vulnerable position again.

'Toots and I are taking a stroll into town, and we'd be honoured to escort you,' Selwyn said.

'Sure thing,' Toots agreed as both men stood on either side of Jane and held out their arms.

'Oh heck,' Jane whispered as they set off. She'd have a few words to say to Kath when they all returned to the ship, but in the meantime, Jane willed herself to act as though she was used to the company of two handsome men.

Toots wore shorts and a T-shirt, and his dreadlocks were encased in a colourful tam. He explained that he had grown up in Saint Vincent before his family relocated to England and was happy to point out to Selwyn and Jane many of the attractions of Kingstown. 'But first,' he said, guiding them along a short walk from the port, 'we must stop at the Sunbeam Bakery.'

Jane had eaten breakfast, but she felt her mouth water as they stepped into the small shop, where a delicious smell of toasted coconut and warm sponge emanated from the kitchen behind the counter. Toots pointed to a glass-fronted cabinet and ordered three Red Bellys.

'This is the island's favourite snack,' Toots said. 'They sell fast, we're lucky to get them.'

Jane wondered what could be so good about the shapeless, green-tinged cake that he thrust towards her, wrapped in a paper bag, but as she bit into the semisweet sponge and tasted the soft shaved coconut filling, she closed her eyes and wondered if she'd died and gone to heaven.

Kingstown was surrounded by steep hills, and as they continued, Toots pointed to a fort that overlooked the town on the north side. He explained that Fort Charlotte was built by the British in 1763 and has a lighthouse that acts as a beacon at the entrance of Kingstown Bay. The fort had been used for several purposes over the years, including a poorhouse, a leper colony, and a mental hospital. It had even been used as a prison.

To her surprise, Jane found that she was beginning to enjoy herself. The Red Belly cake had left her with a delicious feeling of contentment, and Toots was an excellent guide. Instead of feeling uncomfortable, she liked the attention she was receiving.

Selwyn watched the boats in the water and asked about

the harbour's lively activity. Toots said it was the main commercial port of the Grenadines and the centre of the island's agricultural industry. Jane felt history ooze from every brick of the impressive colonial buildings as she stared at the ancient warehouses, which seemed to come alive as Toots described what the bustling area would have been like centuries ago. She imagined being a visitor to Kingstown in the 1700s and witnessing the varied lives of its inhabitants. Goods such as sugar, rum, tobacco, and coffee would be packed into barrels and loaded onto ships bound for Europe and North America. Toots said that the port had been home to sailors, shopkeepers, merchants, and artisans, and Jane could almost hear the hustle and bustle of ghosts from a bygone age.

She was silent as Toots described how over four million Africans were brought to the islands of the Caribbean. She gripped Selwyn's arm when Toots told of newspaper advertisements announcing the arrival of shiploads of Africans who were unloaded into holding facilities on the quayside. Jane could almost hear their haunted voices crying out. She visualised the human prisons and felt tears falling onto her cheeks as she thought of the terrified arrivals awaiting their fate.

Silently, Selwyn touched her cheek and gently wiped her tears away.

They walked through dark winding alleys to the centre of the town, and again, Jane felt pleased that she wasn't alone. Kath had been right.

Soon, they were in the market square, where an eclectic

display of stalls spread out to all corners. Jane was in awe as she walked alongside mountains of colourful fruit and ripe vegetables stacked in crates and displayed on tables, spilling onto the ground. Eddoes, sweet potatoes, yams, breadfruit, and guavas sat alongside coconuts, passion fruits, fig bananas, and pineapples. Toots told her that the island's rich volcanic soil was perfect for growing produce, and the crops had recovered quickly after the volcanic eruption earlier in the year.

'Nature is miraculous,' Jane said and marvelled at its restorative powers as she studied a large selection of differently shaped bananas. Toots explained there were more than a hundred and twenty varieties.

A lady wearing a hessian apron over a cotton dress sat by a cart loaded with herbs and spices. Her head was wrapped in swathes of vibrant fabric. 'Yo! Lady!' she called out and, waving her fleshy arm, insisted that Jane smell and taste her produce.

'I'm tempted to buy one of everything,' Jane said to Selwyn as she made her purchases. 'It's all so fresh.' She watched as the vendor weighed cardamom, sage, and cinnamon, then twisted the items into little parcels.

'I think that you are a very good cook,' he replied, 'your friend Kath has told me that you were excellent at your job. It must have been fascinating to work in television with so many famous chefs.'

Jane wondered when Kath had found the time to have such an in-depth conversation with Selwyn. He seemed to know far more about her circumstances than she remembered telling him.

'I hope you'll cook for me one day,' Selwyn said.

It wasn't a question, more of an observation, as though Selwyn took it for granted that their paths would cross again after the cruise. Flustered, she packed her purchases into her bag as the butterflies began to dance in her stomach. Jane's face flushed, and she turned away.

'I fancy a rum,' Toots announced.

'Sounds good,' Selwyn agreed.

Jane wasn't sure that rum in the morning would be good but, not wanting to part from her guides, she stood alongside as Toots asked a local where to go.

'Go all the way down de alley, till you get to four rude boys liming on de block,' the wizened old man explained. 'You'll see a garage, don't turn there, make a right and you'll see a green door. That's not it. Go straight. It's the red house with a dunk tree out front.'

Jane was goggle-eyed. She hadn't a clue about what the man said, but Toots seemed to know where they were going. She clutched Selwyn's arm as they set off and felt hot and uncomfortable when they picked up their pace. What must he think of this lumbering woman hanging on to his arm?

The street was dark and claustrophobic, and rubbish littered the pavements. Several mangy cats scrapped on fish carcasses from an overflowing bin. A woman in a leather miniskirt stood in a doorway. She was smoking as she watched them approach and Jane noticed that the woman's wig hung to one side, and her lips were smudged with deep red gloss. She made a clicking noise with her teeth as they went by.

A Rastafarian stepped out from behind the woman and fell into step with Toots. They spoke quietly, and Jane couldn't hear their conversation. In moments they arrived back at the harbour, on the industrial side, and were guided into a little bar, where they sat on plastic chairs around a rickety table. Jane stared at her surroundings through a smoke-filled haze. The bar was dark, and Toots explained that the owner didn't put the lights on to save money. She realised she was still holding onto Selwyn's arm, but as he adjusted his position, his hand slid into her own.

'The real Kingstown,' he said and smiled. 'Don't worry, you're quite safe.'

Selwyn's hand felt warm and strong, and despite the instinct to pull away, Jane gripped it tightly.

A man approached. He had long grey dreadlocks and a goatee beard and walked barefoot with a crooked limp. Tattoos covered most of his skin. Fist-bumping Toots, he said his name was Spirit and announced that he was the unofficial marijuana ambassador for Saint Vincent and the Grenadine islands. His voice was low and husky. Pulling out a chair, he sat down to explain that a bullet had lodged in his throat during an assassination attempt on the Attorney General. It was still there. After a spell in prison, his innocence was proved, and he opened this rum shop.

Jane was gobsmacked. Spirit's frankness felt like too much information, and her mouth fell open as she studied the jagged scar on his neck. He wore shorts to his knees, and a cut-away vest and Jane stared at the tattoo on his back. It was the head of a lion and beautifully etched, the eyes soulful and soft. She watched as he summoned the Rasta who'd led them to the bar. A tray of drinks was produced, and they all took a glass.

'This rum is the finest in the Grenadines,' Spirit said. 'It's called Sunset, and it's illegal to sell it off the islands.'

Jane watched as Selwyn, Spirit, and Toots drank a shot. She held her glass to her nose. The rum was dark and velvety and wanting to keep up with her companions, Jane raised it to her lips and knocked it back.

Time seemed to stand still. For what felt like an eternity, Jane's body was paralysed.

'Dear God...' she whispered to Selwyn as her blood began to flow again, '*what* was that?'

'Sunset is eighty-seven per cent proof,' he replied, 'which is why it can't be exported.'

'For a moment I thought I'd experienced my final sunset,' Jane muttered.

'Go easy, have a soft drink next or we will be carrying you back.'

Jane thought it would take more than Toots, Spirit and Selwyn to carry her back and grinned as she imagined Kath's and Anne's faces.

Spirit was handing round a spliff, and Jane, now mellow, reached out. Her limbs felt like liquid honey, sweet, sexy, and supple.

'Are you sure?' Selwyn asked.

'Absolutely,' she lied. 'I puff the stuff all the time.'

Jane had never smoked in her life, and as she dragged deeply, she felt her eyes bulge, her heart pound, and her chest expand as though it was about to explode. Music began to play, and she recognised the beat of a reggae song. In a trance, Jane rose to her feet and, handing the spliff to Toots, began to sway. She rocked her hips from side to side and, closing her eyes, began to dance. The feeling was incredible, and her body had come alive! Why had she never listened to reggae music before? It was the most delightful sound, and Jane's sense of well-being was unlike anything she'd ever known. She reached out and, taking the fabric of her dress in both hands, moved away from the seated group.

'The thing about reggae is that when it hits you, there's no pain, physical or emotional,' Selwyn said to Toots as he watched Jane dance.

Jane sang along with the music and began swirling the flowing, flamboyant fabric. She was oblivious to her surroundings and totally immersed in the beat.

Selwyn smiled. He was fascinated to watch Jane come to life and resisted the urge to jump to his feet and join her. This was her moment, and nothing should break the spell.

Caught up in the moment, Jane didn't notice that Selwyn had reached into his pocket and pulled out a plastic pouch. Opening it carefully, he waited until all eyes were on Jane, then scattered the contents on the sandy floor. Flo had never liked dancing. She was happy to sing and clap her hands in the church choir, but dancing was the devil's work to be avoided at all costs. Ash mingled with dust, and Selwyn thought he could hear Flo cussing him for placing her in such a den of iniquity.

'Dance like no one is watching, my dear,' Selwyn whispered.

Pushing thoughts of Flo to one side, he turned back, his eyes following Jane's every move. The woman was confident and carefree in a world of her own, and he remembered the painting. The artist's words rang in his ears, 'Maybe it's the woman of *your* dreams?'

Yes! Selwyn realised, it was Jane! Every brush stroke replicated the vision before him. Why hadn't he seen it before? Selwyn's heart felt full, and he was suddenly moved by a surge of emotion as he realised – *he was falling in love!*

But, as Selwyn took a deep breath, he knew that she would be a challenge, and he determined to make it his mission to bring Jane out of her shell to blossom and live her life to the full.

'Every little thing gonna be all right!' chanted Selwyn, Toots and Spirit as they sat back to smoke, drink, and enjoy the whirling mass of moving colour before them.

Chapter Sixteen

Anne had enjoyed a wonderful day in the company of Dicky as they'd toured around the island of Saint Vincent. She felt exhilarated as she walked through the ship and into Hibiscus, where she found Kath sitting in the shade of the balcony. She was reading a book.

'Hello,' Anne called out as she tossed her damp beach bag onto the bathroom floor, 'have you had a lovely day?'

'I certainly have,' Kath replied, looking up from the open pages as Anne joined her, 'Brigette was a knowledgeable guide and knew everything about conservation and plant history.'

'Was her talk interesting?'

'Yes, fascinating. The botanical gardens are massive and one of the oldest in the world. We saw the famous Saint Vincent parrots hiding between bunches of breadfruit in the boughs of the trees. It was quite a sight.'

'I had a budgie once.' Anne frowned. 'I accidently opened a window, and it flew away.'

Sensing that Anne had more interest in budgies than botanical gardens, Kath didn't want to hear about Anne's escapee. 'But how was your day?' she asked. 'Did you enjoy yourself?'

'It's been brilliant, I haven't had so much fun in a long time.'

'How was the movie set?'

'Stunning, they've transformed Wallilabou Bay into a studio backlot to make it look like Port Royal in Jamaica. That was where the first *Pirates of the Caribbean* film was supposed to have been located.' Anne flopped down on a chair beside Kath and stared at the calm sea.

'You've caught the sun; your skin looks baked.'

'We've been swimming for most of the day. It was marvellous.' Anne grinned. 'Dicky pretended that he was Captain Jack Sparrow and stepped off a sinking boat to capture a drowning damsel, who was me.'

'My word, he's quite a hero.' Kath's eyebrows were raised, and she tapped the book. 'I'm sure he lives up to some of the escapades he describes in his novel.'

'It's not a novel, it's his autobiography.'

'It reads like fiction to me,' Kath replied. She closed the pages of *Dicky Delaney – My Life in Show Business*. 'What else did you get up to?'

'We went to the heritage park and swam under the waterfalls. Then we were taken to Buccament beach, and oh, you should have seen the water.' Anne sighed. 'It was crystal clear, and our guide threw pieces of bacon to encourage the turtles to swim close.'

'I'd love to see turtles,' Kath said.

'They were so tame.' Anne leaned in, her voice a whisper. 'And I actually touched one.'

'Lucky you!' Kath's eyes were wide.

'I know, it was quite thrilling, then we ate lobster and drank a bottle of expensive French wine, at a beach bar, and had another swim before coming back to the ship.'

'It sounds like the trip was good value for money if you managed to eat lobster, drink wine and fit so much in.'

'Well,' Anne paused, 'there was a fee at the heritage park and of course lunch wasn't included.'

'No doubt Dicky treated you from his winnings?'

'Unfortunately, he'd forgotten his wallet, but I told him not to worry and he said he'd pay next time.'

Kath stared at Anne. Surely she hadn't coughed up for Dicky all day? She wanted to press Anne further, but they were suddenly interrupted as Jane bounced in.

'Hi there!' Jane called out. 'Anyone fancy a livener? The sun is over the yardarm.'

Anne and Kath peered through the balcony door to see Jane sifting through the bar's contents. She grabbed a bottle of wine and gripped a packet of chocolate candies between her teeth.

'Hungry?' Anne asked as Jane placed the bottle on the table.

'Starving, I need sugar.' She disappeared and returned

with three glasses. Ripping the packet open, she tossed a handful of candies into her mouth and began to hum.

Anne poured their drinks and watched Jane. She noticed that Kath was staring, too and wore a puzzled expression as Jane swayed and began to dance. They exchanged baffled glances, and Kath shrugged her shoulders.

'Are you feeling all right?' Anne asked.

'Never better,' Jane replied. With her arms raised, she bent her knees and moved her hips from side to side, then began to sing as she danced around the decking.

'Have you been on the whacky baccy?' Kath sat upright and tutted.

'I may have had a little toot.' Jane smiled.

'Oh, dear, it's a good job you weren't checked as you came back on board, you smell like Errol's weed wagon.'

'I'll have a large portion of whatever she's on.' Anne laughed and kicked off her sandals as Jane wound around her friends.

'I suppose Selwyn is responsible for this?' Kath asked.

'Chill, man, chill.'

'I hope you haven't got any contraband on you. We might get thrown off the ship.'

'Safe, man, safe...'

'I think Jane is telling you that everything is fine. She's had a wonderful day and now feels like dancing.' Anne giggled as Jane opened her eyes and gave a thumbs-up before grabbing hold of her dress and swirling it in the air.

'It's most unseemly for a woman of our age,' Kath grumbled. 'Getting stoned at sixty-three is senseless and isn't something we discussed when arranging this cruise.' Kath removed her glasses and pushed her drink away. 'I think I need to have another word with Selwyn. I didn't expect him to lead you astray.'

'He can lead me astray anytime,' Anne said. Throwing back her chair, she grabbed Jane's hands and twirled with her. 'I've never seen you so happy,' Anne called out as Jane sang louder. 'And I'm so pleased,' she said as Kath stood at the balcony door, watching their antics.

Suddenly, Jane stopped dancing. She stood by her bed and, with a heavy sigh, collapsed onto the mattress. In moments, she was asleep.

'Well, that's Jane out for the count,' Kath said.

'I don't suppose she'll want any dinner?'

'Hardly,' Kath said, raising her voice above the loud snores from Jane's slumbering body. 'But I'm not going to miss a meal, and this wine is getting warm.' Kath turned. A smile had crept across her face. 'Shall we toast Jane's awakening?' she asked, 'I have a feeling she's coming out of her comfort zone at last.'

'It's cause for a celebration.'

They stood on the balcony and watched the sun collapse beyond the horizon in colours of orange and gold, the last rays before twilight called on the stars.

'This cruise is heavenly,' Anne said. 'I feel so relaxed, it's as though all my cares have ebbed away.'

'Like someone turned on a light in your life?' Kath asked.

'Exactly, and we have to make the most of it because none of us know when our lights will be extinguished.'

Kath linked her arm through Anne's and stared at the darkening sea. Had Jim known that his light would be snuffed out when he stood on the steps? Did he have any regrets or time to think of the wife who'd been loyally beside him for so many years? Probably not, Kath mused. Life can change at the flick of a switch, and her life had changed beyond recognition in the last few days. She nodded slowly and determined not to waste a single moment of whatever she had left.

'This sunburn is killing me,' Anne said and touched the tender reddening skin on her arm. 'I don't think I'm going to manage any dinner.'

'I'll have something for it in my bag.' Kath began to rummage and soon found some lotion. Handing it to Anne, she suddenly announced, 'I think it's time we had our hair re-styled, what do you say? My treat.'

'I'd say that would be fabulous.' Anne cocked her head to one side and studied Kath. 'What do you fancy?'

'I'll have the ten-years-younger colour and cut.'

'Then I'll go for a tousle and tease, something to encourage Dicky.'

'He doesn't need encouragement.'

'But what about Jane? Do you think we can coax her into a new style?' Anne turned and peered at their sleeping friend. 'Getting rid of that short crop would take years off her, but I'm not sure how it could be styled with so little to go on.'

Kath walked ahead and picked up the phone. She pressed the salon extension. 'I'll make appointments. We'll frogmarch Jane there if we have to.'

Anne raised her glass, 'I'll drink to that,' she said, 'and to the revitalised you!'

Dicky sat in his dressing room and stared at his face in the mirror. His skin was as red as a rooster, and he knew that he'd foolishly overdone things whilst larking about in the sun all day. He glanced over to where Melissa Montana's makeup was scattered haphazardly and wondered if she had anything that might cool his burning skin and calm the redness. He'd look a complete tit on stage tonight if his face was on fire; the spotlights were hot and would exaggerate his problem.

'You can keep your grubby paws off my stuff,' a voice called out as the door opened, and Melissa strode into the room. She was appearing in the Neptune Lounge that evening and needed to prepare for her act. 'Don't think you can nick anything that will turn a frog into a prince,' she added.

'Good evening,' Dicky said, deciding to be civil as he patted his skin with an ice-pack cloth.

'Blimey, what have you done?' Melissa laughed as she fastened a silk kimono, took a seat, and stared at Dicky. 'You look like you've dipped your face in a deep fat fryer.'

'Very funny,' Dicky said, his voice muffled by the ice. 'If you had a heart, you'd suggest something for this sunburn.'

'A trip to the infirmary?' Melissa said. She ignored Dicky and, scraping her hair into a band, began to apply foundation to her face.

'I don't know what to do, I've got quiz night and bingo in the Mermaid Theatre followed by a late-night show in the Neptune Lounge.' He peeled back the cloth and winced at his reflection. His eyes were puffy, his head ached, and he was clearly suffering. 'I'm not sure if I'm going to be able to get through it all.'

'I'm sure you'll manage. If you don't, Peter will say it's self-inflicted and reduce your contract fee.'

'Like hell he will, I've got to do something, but I don't know what, I've only got half an hour before I'm on stage.'

Melissa continued to ignore Dicky. She had no sympathy for the philandering comedian. She knew he'd spent the day on an island excursion with one of the passengers, most likely at the lady's expense. Melissa knew all of Dicky's scams, having worked on previous ships where they'd provided entertainment. She foolishly had a fling with him on a two-week cruise in the Canaries. But as she began to apply eyeshadow and false lashes, she furtively glanced at his face. He was obviously in pain and floundering like a fish as he tried to work out what to do. She'd done many silly things and imagined herself in a similar position.

Melissa knew that the show must go on and felt sympathetic. She reached into her bra, produced a little key, and sliding it into the lock, opened a drawer and felt for a jar of cream. 'Here,' she said, 'use this. I got it from an old lady in Barbados who mixes up pills and potions. You can't get this on the NHS, but it should do the trick.' Melissa leaned in and gently removed the cloth from Dicky's face. His eyes were closed, and trustingly, he tilted his head back.

She began to gently apply the sticky brown gunk to Dicky's skin.

'Bloody hell, that hurts!' he cried out, his eyes wide. 'What on earth have you done to me?' Dicky leapt from his chair and began to pace the room as the cream burned through layers of fiery skin.

'Man up,' Melissa barked. 'If you give it a moment it will calm down.'

And, as good as her word, Dicky felt the heat reduce as the cream cooled his sunburn within minutes.

'You can wash it off now, and take a couple of these.' She opened a little box and pulled out two orange tablets. 'They'll stop your headache and any sunstroke symptoms, *and* they'll perk you up.'

Twenty minutes later, Dicky was ready for action. Dressed in his stage outfit, with minimum makeup, he felt on top of the world. 'Melissa, darlin', you are a wonder, and I owe you one,' he said and hugged her.

'Watch out … you'll ruin my hair.' Melissa darted away and reached out to secure her blonde wig. 'And you owe me plenty,' she said.

'Break a leg!' Dicky called out as he left the dressing room, shoulders back, head held high, to make his way to the Mermaid Theatre.

But the unsuspecting Dicky had, at that moment, no idea that Melissa's magical medication would create additional symptoms that were about to make themselves known.

———

Kath had enjoyed her meal in the Terrace Restaurant and found a place in the Mermaid Theatre after an after-dinner peppermint tea. She joined Harold, Nancy, Bridgette, the Captain, and Selwyn at a table close to the stage.

'Where are your friends tonight?' Harold asked as he settled with Nancy and ordered their drinks.

'Anne had a hectic day but spent too much time in the sun,' Kath replied and thought about Anne's naked body, burning up and lying prone on her bed, covered in calamine lotion. As Kath crept out of Hibiscus, her friend appeared mummified, and Kath heard Anne groan that she'd never, ever go in the sun again.

'Is Jane all right?' Selwyn asked, his face showing concern.

'Perfectly,' Kath snapped, 'just tired from traipsing around Kingstown.'

She wanted to tell Selwyn that she thought he'd been most irresponsible and had taken Jane down a path that would only lead to trouble. But as she looked into his dark eyes, sincere in their questioning, she knew she couldn't be cross with him. After all, he'd got the wayward Jane safely back to the ship, and if Kath was truthful, her friend appeared to have had the time of her life.

'Should I go and make sure that she's all right?' Selwyn asked.

'I wouldn't, you won't get a peep out of her.'

'Sleeping the sleep of an angel,' Selwyn sighed.

Kath was about to say that Jane was hardly an angel. In fact, after today's outing, she seemed to have the devil in her, but Peter was on the stage, and the band had begun to play the theme music from *Who Wants to Be a Millionaire?* The curtains drew back, and Peter introduced Dicky, who ran onto the stage to applause.

The comedian appeared to have an extra spring in his step as he took the microphone and asked, 'Who wants to be a millionaire?' Dicky cupped his ear and looked at the audience. 'What's that? *None of you*? You're all millionaires already?'

'I wish!' Harold called out.

'Me too,' yelled another passenger.

Dicky shook his head. 'Nothing for me to do tonight then...' He turned as if to leave the stage. But the audience was eager for Dicky to present the show, and they began to clap and cheer. 'All right.' He held up his hand. 'Is there anyone out there who would like to play the *Diamond Star* version of the *Millionaire* game?'

Like a Mexican wave, hands shot up.

Kath was fascinated. She'd never been to a game show before, but she'd watched *Who Wants to be a Millionaire* on television countless times. Quiz shows, like crosswords, were one of her favourite pastimes. Together with Jim, she nearly always got the questions right. She remembered watching a contestant, an army major, who'd been involved in a coughing scandal after he'd won the top prize. Jim had been convinced the major was guilty, and Kath had been inclined to agree.

'We have a wonderful prize,' Dicky began, 'and the lucky winner who answers three questions correctly within ten minutes will get a complimentary treatment in the spa to make them feel like a millionaire.' Dicky reached into his pocket and produced a piece of paper. 'The rules are easy,' he said, 'the contestant has four multiple-choice answers to each question I read out.'

Kath thought it all seemed straightforward and settled back to enjoy the quiz.

'Our first contestant has been drawn randomly from the passenger list.' He looked up. 'And I hope she's here tonight.' Dicky paused, letting the tension build. 'The lucky lady's name is...' There was a drum roll before he announced, 'Kath Taylor!'

Kath heard a name called out but thought she'd misheard and looked around the room.

'Is the lady here?' Dicky asked.

Kath gripped her bag and waited for someone to stand up and head to the stage. After a few moments, she couldn't understand why Harold, Nancy, and Selwyn were staring at her.

'It's you.' Selwyn smiled and took hold of Kath's arm. 'It's *your* name that's been called out.'

'Don't be so daft,' Kath said, suddenly flustered as a spotlight panned around the room and shone in her direction.

'I'll watch your bag,' Nancy said, and Harold stood up to assist Kath.

'Go on,' Selwyn urged.

The audience began to clap, and Dicky came forward. He took Kath's hand and guided her to a seat as one of the band members placed a large clock on the stage.

'Oh, my goodness,' Kath said, straightening her glasses as she sat down. 'I'm quaking.'

'Well, let's hope your nerves help you. The rules are straightforward, answer three questions correctly within the time limit and win the wonderful prize.'

Dicky stared at the woman and told himself she looked clueless. He should be able to get plenty of gags in to use up the time while he waited for her to try and answer at least one question correctly.

Kath's fingers fidgeted as she watched Dicky walk over to the clock.

'The quiz starts now,' he said. 'Here we go!'

She heard the clock begin to tick and felt vulnerable without her bag on her knee, sitting alone on the stage.

'Which Caribbean island has the oldest rum distillery?' Dicky asked, but before he could give Kath options, she called out her answer.

'Barbados. Next question, please.' The question was simple, she'd learnt about the distillery from Errol during their tour of Barbados.

'My goodness – Kath is correct,' Dicky said, and the audience applauded. The clock was only fifty seconds in. He began to pace the stage, but Kath refused to be stalled.

'Next question!' she demanded.

'Let's see if she is as quick with this one.' Dicky winked at the audience. 'What is the largest island in the Caribbean? You have a choice of A, Antigua, B...'

'Cuba,' Kath said without waiting for Dicky to finish.

Dicky had begun to sweat. Peter had given explicit instructions to make the quiz last ten minutes with each contestant. He was to engage the audience by getting them involved too. 'Are you sure?' he asked, already knowing that Kath was correct. 'Wouldn't you like to ask the audience?'

'No.' Kath was adamant. 'Next question.'

'Well...' Dicky hesitated. 'That is, in fact, the right answer.' He flicked through the cards in his hand, searching for the most challenging question. Turning to the audience again, he said, 'I trust there are no army majors out there, and if so, no coughing, please, as we wait for Kath to answer this question.' One or two guests sniggered, and Dicky laughed.

As the clock ticked down, the audience shouted encouragement to Kath, knowing she was one question away from a prize and with plenty of time left.

'Stop talking and ask the next question,' Kath demanded.

Dicky gritted his teeth and held up a card. This will stop

the old bag in her tracks! He grinned. 'Kath, the French never ruled which of the following islands? A, Dominica…'

'St Croix,' Kath called out before Dicky could finish.

The audience was silent as they waited for Dicky to respond, and Selwyn, Harold, and Nancy sat forward in their chairs.

'Wouldn't you like to phone a friend or ask the audience?' Dicky stalled, glancing at the clock, and realising they had many minutes left to fill.

'No, I don't need to, St Croix is right.'

Dicky stared at Kath and wondered if she could somehow read his card but knew it was impossible. He began to pad out the answer. 'Well, one island was colonised by the Danish in the 17th century,' he read, 'but purchased by the United States in 1917. French place names still linger on Saint Lucia…'

'Stop waffling,' Kath said. 'Have I won?'

'Er … well, Kath.' Dicky paused. 'St Croix is … in fact … the correct answer.'

Kath was on her feet, and the audience was cheering. Dicky nodded as though pleased for her win. A spotlight shone on Dicky and Kath just as the ship's photographer took a photo of the prizewinner and host. When the applause died, Dicky asked Kath if she was happy with her prize.

'Oh, yes,' Kath said. She stood next to Dicky and stared at his face, her eyes studying the large orange blotches that had suddenly appeared all over his skin. 'But I think you need a spa treatment far more than I do. In fact, I hope that whatever is wrong with your face isn't contagious.'

Peter heard the word 'contagious' and rushed forward to Dicky, who stood glued to the stage. 'Get off!' Peter hissed, stumbling away from Dicky, and shaking his head back and forth. He grabbed the microphone from Dicky's hand, where the skin was also glowing with orange blotches.

Melissa's pills had paralysed Dicky, not perked him up, and he also appeared to be experiencing an allergic reaction. Dicky glanced at his hands, then felt the bumps on his face, and as the photographer snapped again, his eyes were wide with horror. Kath reeled back and held up her hands, making it clear that she didn't want to catch anything.

'*Off!*' Peter snarled and shoved in front of Dicky to take over.

Dicky left the stage, where he saw Melissa darting behind a curtain. 'Come here!' he yelled to her disappearing body. Stagehands stood back, heads turned, and palms raised as if to push Dicky away. 'Melissa!' Dicky screamed, his face distraught and angry. 'Just wait till I catch you.' He shook a blotchy fist. 'Your meddlesome magic potions have ruined my career!'

Chapter Seventeen

T he following morning as the ship docked, the
Diamond Star Marine & Wellness Spa hosted three
eager new clients. Wearing comfortable robes and towelling
turbans, Kath, Jane, and Anne sat with their feet resting on
footstools, enjoying a manicure and pedicure.

'Isn't it heavenly to have all day to relax before we
sample a festive feast in Martinique?' Anne said. Her
sunburn had settled down, and they had decided to skip a
beach excursion and opted out of a trip to another rum
distillery.

'It certainly is. This was a great idea of Kath's,' Jane
agreed. She studied a Christmas tree decorated with plastic
globes that held samples of the spa's creams and lotions,
tied with silver and red ribbons. Picking up a list of
treatments, she read, '"The spa is an oasis of calm and uses
marine active products that will heal, revitalise and
rebalance your life."' I'll have a double dose of all that.'

'I've never known such luxury, and I love being pampered.' Kath smiled. She'd opted for the De-stress & Revive treatment which began with an energising plasma shot followed by a body scrub using brown sugar and citrus oils. 'My skin feels years younger and silky smooth,' Kath said as she sipped bitter orange tea and studied a copy of the *Diamond Star Daily*. She gazed in wonder at the headline on the front page.

Mrs Taylor Wins a Diamond Star *Treat!*

For the fourth time that morning, Kath re-read the article that supported the headline, and a relaxed smile crossed her face as her cheeks turned pink with pleasure. She carefully ran her fingers over a photograph to avoid smudging her newly polished nails. Her own image beamed back as she stood beside Dicky Delaney. To everyone's astonishment, Dicky appeared to have contracted some sort of disease. His skin was the colour of custard, and vivid orange blotches covered his face.

'Do you think that's what the plague looked like?' Jane leaned over Kath's shoulder to study Dicky's face. 'He looks close to death, if you ask me.'

'I spoke to him this morning and he said he has an allergic reaction to a painkiller,' Anne said.

'Severe enough to be put in isolation in the infirmary.' Jane giggled. 'That buggers up the rest of his cruise.'

'Not at all.' Anne shook her head. 'The doctor thinks it

will settle down today and he'll only be out of action for forty-eight hours.'

'I thought Peter was going to faint last night, when he saw Dicky's face,' Kath added. 'It was as though a dreaded lurgy was about to sweep through the ship.'

'Which would have cost the company a fortune.' Jane nodded. 'No wonder he was upset.'

'Dicky will be fine.' Anne was adamant. 'Hopefully, he will return to host the cabaret on Christmas Day.'

'He could have a part in a pantomime,' Jane said, 'as Captain Hook without the need for makeup.'

'Very funny.' Anne sighed and reached out to finish her blackcurrant tea.

'I can't believe I'm in print.' Kath ignored her friends' banter and re-read the article. 'It says, *"Mrs Kath Taylor, from Garstang in Lancashire, is the first Diamond Star Millionaire quiz contestant to get three correct answers in a record time."'* Kath's eyes gleamed. 'All those wretched quizzes on TV that Jim insisted on watching have paid off.'

'You were lucky to receive such a lovely prize,' Jane said, nodding, 'and it's very kind of you to invite and pay for Anne and me too.'

'Isn't it great? I feel like a millionaire after the facial, and I want you both to enjoy and share the experience with me.' Kath touched her skin and ran her fingers lightly over the faint lines around her eyes. 'I'm polished and plumped and totally hydrated.'

'You look ten years younger,' Anne said, 'and I feel

fantastic after my anti-ageing treatments, especially the massage with aloe vera, which has soothed my sunburn.'

'I think you're bonkers having Botox,' Jane said with a shudder, 'and injecting all those chemicals into your body.'

'No worse than the craving you have for sugar,' Anne retorted, 'which is known to be as addictive as cocaine.'

'Each to their own.' Jane stretched out her arm and reached for a fruit flapjack. 'But after my Slim & Tone treatment I feel like I've lost pounds.'

Kath and Anne exchanged glances and shook their heads as they watched Jane devour her snack.

'What was so special about the treatment?' Anne asked.

'I was wrapped in some sort of foaming substance on my thighs, hips and tummy then had another wrap of something called Frigi-Thalgo, to eliminate toxins and excess fluid.' Jane patted her stomach.

Kath interrupted as the manicurist gave the finishing touches to her pearly pink toenails. 'We're having our hair done next, and I can't wait to see what the stylist suggests.'

'Did someone call for a stylist?' A voice called out, and the three friends turned to see a lean and muscular man walk towards them. 'Philippe to the rescue! News on the ship's grapevine tells me that this is an emergency,' he said.

Kath, Jane, and Anne stared as the tattooed apparition, wearing patchwork harem trousers and a Nehru shirt, stood before them. Jane gripped the arms of her chair and was about to bolt, but Kath and Anne tugged on her robe, forcing her to remain.

'All beads, bangles, and Buddha,' Jane whispered. 'He's not touching my hair.'

'Admiring the sleeve?' the man asked, thrusting his arm out. He rolled his shirt to reveal the full extent of his vivid tattoos. 'Tribal graphics,' he said, 'I know a man in Martinique. If you're going ashore later, he's very quick.'

'No thank you,' Kath said and folded her arms. 'Not for me.'

The man clapped his hands. 'Let's get to work,' he announced. 'I haven't been called in from my mindful meditation to stand here chin-wagging.' He reached out and pulled Kath's turban off. As her hair sprang out, he ran his fingers through the greying mass, 'Hmm, dry, dreadful and dull.' Shaking his head, he turned to Anne and, repeating the process, sighed, 'Over-bleached, split-ends and done up like a dog's dinner.' He ducked as Anne's arm swung out.

Looking down, Jane removed her turban and gripped it in her hands. She knew what was coming. His comments would reflect a terrible masculine cut and ageing white hair that had never seen a stylist's scissors.

'Now, dear,' he said and softly caressed Jane's head, 'we're going to make you look beautiful.'

Jane wondered if Philippe was on drugs and winced away from his fingers.

Kath had heard enough and decided to take control. 'Philippe,' she began and sat forward. 'My dear friends and I are at a time in our lives when heads fail to turn.' Knowing that Jane was about to interrupt and say that heads had never turned for her, she held a finger to her lips. 'We hate to admit that we won't see sixty again and perhaps we could have tried a little harder with our hair, in the past.'

Anne's head jerked up. 'Speak for yourself,' she said.

Kath ignored Anne. 'But I have it on great authority that you are one of the most respected stylists in the north of England, having a residency at the famous Sparadise Spa in Lancashire. We are indebted to you for your time today.'

Philippe's pearly white veneers shone like a dental advert as he touched his hair and preened.

'We want people to sit up and notice us,' Kath said. 'Can you make our days of disappearing into the wallpaper a thing of the past?'

Philippe's hand flew to his luscious thick locks, and they saw a flash of gold from a bracelet amongst layers of leather and beads twisted around his wrist. His dark eyes shone as he flicked back chocolate-tinted curls. 'Challenges like this are as rare as a four-leaf clover,' he said, 'but it is a challenge that I accept.' He clicked his fingers, and an assistant appeared with gowns. 'Are you ready?' he asked, looking from one to the other. Trance-like, Kath, Anne, and Jane nodded.

Philippe turned on his heel, and, following in his wake, the assistant guided the friends through to the hair salon, where they sat in a row, staring at their reflections in a mirror.

'You are to put your complete trust in me,' Philippe said. He had a wicked gleam in his eye as he raised knife-like scissors in one hand and a long-tailed comb in the other. Kath, Jane, and Anne shrank low in their chairs. 'Let the magic begin!' Philippe whispered and, wasting no more time, began his mission.

On the south side of the island of Martinique, Selwyn stood on the beach at Grande Anse des Salines and watched hundreds of holidaymakers. Many were from the *Diamond Star*, enjoying the sun and sea in one of the most iconic locations in the Caribbean. He stood with his hands in the pockets of his bright scarlet swimming shorts and wished there were fewer people on the beach but knew it was a downside of high season. The cold winter evenings he'd left behind in Lambeth felt like a million miles away as he felt the sun heat his skin. How many nights had he sat alone and dreamt of clear turquoise waters, long stretches of white sand, and overhanging coconut trees?

Despite the heavily populated beach, Selwyn appreciated the beauty of his surroundings. It was a bright clear day, and in the distance, he could see the island of Saint Lucia. Jutting out of the water, in the channel between the islands, Selwyn saw the famed Diamond Rock glittering in the sunlight. The tiny inaccessible island was covered in thick vegetation and had an imposing peak. He remembered reading that at certain hours during the day it looked like the jewel it was named after.

'Martinique is one of the few Caribbean islands that still grows sugar cane...'

Selwyn turned to see Bridgette walking towards him.

'Christopher Columbus landed on the island in 1502, but the French eventually took ownership,' Bridgette continued, 'and since the 1970s, it's officially a region of France.' Bridgette's little bare feet hopped up and down on the hot sand. 'Christopher Columbus once said, *"You can never cross the ocean unless you have the courage to lose sight of the shore,"* and I've always thought that made a lot of sense.'

Selwyn agreed. It was an interesting quote. Still, he didn't need a history lesson and had spent considerable time reading his guidebooks. But as he looked down at Bridgette, he was pleased to have her company and decided to indulge his new friend. 'Did you know that Napoleon's Empress Josephine was born on the island?' he asked.

'Of course,' Bridgette replied. 'She was revered for her fame but reviled for propagating the trade of slavery. In the 1990s, the locals became angry that she'd been pro-slavery and destroyed her statue in the capital, Fort-de-France.' Bridgette shook her head. 'And I can't say I blame them.'

'Are you going to have a swim?' Selwyn asked, noting that Bridgette was wearing a poppy-patterned, skirted swimsuit.

Placing her hands on her hips, she glanced up and down the beach, 'I'd rather hoped to get to the naturist section, but I'm not sure I can manage the Captain all that way.' Bridgette stared further down the beach where the shoreline curved, and the trees were lusher. Like Lowry's matchstick men, darkly tanned sunbathers milled around.

Selwyn turned to look at the group of passengers he'd travelled with from the ship to the beach. Bridgette had insisted that the Captain have a day out. She was determined to get him off the ship and away from the bar. Now, the old boy sat on a deckchair under the shade of a tree and waved his stick at everyone passing by.

'You're very kind to have accompanied him,' Selwyn said. He thought of Bridgette's care when demanding that a wheelchair be made available for her to transport the Captain from the ship to the coach. Selwyn had assisted.

'I'm very fond of him. We've had fun over the years on cruises. He hasn't always been so absent-minded and was hugely entertaining in his day. Quite a Romeo with the ladies too.' Bridgette looked thoughtful, as she raised her hand and the Captain waved his stick. 'He's always supported my talks, and when Hugo came with me they'd chat for hours in the bar.'

'You must see a big change in him?' Selwyn asked.

'Of course, ageing is cruel, and would you want to be stuck on the ship all the time, when there is so much beauty everywhere?' Bridgette looked around. 'In fact, I think a sea bathe would do the Captain good – will you help?'

And that is how Selwyn found himself carrying a slight, eighty-eight-year-old man across a crowded beach and lowering him gently into the water. Harold, wearing minuscule trunks, was drinking beer at a nearby bar and strolled over to assist. Nancy, cosy in a capacious kaftan and sipping a pina colada, looked on.

The Captain lay on his back in the sea. He wore Union Jack swimming shorts that floated like a flag around his withered body. Selwyn and Harold each held his hand while Bridgette swam with dainty breaststrokes, circling the trio.

'Sharks!' The Captain called out, kicking his legs and splashing before hooting with laughter.

'He's enjoying himself,' Bridgette said as she paused to catch her breath. 'The swim will be so beneficial for him.' She moved towards the Captain. 'I've got him.' She took the Captain's hand and shooed Selwyn away. 'Off you go and have a swim too.'

Selwyn dived beneath the surface and powered away from the shore. His strokes were rhythmic, and he felt a sudden sense of freedom, almost a weightlessness of both body and mind. Years of denied holidays and pent-up frustration gave him energy in the silky warmth of the water. Swimming was such an excellent exercise, he thought as he surfaced and looked back at the beach. His early morning swims at Brixton Leisure Centre didn't compare with the calm Caribbean Sea. Still, they kept him fit, as did the open water pool at Brockwell Lido, where he spent many hours in the summer months. Flo had never gone with him unless it was to sit in the café drinking tea and eating cake. He'd never been able to persuade her to take swimming lessons, and she refused to put any part of her body in the pool. Beach holidays had been out of the question.

Selwyn turned to float and stared up at a sky as blue as his mother's eyes. How much Flo had missed in life ... and how much had he missed too? Her life revolved around the church, Pastor Gregory and the congregation, and Selwyn had allowed it. Perhaps he should have been firmer and insisted they break out of life in Lambeth. But in his heart, Selwyn knew the only way out would have been to leave Flo, and for their daughter's sake, it was a route he'd never chosen to take.

Reaching into a pocket, Selwyn removed a waterproof pouch. Holding it up, he lay back and watched Flo's ashes catch on a wisp of breeze, twirling heavenward like smoke. He smiled as he watched the grey cloud disperse. 'Fly high, my dear,' Selwyn whispered.

An image of Jane dancing in Spirit's bar came into his thoughts. She'd twirled her body and moved freely as though a key had unlocked her inhibitions. Selwyn wondered why Jane disliked herself so much, for, in his opinion, she was a fine, independent woman. But somewhere along life's highway, she'd lost her confidence. How could he help her to find it? As he lingered lazily in the water, it was an enjoyable problem to ponder. Selwyn remembered Bridgette's quote, *'You can never cross the ocean unless you have the courage to lose sight of the shore.'* Would Jane ever cross her own ocean? But his dalliance with improbabilities was short-lived as he heard Bridgette's voice. Turning to face the shore, Selwyn could see her waving.

'Give me a hand?' she yelled. Her little body bobbed about, and together with Harold, she clutched hold of the Captain's hands. The old boy was upright, his wispy white hair plastered across his head.

In moments Selwyn was by the Captain's side. 'Now, sir,' Selwyn said, 'if you're all ship-shape and ready, it's time to get you back on board.'

'Whales!' The Captain called out as Selwyn lifted him into his arms, 'marooned, get help!'

Selwyn safely crossed the beach with his fragile consignment.

'Fancy a livener?' Bridgette asked Selwyn as she finished towelling the Captain. She placed a T-shirt over his head, pulled it onto his body, then settled him comfortably in a shaded spot by the beach bar, where Christmas calypso songs played.

'Beer for me,' the Captain told no one in particular as his cloudy eyes started to close.

'My round,' Harold said and went to order. 'Another one of those, Nancy?' he asked as he danced to the music and jigged across the sand to rejoin his wife and point to her empty glass.

Selwyn helped Bridgette onto a stool. The crowd at the bar seemed companionable. Most of the drinkers were from the ship. Familiarity flowed as fast as the drinks, and the conversation became lively.

'Have you read that comedian's book?' Nancy asked as

she took a cocktail umbrella out of her pina colada and bit into a cherry.

'Which comedian?'

'You know, the one who's broken out in orange spots.'

'He was on the front page of the *Diamond Star Daily* today,' Harold added.

'Oh, you mean Dicky Delaney.' Bridgette nodded. 'No, I haven't, is it any good?'

'No idea,' Nancy said, 'but we got a copy of it for half the price you pay in the shop.'

'How did you manage that?' Selwyn asked and took a sip of his beer.

'Dicky will come to your cabin, if you pay him cash,' Nancy said as she sucked on her straw.

'He'll personally sign it too.' Harold smiled. 'We're going to give it to our son, it's his birthday next month.'

Selwyn had finished Dicky's book the evening before and could think of better birthday gifts. He wondered if Diane, the shop manager, knew that Dicky was flogging his books on the side? Not that it was any of his business.

'Transport for the *Diamond Star*!' A driver stood at the bar's entrance to round up his passengers. 'Anyone responsible for this person?' he pointed towards the Captain, who was sleeping soundly. The logo on his T-shirt read *If Lost, Please Return to the Ship*.

'Another day in paradise,' Selwyn said as he and Harold helped the Captain onto his wheelchair, and Bridgette began to push.

With the Captain on the coach, Bridgette sat beside

Selwyn. 'Are you going to the festive meal in Fort-de-France this evening?' she asked.

'Yes, I like French food and Diwa recommended it.'

'Jolly good, me too.' Bridgette's face softened, and she sighed. 'Hugo and I had some wonderful holidays in Brittany. I do miss him.'

Selwyn was about to ask Bridgette about her late husband, but her eyes had closed. Her head drooped onto his shoulder and in minutes, Bridgette was sound asleep.

Chapter Eighteen

I n cabin 1101, every little thing was far from all right. Dicky, who'd spent the night in the infirmary, lay on his bed cursing the day he met Melissa Montana. Whatever he had taken, which she'd willingly given, had severely reacted with his skin. Although the blotches had begun to fade, his skin was now a vivid shade of orange. He'd overheard a nurse sniggering that the comedian looked like a giant space hopper, which, she suggested, might improve his comedy act. Neither was the doctor sympathetic; he scolded Dicky for taking unprescribed medicines and threatened to keep him in quarantine for the rest of the cruise.

But Dicky's pleas were persuasive. As he posed no immediate threat to the passengers, he was dispatched to his cabin to remain in solitude for the next forty-eight hours. At that time, he would be reassessed before returning to duty.

His condition meant he would miss performing and, at best, only be allowed back for the concert on Christmas Day. During an uncomfortable conversation with Peter, he learnt that, for the time being, Melissa would be taking over Dicky's schedule.

'To hell with you, Melissa,' Dicky cursed.

When questioned, Melissa denied giving Dicky the medication. She said that he must have got hold of it in Saint Vincent. To make matters worse, Peter reminded him that due to a clause in his contract that Clive had agreed to, his self-inflicted sickness would automatically trigger a salary reduction.

'Shite,' Dicky exclaimed as he lay staring at the ceiling. Clive would have a fit if his agent's commission tumbled too. Dicky closed his eyes and thought of the money he'd miss from illicit sales of his book and DVDs. Would his winning streak in the casino now be jinxed? Other crew members were stacked like cards to take Dicky's place in the wooing of wealthy widows. Nathaniel, the restaurant manager, would soon be wearing a Tag Heuer watch if Dicky didn't get his act together and fast.

Dicky leapt off the bed and began to pace. His brain was racing, and he fantasised about hanging Melissa off the ship's bow and dropping her slowly into deep and deathly waters, never to sing at sea again.

But at least Anne had been on his side.

Faithful to her new acquaintance, she'd phoned and asked if Dicky was all right. Her soft voice assured him that everyone was missing him, and Melissa would not be a match for his talent. Dicky was the star of the show. He reached for a bottle of scotch and poured a stiff measure, and as the rich amber nectar slid down his throat, he began to feel calmer. All was not lost. Anne was an attractive woman and if she could afford to stay in the Hibiscus suite, she must have money. Lots of lovely lolly could quickly come his way if he upped his game. It wasn't difficult. He'd need to increase the charm, take her to bed, fill her pretty head with pillow talk, and then invent a sob story of monumental proportions. It would ensure that Anne's bank transfer arrived in his account before they returned to Barbados.

Dicky stood in front of the mirror and leaned in to examine his face. As he turned from side to side, he saw that the blotches were less pronounced, and the livid colour would fade with any luck. He might even be able to tone it down with Melissa's makeup. It was the least she could do to let him use her products. He glanced at his watch and knew that the passengers had returned from their excursions and would be getting ready for dinner. Peter had arranged a meal in Fort-de-France, and he was sorry to miss it. French food was his favourite, and it would have been easy to tag along, crack a few jokes and let someone else pick up the tab.

With a sigh, Dicky strolled over to the porthole window. He stared out at the sky where the sun was sinking like a stone over the horizon. Dicky marvelled at how this happened in the Caribbean. One moment the sky was a mass of rainbow flames of red and gold, and the next, velvety night. Sometimes, he'd witnessed the extraordinary flash of green light at sunset. As Dicky held his forehead to the glass, his eyes lit up as a brilliant emerald burst of dazzling light momentarily lit up the sky.

'Wow,' Dicky breathed, 'that's lucky!' He remembered his day with Anne at Wallilabou Bay on the *Pirates of the Caribbean* set. The guide had told them that the pirates referred to this phenomenon as a soul coming back to this world from the dead and that person would be successful in matters of the heart.

Feeling cheered by the sighting, he poured another scotch. Sitting comfortably on his bed, he whispered to himself, 'Well, Dicky, that's a sign of you coming back from this experience and winning the heart of Anne.'

At that moment, the phone beside his bed began to ring.

'Hello, Dicky Delaney speaking.'

'Dicky, it's Anne.'

Yes! Dicky punched the air.

'How are you feeling?'

'Oh, you know, up and down.' Dicky rolled his eyes and took a slug of his drink.

'I've left a tray outside your door, with sandwiches, savouries and a bottle of wine.'

'You didn't need to do that.' Dicky grinned and rubbed his stomach.

'Everyone is missing you and hopes that you'll be back in action very soon.'

Dicky nodded his head. He had every intention of being back in action sooner than Anne might think and decided to begin his charm offensive straight away. 'Enough of me,' he said. 'Tell me, lovely lady, what have you been up to today?'

'Not a lot, really, I've been very lazy and had a pamper session in the ship's spa. It's been a relaxing day.'

'You don't need any pampering and if you do, I will be the one to administer it.' Dicky finished his drink and listened to Anne's girlish giggle. 'I think we should celebrate with champagne when we meet again, maybe a candlelit dinner for two?'

'That sounds lovely, I'll look forward to it, Dicky.'

'What are your plans for this evening?'

'I'm going ashore with my friends. There's a festive meal at a restaurant in Fort-de-France – it should be good.'

'If only I could be with you, but I'll be beside you in spirit.'

'Please rest up and if you need anything just leave me a message.'

'Don't think about me, go and enjoy yourself. Bye-bye, sweet girl.'

As Dicky ended the call, he punched the air again. 'Cracked it!' he called out and, rising to his feet, danced to the door to retrieve the tray that Anne had left.

In Hibiscus, Kath and Jane put the finishing touches to their outfits. There was much hilarity as the two stood in the bedroom, staring with wonder as they admired themselves in the floor-length mirrors that lined one wall. In the lounge, Anne sat on a sofa in conversation with Dicky. As she ended the call, she stared at the phone, her brow furrowed as she heard his closing sentiment.

'Bye-bye, sweet girl…' Anne spoke out loud, '*Sweet girl?*' she repeated and shook her head.

'Who's a sweet girl?' Kath asked, stepping into the lounge.

'I am, it seems.' Anne pulled a face. 'But to be honest, I'd prefer to be anything but "sweet" – maybe sexy, seductive, stimulating, or spicy? "Sweet" makes me sound like a goody-two-shoes.'

'Husband-hunting doesn't always run smoothly, sweet girl.' Jane grinned. She headed to the bar and poured ready-mixed cocktails into glasses, adding chunks of ice. 'Surely you don't still have Dicky Delaney on the list?'

'He's sort of hovering,' Anne replied, taking a sip of a delicious mojito.

'He looked a complete tit and deserves to be in quarantine for the rest of the cruise.' Jane giggled. 'You're lucky you haven't caught anything from him.'

'It wasn't his fault, he thought he had a remedy for his sunburn.'

'I think he needs to be more careful about what medicines he takes.' Kath was cautious in her opinion. 'Things like that can be harmful.'

'He must have plenty of money.' Anne changed the subject. 'He tours all over the world.'

'And tells you that he is single and lives in a big debt-free house?' Jane asked.

'He's not said as much but I'm sure that's how things are.'

Anne wasn't sure about Dicky's finances, or his marital status and also agreed with Jane that Dicky had made a fool of himself. But she'd worry about that in the morning. They had an exciting evening ahead.

'Well, I think that we've had a successful day at the spa and hair salon,' Kath announced, 'and we should toast ourselves for being brave and coming out of our comfort zones.'

'Do you think anyone will notice a change?' Jane asked.

Kath and Anne did a double-take and stared at Jane.

'Shall we find out?' Anne rose to her feet.

Kath held up her glass. 'Before we go, I propose a toast to my two wonderful friends,' she began. 'I want to thank you both for helping me to enjoy this holiday.' Kath was misty-eyed. 'You've made me realise that I'm not ready for a care home, walking aids, or anything related to getting older. I'm a woman of a certain age who doesn't give a damn about the number of her age.'

'And my number is ex-directory,' Anne added.

'Hear, hear.' Jane rubbed her tummy. 'But I'm starving so I suggest we get a move on.'

They left the suite and headed through security until they reached the gangway. Dressed in bright casual clothes, Peter stood tapping a pen impatiently against a clipboard.

'You're late,' he admonished and checked their names on a list. When he looked up, his head jerked, and he shuffled back a step or two. 'My word,' Peter said, 'I must say, you all take my breath away.' Spreading his fingers in a fan against his breastbone, he continued, 'As you've made such an effort with your appearances tonight, you are forgiven.' Peter's smile was wide and warm. 'The others have gone ahead, and I have a vehicle waiting to whisk you to your meal at the La Cave au Coq.' He stood to one side. 'Please, follow me.'

Away from the breeze on the ship, the night air was humid and hot. A nocturnal chorus of cicadas and crickets, their chatter a pulsating crescendo, greeted them as Peter settled the passengers into a taxi and then took his place beside the driver.

'An interesting name for a restaurant,' Anne commented as they set off.

Jane held her fan to her face and puffed out her cheeks. 'I hope that there's air-conditioning.'

After driving slowly for a few blocks, where they stared at stylish resort wear in the famous department store Galeries Lafayette, they entered Rue Victor Hugo. Their eyes widened as the vehicle cruised past the Caribbean's most fashionable shopping thoroughfare, where windows displayed the latest fashions from Paris and the French Riviera. Luxury items by Cartier, Baccarat and Lalique proudly flaunted French design.

'We've arrived.' Peter stood to one side as the driver opened the door and Kath, Anne, and Jane alighted. 'La Cave au Coq,' Peter said.

He led the way to a large wooden door and pulled a cord. A bell rang in the distance, and after a few moments, a face peeked out and invited them in. Madame Rochelle was an elegant woman dressed in scarlet and black lace. Her jet-black hair was styled in a taut chignon, and she rocked on the highest of heels.

'Zeez way,' she said and led them through a shop stacked with chocolates and fine wines.

Jane stopped to study a display of hand-made delicacies, but Kath grabbed her arm. 'We can have a look later,' she whispered.

They climbed a narrow stairway, and Madame Rochelle drew back a heavy velvet drape. 'Enjoy ze evening,' she said and ushered the latecomers forward.

The room was candle-lit and filled with murals of the French countryside under a glass domed ceiling. Stars twinkled in the sky alongside a silver slither of a new moon. A Christmas tree covered in tiny lanterns lit up a far corner, and festive ribbons and garlands adorned every nook and cranny. An enormous gold chicken sat on a pedestal in the centre of the room.

'Wow!' the three friends gasped.

'It's magical,' Kath breathed as her eyes took in gold candelabras, glistening cut glass and starched white linen.

'Like a weird French café,' Jane said.

'I think it's marvellous,' Anne whispered. 'So now that we've found La Cave, this must be Le Coq?' she said and stepped forward to touch the golden chicken.

The room was full of passengers from the *Diamond Star*, and they chattered animatedly.

'Oh, look, here's our crowd.' Kath pointed to a circular table in one corner.

Heads began to turn, and conversation stilled as Madame Rochelle led the three friends. As if seeing the three newcomers for the first time, Bridgette, Selwyn, Harold, Nancy, Diane, and the Captain stared wide-eyed, and Peter beamed. They pushed back their chairs to stand, then slowly began to applaud.

'My goodness,' Bridgette exclaimed, 'you have been busy, I hardly recognised you.'

Selwyn was silent as he drew out a chair for Jane. Harold indicated that Kath should sit beside him, and Anne took a seat by the Captain.

Wearing a T-shirt with the logo *Vive la France!* the Captain banged on the table with a spoon and called out, 'Mangez bien, riez souvent, aimez beaucoup!'

'Quite right,' Bridgette said as Madame Rochelle filled everyone's glass with champagne. 'We should all eat well, laugh often, and love abundantly.' She smiled at the Captain. 'Bon appétit, everyone.'

'Bon appétit,' they chorused in reply.

Chapter Nineteen

The following morning, the skipper of the *Diamond Star*, Captain Kennedy, announced their scheduled stop in Guadeloupe had unfortunately been cancelled. Due to recent social turmoil on the island, it was his responsibility for the safety of his passengers not to dock there. There would now be two sea days before arriving in St Maarten early on Christmas Day.

Kath, Jane, and Anne sat at a table on the balcony in Hibiscus and tucked into their breakfast. 'I read about the unrest in Guadeloupe,' Kath said, 'and wondered if we would be giving it a miss.'

Jane munched on sweet red apple, 'What happened?' she asked and licked her fingers.

'The French Government stated that all workers in French territories had to have the Coronavirus vaccine, it is compulsory,' Kath replied. 'Many people objected, and there's a big anti-vaccine movement on the island. There were rioters torching cars and looting shops.'

'Crikey,' Jane gulped. 'That won't be good for tourism.'

'It's probably calmed down now, but I'm sure that Captain Kennedy doesn't want to take any risks.'

'Well, it doesn't matter to me,' Anne chipped in. She cradled a glass of orange juice and stared out to sea. 'Just look at this beautiful setting. We've got loads to enjoy in our floating hotel, before we reach land again.'

'Oh, but I so enjoyed last night.' Kath sighed. 'It was a wonderful evening.'

'The best so far,' Anne agreed.

'I think we surprised people with our appearance.' Jane smiled. 'I thought everyone was going to fall off their chairs when we walked into the dining room.'

'We certainly made an entrance,' Kath agreed. 'Selwyn seemed the most surprised.' She turned to Jane. 'Especially with your new image, he couldn't stop looking at you.'

Jane sat up straight. She stretched her neck, then shook her head and grinned as she felt the heavy length of hair extensions, weaved into tiny plaits, fall around her shoulders. 'I love my hair,' she said, reaching out to caress dozens of coloured beads threaded into narrow plaits. 'I thought Philippe might have suggested a tint or new shade, but he's matched the white extensions perfectly.'

'He's made it look so natural, and it really suits you,' Anne said, 'especially with the tan you're developing.'

'I never thought I'd see you wearing tinted moisturiser

and lipstick,' Kath added. 'I don't think you realise how pretty you are.'

Jane poured a coffee and thought about Selwyn. Had he really been surprised when she sat down beside him? As their first course was served, he'd whispered, 'You look lovely.' The butterflies in Jane's tummy began to dance and continued throughout the evening, right up to the point when they descended the stairs, and Selwyn insisted on buying a box of chocolates.

'For having the courage to make a change,' he said and presented the perfectly wrapped package to Jane.

'You *do* know that you have an admirer?' Kath looked at Jane and saw her friend's cheeks flush. 'Selwyn is smitten with you.'

'Don't be ridiculous,' Jane replied, 'he's just a generous person, a gentleman, someone who wanted to congratulate me for making a change. Don't forget that he lost his wife earlier this year and is on holiday to get over her passing.'

Kath and Anne looked at each other and shook their heads. 'You can deny it all you like,' Kath said, 'but one day you might wake up to the possibility that a man finds you attractive and it may pay you to gamble on Selwyn.'

'I don't gamble and I'm one of life's losers when it comes to relationships.' Jane was adamant. 'So please stop trying to push me towards a stranger that I know nothing about.'

Kath knew it was useless to argue further, and, still shaking her head, she filled a bowl with cereal and began to tuck in.

Jane sipped her coffee while Kath and Anne chatted. She was miles away. She remembered Selwyn's hand taking her own as he gave her the gift. His skin felt warm, and her fingers tingled at his touch. His eyes were so dark and penetrating that she'd had to turn away, mumbling her thanks as she hurried out of the shop to the waiting transport.

Finishing her cereal, Kath dabbed at her mouth with a napkin. 'I love my new look,' she said, 'I've never had so many compliments.'

'Your hair is fab.' Anne reached out and stroked Kath's shiny hair. Gone was the dull, dry salt and pepper of the past. Kath's hair fell perfectly into place, cut into a side-swept pixie. 'Philippe is a genius and the chestnut colour has taken years off.'

'I think tons of marine cream and a bucketload of new products are contributing to that.' Kath hardly dared think of the money she'd spent in the salon. Jim would have been incandescent with rage at her extravagance. Her visit to the ship's boutique also produced a staggering bill. Kath never dreamt that she would wear a jewelled jump-suit nor toss her plain old pumps into the sea. But from now on, she determined, she would spend whenever she liked. To hell with the haunting memories of life before Jim's death.

Anne touched her face with her fingers. 'I'm smooth and wrinkle-free,' she said, catching sight of her reflection on the balcony door.

'Not a muscle moves, your skin is as velvety as a new-born,' Jane commented. 'If you look any younger, you'll be sucking a dummy.' She grinned. 'But I still don't know how you can bear to have stuff injected into your face and lips.'

'No pain, no gain. My wrinkles are hardly noticeable,' Anne replied, 'and it really doesn't hurt, plumper lips make me more youthful and desirable.'

'To a trout, perhaps…' Jane teased and ducked as Anne's hand flew out.

Anne patted her hair. 'I love this style. Philippe called it the Wolf cut.'

'In my day it was called the Shullet,' Jane grinned.

'What's that?'

'A cross between a shag and a mullet.'

Anne laughed and stroked the tendrils that fell softly around her face, 'Well, I love it, and I think it's very glam-rock.'

'We all look glamorous, with our make-overs, and I'm ready to rock into whatever activity you two girls fancy today.' Jane picked up a copy of the *Diamond Star Daily* and began to browse. 'Does anyone feel like a ukulele lesson?' She grinned. 'Or alternatively, Bridgette is hosting a talk in the Neptune Lounge, *From Your Garden to Show Garden*, which should suit Kath.'

'My garden is badly neglected,' Kath said. 'It would take more than a talk from Bridgette to get it looking tidy again.'

As she listened to Jane call out the events scheduled for the day, Kath remembered Hugh and Harry telling their mother off for neglecting the garden since their father had died. She knew they didn't want the property to devalue and would be pressing her to sign it over to them as soon as she returned. They'd assured Kath that she'd be comfortable in the annexe at Harry's home, where, they said, she'd be safe, and they would manage her money and keep an eye on her.

Pah! Kath thought. She would not be cooped up with either of her sons. If her money was invested in their future, Kath knew that a council nursing home would be her next port of call, and she was determined not to let it happen.

'I fancy the dancing class. Why not try our hand at merengue and mambo?' Anne was on her feet and sashaying around the room.

'The only meringue I would like is the one on top of a lemon pie,' Jane snorted. 'I'll give dancing a swerve.' But as the words left her lips, Jane thought of how she'd danced in Spirit's bar and how free and alive it had made her feel. Was she brave enough to go and learn something new with a crowd of complete strangers? They'd all be as thin as rakes, and no one would want to partner her. Did she really want to embarrass herself?

Anne was moving back and forth. 'I learnt how to mambo when I was in South America, in Rio, on a stop-over. The time I spent in Rio was wonderful, all sun, sea, romance and dance...'

'Does it make you want to turn back the clock?'

'Not really,' she said and stopped dancing. 'I have to face up to the future, not live in the past.'

Jane flung the *Diamond Star Daily* to one side. 'That's me sorted,' she announced. 'Jaden Bird is demonstrating in the cookery theatre, *Treats of the Islands*, and there's a front-row seat with my name on it.'

'Then I'll go and support Bridgette,' Kath said, 'I'm sure I'll enjoy her talk.'

'And I'll give ukulele a go, you never know who might be there.' Anne reached for a lipstick and smoothed it over her pout.

'Shall we meet up later for afternoon tea?' Jane asked.

'Good idea.' Anne stood in front of a mirror and adjusted the straps of her sundress as she admired her reflection.

'That sounds lovely,' Kath said. 'but I've put my glasses down somewhere and I can't find them.' She poked through her bulging bag.

Kath's glasses were beside her at the table, and Jane held them up.

'Oh, thank you, I'd forget what day it was if you weren't here to remind me.'

'What day is it?' Anne asked.

'The twenty-third of December,' Jane said. 'Almost Christmas and halfway through our holiday.'

'Then let's continue to make the most of it,' Kath stood. She took hold of her friends' hands and marched them out of the suite.

Chapter Twenty

Two glorious days at sea passed pleasantly for the passengers of the *Diamond Star* and, with an extra day to accommodate, the crew were kept busy providing additional activities to entertain their guests. One afternoon, an impromptu concert took place around the pool when the Marley Men provided calypso and reggae music, and rum punches flowed freely.

Harold, now accustomed to the sun, and wearing the shortest of shorts, threw himself into the limbo competition. Lubricated by several rum punches and ignoring Nancy's cries of 'Mind your lumbago!' he was determined to limbo under the lowest horizontal bar.

Peter compered the competition and assured everyone that it was just for fun, as competitors stretched, flexed, and waited for their turn. The Marley Men played 'Limbo Rock' and chanted, 'How low can you go?' as Harold took his place in the final. Determined and with his face set, Harold eased back and bent his body under the bar. But he stopped halfway, and several guests said that they heard the bones creak in Harold's back from the other side of the pool. His guttural cry of pain was heard throughout the deck.

Nancy fell into a faint, and it took Armani and three lifeguards to get her back on her feet as Harold was placed on a stretcher.

Bridgette, an observer, told Selwyn that Harold had been foolish to attempt such a feat. A man of his age should know better. The unbroken world record for the lowest game of limbo, she informed, belonged to one Dennis Walston, who, in 1991, squeezed underneath a bar six inches from the ground. This eye-watering information made Selwyn vow never to indulge in such a practice.

He'd stick to dancing and joined in with the Marley Men.

Before getting ready for dinner, Selwyn stood on deck and reached into his pocket. He stared out at the distant horizon as he emptied the contents of his plastic pouch into the sea. Flo had never liked to dance, but with her ashes in Selwyn's pocket, unwittingly, she had.

As the ship headed north that night and darkness gave way to a new day, passengers woke to another packed schedule. Quoits, shuffleboard, and skittles took place on an upper deck, and a watercolour class encouraged budding artists to sit at easels and paint nautical scenes in a light-filled studio.

Guests in the Neptune Lounge attended talks that included 'An Audience with Our Crew,' where key crew members explained what it took to sail a cruise ship around the world. The Captain sat in the front row and cheered as he recognised the countries he'd visited.

Dancing classes were popular and attended by many, including Jane, who was surprised that she had more rhythm than she'd bargained for.

While Kath went to ukulele lessons, Anne, frustrated by not seeing Dicky, sat through a classical recital and joined Jane and Kath for a cheese and wine experience. As they dressed for the evening entertainment, the three friends were delighted that housekeeping had sculpted Christmas trees out of the towels at the end of their beds and little boxes of liqueur chocolates had been placed on their pillows.

'These are divine,' Jane exclaimed as she popped a mini chocolate rum log into her mouth and they set off to watch Melissa Montana fill in for Dicky.

On Christmas Eve, the friends enjoyed mulled wine and mince pies and stood around the giant yuletide tree in the vestibule to sing carols by candlelight. They linked arms as they were joined by the other passengers, remembering Christmases past as a string quartet accompanied the singing. A buffet in the Terrace Restaurant followed and was laden with festive dishes with a roast suckling pig at the centre. The Neptune Lounge filled up for the evening's entertainment, and at midnight many guests attended mass in the chapel.

When dawn broke on Christmas Day, the *Diamond Star* shone like a giant gleaming globe as the sun rose and the ship sailed silently through tranquil waters.

'Good morning,' Captain Kennedy's voice was heard throughout the ship as guests woke. 'It's Christmas Day and I am pleased to tell you that we are now arriving in St Maarten on a beautiful, sunny morning.'

He described what he could see from the bridge and the activities that would soon take place. His velvet voice concluded with his message for the day.

'Fellow travellers, may I be the first to wish you all a very happy Caribbean Christmas and I hope that today is, for you all, a most memorable day.'

Chapter Twenty-One

'Wake up! Santa's been!' In Hibiscus, Jane stood at the foot of Kath's bed and, reaching out, grabbed her friend's toes. 'Come on, sleepy head, wake up.' She wore a giant onesie patterned with Rudolph and Santa's reindeer and marched over to Anne's bed to lean close to her ear. 'Jingle bells, jingle bells, jingle all the way!' she sang.

'Bugger off!' Anne hollered and, grabbing a pillow, hurled it at Jane.

'Now, that's not very nice.' Jane laughed and ducked out of the way. 'Naughty children don't get stockings from Santa.'

'All I want for Christmas is two aspirins and a gallon of water,' Anne groaned as the night before flashed through her mind.

She remembered dancing in the disco with Bridgette until the early hours. The Captain, perched on his regular stool at the bar, had been delighted to supply a never-ending range of cocktails as he watched the women twirl and twist under a giant glitter ball. Waving his stick and raising his hat, he'd shimmied his shoulders and joined in. Anne had a hazy recollection of the disco closing and, with the Captain ensconced in his wheelchair, together with Bridgette, and considerably worse for wear, they'd negotiated their way to his suite to continue to party.

'I imagine that Bridgette is suffering as much as you are today,' Jane said.

'Don't think so,' Anne mumbled, 'she was sharing space cake with the Captain when I left them.'

'*What?*' Kath and Jane exclaimed.

'She said she bought it in a bakery in Saint Vincent, and cannabis cake is known to combat the effects of excessive alcohol and make you feel good.'

Jane remembered the delicious Red Belly cake she'd eaten with Selwyn and Toots. No wonder she'd experienced a sublime calm that day. Not to mention Spirit's lethal spliff. She was hardly able to criticise Bridgette.

Kath was out of bed. Wearing a reindeer-patterned nightshirt, she picked up a Santa hat and pulled it on, then stood beside Jane and stared at Anne's huddled body. Turning to Jane, they both nodded and pulled back the covers to jump in Anne's bed.

'What the hell...?' Anne raised her tousled head and removed her eye mask, peering with one eye closed, 'What on earth are you doing?' she asked.

'We are your rescue Santas.' Jane laughed, wriggling her

body further into the bed. 'And if you care to sit up and see what Santa has left in your stocking you might feel a great deal brighter.'

'What stocking?' Anne asked and eased into a sitting position.

'This one.' Jane handed Kath and Anne a bulging stocking, cut from her heavy denier tights. 'When I was a kid, my mum used to leave a filled stocking at the end of my bed. It was always one of her Pretty Polly American Tan nylons, usually full of ladders and worn at the toe.'

'I had one of my father's old socks.' Kath smiled. 'There would be a tangerine in the bottom, a bag of gold-covered chocolate coins, and a small wooden toy.'

'Or a bag of jacks.' Anne, suddenly brighter, was upright. 'I spent hours playing the game, sitting cross-legged, bouncing the ball in our hallway, and scooping the metal jacks against the tiles. It used to drive my mother mad.'

'Well, your stocking contents have been updated this year.' Jane grinned. 'I hope you appreciate my sacrifice of cutting the legs out of my tights.'

'Shall I sew them back on?' Kath asked. 'I've got a sewing kit in my bag.'

Ignoring Kath, Anne reached into her stocking and unscrewed the top of a miniature bottle of prosecco. 'Perfect,' she said and sipped the contents. 'The hair of the dog. Santa is a life-saver.'

Kath unwrapped a tube of La Prairie hand cream. 'My goodness, Santa *has* been generous,' she exclaimed. Soon the bed was covered in discarded paper, and they laughed as each of Jane's gifts was unwrapped.

'This is wonderful!' Anne crawled over Jane and slipped into a silky La Perla nightdress. 'And Kath got me matching bra and knickers.' She held up a wisp of lace in each hand.

'We consider the gifts an investment,' Kath said.

'To ensure that your husband-hunting mission is successful,' Jane added. 'Strut your stuff in that lot and you'll be walking down the aisle in no time.'

'I do love you both,' Anne said, embracing her friends.

'Where's my bag?' Kath asked and, finding it by her bed, reached for her glasses and began to rummage. 'A little something for Jane,' she said and held out a beautifully wrapped box.

'Chocolates?'

'Open it.'

Kath watched as Jane carefully undid the ribbon and opened the gift. Lying on a bed of silk lay an exquisite enamelled turtle pendant on a silver chain. Two little diamonds represented the turtle's eyes.

'Oh...' Jane breathed, 'it's superb.'

'The turtle represents new beginnings and I thought it an appropriate gift.'

'I shall wear it always,' Jane said, fastening it around her neck. Stroking the beautifully crafted jewellery, she turned to a mirror. 'It's the most gorgeous thing I've ever owned.'

'Now, Anne, this is for you.' Kath handed Anne a package.

Anne opened her gift and gasped when she saw a ring.

'The stone is Larimar,' Kath said. 'It's a unique blue gemstone, found only in the Caribbean.'

'The colour is like the blue of the sea and the sky,' Anne said as she slid the ring onto a middle finger.

'Exactly. A reminder of our holiday, but also a reminder of our life-long friendship too.'

'Oh, Kath.' Anne and Jane were tearful as they hugged Kath and thanked her for her memorable presents.

'Now, it's my turn.' Anne opened a drawer and pulled out two packages. 'It's the thought that counts,' she added as she handed them out.

Jane tore the paper and shook out an oversized T-shirt. As she read the logo, she giggled. *Your First Mistake Was Assuming I'm An Old Lady*.

Kath whipped her nightshirt off and pulled her T-shirt over her head.

'What does it say?' Jane eagerly asked.

Kath thrust out her chest. 'It says, *"Do You Know What I'm Thinking? Because I Forgot"*.'

'Yeah!' Jane punched the air. 'These are hilarious, Anne, thank you so much.'

'Look.' Kath pointed and reached out to turn up the volume on the television. On the ship's channel, carols were being sung in the chapel. The camera focused on a nativity scene as a choir sang 'Away in a Manger'.

'Happy Christmas, my dearest friends,' Kath said and they all hugged as they joined in with the carols.

On Christmas morning, in his cabin on a lower deck, Selwyn sat up in bed and opened two cards. The first was from his youngest daughter Gloria and her partner Gwen. It depicted a snow scene of Lambeth Town Hall, and turning it over, he recognised the signature and realised that Gwen had drawn the card. A reminder of home. Selwyn studied the beautifully depicted Grade II listed building, a familiar landmark, and admired how Gwen had captured the fine example of Edwardian Baroque architecture. He smiled as he read the inscription.

Happy Christmas Dad
We hope you are enjoying your holiday
With all our love from
Gloria & Gwen xx

Selwyn nodded as he read the words and thought how sad it was that only after Flo's death had Gloria been able to tell him about Gwen. Knowing that her mother would have disowned her eldest daughter for loving a woman, she'd lived with her secret all this time. Selwyn wondered what sort of father he'd been to not know how his daughter felt. But he'd embraced Gwen into the family and vowed to make it up to them both.

The other card was from Susan, and the cheap paper contained sparse words.

From Susan, Raymond & Charlene

Susan was as frugal as her mother and the living duplication of everything Flo believed in. Namely, the Baptist Church in Lambeth. Susan and Raymond spent more time in church than Flo, and Selwyn felt the distance grow greater between himself and his eldest daughter. Charlene, however, was Granddad's delight and Selwyn adored the little girl. He knew that his regular gifts were far too extravagant, but the toddler was the apple of his eye, and he relished the precious hours spent with her.

Selwyn turned up the volume on the television. On the ship's channel, a nativity scene was being shown, and the carol 'Away in a Manger'. It reminded him of childhood in the family house, where relatives, friends, and neighbours gathered around the table with his parents and siblings to enjoy his mother's Christmas cooking. Full of fine food, they'd begin with carols but soon enjoy reggae, ska, and calypso as the day progressed into the night.

Selwyn suddenly felt lonely and sank back against the pillows.

It was Christmas, a time of year when families and friends were together. Yet he was alone, in bed, thousands of miles away from home. Should he have been in the church hall in Lambeth? Pastor Gregory would have welcomed him and ensured Selwyn had company.

Selwyn sighed as he touched the cards that lay on his bed. How good it would be to have the company of a woman. Someone he could make love to and indulge. A person he could be proud of and a companion to share the latter years of his life. There were plenty of ladies on the ship who, he knew, would be pleased to make his acquaintance. Selwyn had never been short of admirers and, on occasion, had played away from home. But he'd felt a duty to Flo and would never leave the mother of his children despite the church being a third member of their marriage. Selwyn considered himself a good husband, but it hadn't been the life he'd chosen, and unbeknown to his wife, Selwyn had a secret.

A secret that he hoped one day to share with the right person. Reaching out, he took a sip of water and thought about Jane. 'That woman is complicated,' he sighed.

Selwyn had never met anyone so fixated with their size, and not in a good way. She was obsessed with being overweight, and it affected her confidence. But in Selwyn's eyes, she was gorgeous, and he remembered how freely she'd danced in Spirit's bar and felt his heart beat a little faster. Could she fall in love with him and would he win her over before the cruise ended? Was Jane the woman to share his secret?

He stared at the television. More melodies played, and the day's events ran across the screen, from gingerbread displays in the library, a snow celebration in the atrium, seasonal movies on a screen by the pool and even a Christmas sweater competition. Selwyn had opted for a traditional meal in the Terrace Restaurant that began at three o'clock. Later, in the Neptune Lounge, there was a holiday-themed entertainment show. His reservation for lunch was on his regular table, and his new friends would be joining him. Including Jane. As he swung his legs over the side of the bed, he determined to find her soft spot, the key that would unlock the woman inside.

But in the meantime, how to spend the morning?

Staying in his cabin wasn't achieving anything, and why on earth was he feeling sorry for himself? This was the holiday of a lifetime! He'd get dressed and go out on the deck to enjoy the island of St Maarten. Maybe take a water taxi to the beach. A swim would be great, and he'd be back in plenty of time for the Christmas meal.

Decisions made, Selwyn stepped into the bathroom and sang softly as he got ready for his day.

Christmas morning hadn't started well for Dicky. Despite feeling relief that he'd been given the all-clear from the ship's medic, and would be allowed to leave his cabin, a phone call from Peter had left him reeling. Staring at the itinerary he'd scribbled on a notepad, his eyes were bulging when he checked off the list of activities Peter had planned.

Dicky glanced at his Tag Heuer. He hadn't expected to begin work until the evening, and had anticipated a day delivering books to cabins and whatever else he could conjure up to add dollars to his stash in the safe. But Peter had demanded that Dicky pull his finger out. His debacle with his health had given the comedian two full days of rest while the crew were working around the clock. Melissa had a heavy cold and was confined to quarters. The *Diamond*

Star Dancing Troupe, who also hosted events, were dropping like flies.

'What would you like me to do?' Dick asked as he gripped the phone to his ear and tapped angrily on the pad with his pen.

'You can begin by being Santa at the beach party this morning,' Peter said. 'Then, I want you to host the Christmas sweater competition in the Mermaid Theatre. During the Christmas lunch, you will circulate – telling jokes, taking charge of the raffle, and helping to ensure that everyone is having a great time.'

Dicky wanted to ask Peter if he'd like him to attach a broom to his bottom and sweep up too? But he knew he was on dodgy ground and, taking a deep breath, replied that Peter could count on him to be a team player and help wherever he could.

'Don't forget that the cabaret evening is in the Neptune Lounge, and you must attend a pre-breakfast run-through with the cast before you head off for the beach party,' Peter added.

Dicky wondered if he should offer to steer the sodding ship and stoke the boilers while he was at it? Instead, he bit his tongue and reassured Peter that he was already out of the door and to leave everything to him.

'I sent an email to Clive to let him know that you let us down in the last forty-eight hours so I'm sure you'll be hearing from him,' Peter added before disconnecting the call.

'Hell!' Dicky cursed and threw his pen across the room.

He hoped that Clive was supping a bottle of brandy by a cosy log fire far away from his computer and, with any luck, wouldn't be sober until the new year. By that time, Dicky would have completed his stint so well that any misdemeanours would be forgotten.

As Dicky stood in the shower, he thought of Melissa. 'A heavy cold' generally meant a cast member had a severe hangover. If others were down with it too, Dicky suspected there had been after-hours parties below the passenger decks. He'd seen Melissa in action off-stage, and her ability to dance all night and drink a tray of shots would floor an army of squaddies.

He cursed as he hastily towelled dry. There wasn't even time to call Anne and wish her Happy Christmas.

Still, the show must go on, and it was in his best interests to step up and prove to Peter that he could make it happen. Maybe the entertainment director would ease off Dicky's case, and things could get back to normal. Dicky stooped low in front of a mirror to comb his hair and apply a layer of tinted moisturiser. He shrugged his shoulders and gave himself a pearly white smile.

At least he looked human again.

Chapter Twenty-Two

For a mere seven dollars per passenger, a water taxi could be hired to whisk sunseekers to the glorious Maho beach on the tropical island of St Maarten. Described by Diwa and her customer service team as one of the most unique beaches in the world, it is situated close to the island's Princess Juliana International Airport. Popular with windsurfers and skim-boarders, the stretch of long white beach is edged by bars and stalls selling local crafts.

For Kath, Jane, and Anne, a couple of hours swimming and sunbathing was the perfect way to start their Christmas Day, and the friends were excited as they left the ship. They waited by a jetty, a boat arrived within minutes, and they climbed aboard.

The water taxi driver assisted them onto the beach, and soon, they found a smooth stretch of sand to sit on.

'I'm surprised there are no sunbeds,' Anne complained

as she spread her beach towel out and slipped out of her shorts and top to reveal her pink bikini.

'Enjoy the natural surroundings,' Kath replied. Wearing a large straw hat, she perched sunglasses on her nose.

'I'm not so sure that a beach so close to an airport runway can be classed as natural surroundings,' Jane said. 'Still, as it's Christmas Day, there won't be any planes landing.'

'Ignore the runway and look at the gorgeous sea,' Kath said and slathered lotion on her skin.

The beach formed a semicircle and sloped down to water the colour of emeralds as waves broke in white crests, creating layers of frothy foam that fluttered to the shore.

'Oh look,' Kath called out, 'the crew have brought refreshments.'

A short distance away, Armani and several crew members reached into cool boxes. Dressed in *Diamond Star* vests, shorts, and Santa hats, they summoned other passengers, who'd also arrived at the beach, to come and enjoy a Caribbean Christmas cocktail.

'I don't need to be asked twice,' Jane said and strode over. She wore a bright yellow sarong over her swimsuit and silently thanked Kath, who'd insisted that Jane purchase two from the ship's boutique, and a colourful kaftan. The cotton enveloping her body was crisp and cool, and as it draped over her curves, she knew that it flattered too.

Armani set up a speaker, and Christmas songs began to play above the sound of gently breaking waves.

'It's beginning to look a lot like Christmas!' Kath, Jane, and Anne swayed together and sang as they sat on their towels and sipped their drink.

'What is it?' Kath asked. 'It's delicious.'

'Ponche de crème,' Jane replied, 'a rum and cream concoction.'

'Yummy,' Anne muttered and licked her lips.

'Good grief,' Kath said, lifting the brim of her hat. She squinted and leaned forward to watch passengers step off a water taxi and head up the beach. 'We're being invaded by elves!'

'Got room for a few more?' a voice called out, and Bridgette, wearing a short green and red dress with a matching hat and bobble, bounced towards them. Two spots of rouge coloured her cheeks.

'It's Santa's little helper,' giggled Jane.

Following close behind, in similar attire, came Nancy, her voluptuous dress gathered with a wide belt and buckle. She stumbled as she reached the friends and held her hand to her mouth. 'It's my motion sickness,' she groaned. 'I should never have got in the boat.' Nancy was as green as her elf's hat, and Anne leapt up to hand her a bottle of water.

'How's your back?' Kath asked Harold with concern.

'Clicked in of its own accord,' Harold replied and laid out a towel. 'I'm as right as rain again.'

'You look very fetching,' Jane told Harold as he took a cocktail from Armani's tray. 'I like your costume.'

Harold wore tiny, tight striped shorts in green and red, a

tunic top and pixie boots. 'We thought we'd get in the spirit of things,' he replied. 'Cheers!'

Kath looked at Jane and shrugged. There was too much of Harold on show.

The last to arrive was Selwyn. Handsome in beach shorts and sliders, Selwyn wore little else but a smile and his red Fedora. After Bridgette's protestations, because he had been reluctant to don a Christmas outfit, he'd compromised and accepted her offer of a sprig of mistletoe pinned to his hat.

'I'm first!' Anne called out. She leapt to her feet to stand on her toes and plop a kiss on Selwyn's lips.

Suddenly embarrassed, Jane looked away. She hoped that Selwyn wouldn't do the rounds of the ever-increasing group.

'You're catching the sun,' Selwyn said. He moved beside Jane and chinked his drink against hers. 'It suits you.'

'I look like an overcooked lobster,' Jane replied. 'I don't tan very well.'

'Why do you always put yourself down?'

'Er ... because it's true?'

'No. It's habit.' Selwyn smiled. 'Accept a compliment, Jane.'

'Well, er ... thank you.'

'And I like your hair.' Selwyn touched Jane's braids and caressed a bead between his fingers. 'You look youthful.'

Jane sipped her drink, and as she heard Selwyn's words, she almost spat it out. *Youthful?* She wondered what possessed him to call an overweight sixty-three-year-old 'youthful'. Deciding that he was toying with her, she turned away.

More passengers joined the group and were encouraged by the crew to sing along with the Christmas songs. Several began to dance as Wham! and Mariah Carey whipped everyone into a festive frenzy.

'We just need a visit from Santa,' Jane suggested as Armani produced delicious warm snacks.

Jane was enjoying a conkie, a pumpkin- and coconut-filled parcel wrapped in a steamed banana leaf. She looked up to see a figure lumbering up the beach. 'Blimey,' she gasped, 'Santa's here!'

Santa was dressed in boots, a red jacket, trousers, and a hat, all trimmed with white fur, and his face was covered by a bushy white beard. He carried a bulging sack over his drooping shoulder. 'Ho, Ho, Ho!' Santa called out. 'Merry Christmas, one and all!'

'How wonderful!' Anne jumped up and down, clapping her hands as the suited and booted figure approached.

'He must be roasting with that lot on,' Jane said as Santa swung his sack from his shoulder and placed it on the beach. 'Who would be daft enough to play Santa on a Caribbean beach?'

Unbeknown to the group gathered around, 'roasting' was an understatement and Santa, alias Dicky Delaney, was about to expire. Cursing Peter for making him wear such a ridiculous outfit in thirty-degree heat, Dicky was tempted to grab a couple of Armani's cocktails, but knew he'd probably get fired on the spot.

'Have you all been good little boys and girls?' Dicky sang through gritted teeth and reached into his sack.

'We have!' – 'Most certainly!' – 'All year!' the merry band of elves and sunbathers replied.

Dicky's fingers felt dozens of Christmas-wrapped gifts, and with a sigh, he began to lift them out. There was no sign of Peter, who was probably sitting on an empty deck, feet up, sipping a Buck's fizz, with a telescope poised to make sure Dicky was playing his part.

'Happy Christmas!' Dicky yelled and tossed his packages towards the guests.

Bridgette tumbled over Nancy as she threw herself into the air to catch with one hand. At the same time, Harold adopted a rugby-style tackle on Anne as guests shrieked with laughter and grabbed the gifts. Delighted with the unexpected treats, they ripped off the wrapping to find *Diamond Star* caps and T-shirts amongst party poppers, glow sticks, and paper trumpets.

Dicky sighed with relief as he reached the bottom of his sack and stood upright, longing to find a towel and wipe his perspiring forehead. He couldn't wait to rip the stupid suit off and, away from the guests, dive into the sea. But as he was about to wish everyone a merry goodbye, he heard Armani shriek and saw her run to secure the cool boxes with the other crew members.

'What's wrong?' he called out.

'It's a plane!' Armani shouted and pointed to the sky as she hastily packed beakers and bottles.

'Looks like American Airlines to me,' Harold said, his hand shielding his eyes, 'and it's a big one.'

'No wonder there are no sunbeds,' Anne yelled to Jane as the friends secured their bags and towels. 'I thought you said there wouldn't be any planes landing on Christmas Day!'

'I didn't think there would be, but it looks like it's landing,' Jane called back. 'Brace yourselves!'

Like a monstrous bird, the plane made its descent and now, cruising at less than a hundred feet, began its final approach. The roar from the engines was deafening as passengers plugged their ears and crouched low. Dicky, who'd made his way down the beach, was suddenly engulfed by water as an enormous wave created by the plane's back-blast surged over him. His hat and beard were washed away as he struggled to his feet. Spluttering and coughing, Dicky tried to regain his balance, only to be hit by a sudden gust of sand as the plane touched down on the runway.

Further up the beach, the windswept passengers were all safe and standing, staring at the bedraggled figure on the shore.

'Oh, no!' Anne cried out, 'it's Dicky!'

Wet sand clung to Dicky's face and clothing as he struggled to summon his nearby water taxi.

'He looks like he's been pebbledashed,' Jane giggled.

'The sand will set like concrete in this heat,' Harold added.

As the passengers stared out to sea and Santa's water

sleigh pulled away, Armani reopened the coolers and turned the music back on. 'Half an hour to go, folks!' she said, topping up the drinks, as Noddy Holder belted out a song and everyone joined in.

So here it is, Merry Christmas,
everybody's having fun!
Look to the future now.
It's only just begun.

'Merry Christmas, my backside!' Dicky swore as he hurried down the corridor to his cabin. Stripping the sodden jacket from his shoulders, he hurled it to one side and cursed Peter. He must have known that a plane was due to land that morning. Flight times in St Maarten were always posted well ahead of time. There had been no risk to passengers situated safely by the crew further up the beach. Still, Dicky felt he should have been warned not to go near the water with a jumbo jet ready to land on his head. Why had no one told him the beach was notorious for jet blasts? The water taxi driver laughed at Dicky's dilemma and told him plane spotters and video makers came from around the world to Maho beach to closely view aircraft on their flight path. Reaching his cabin, Dicky peeled off his boots and trousers and dumped them to one side.

Housekeeping could deal with that dripping lot.

But now, he had to scrape the sand off his face, shower,

and prepare for the wretched Christmas sweater competition. Peter had promised that an outfit would be delivered to Dicky's cabin, and as Dicky stepped in, he groaned when he saw a sweater on his bed.

'No!' Dicky roared. 'Absolutely not. Not under any circumstances!' he shouted to an empty room. Hopping on one leg, he stripped off his wet boxer shorts, then stomped into the bathroom. 'You can stuff your Christmas sweater right up Santa's chimney!'

Lunchtime in the Mermaid Theatre was a jolly affair. Having returned from the beach, after briefly freshening up, many guests wore their Christmas sweaters. They took seats to take part in the competition and those not joining in were dressed in Santa's gifts.

The Captain, asleep at a front-row table, gripped a glow stick. His T-shirt depicted a snowman with a beer bottle and the words *On the Piste*.

Harold was the first to join the Captain. His snug red shorts were teamed with a short-sleeved sweater displaying an image of a Christmas turkey and the strapline *Gobble Till You Wobble*.

Kath, Jane, and Anne followed close behind.

'Is Nancy with you?' Kath asked.

'She's not herself.' Harold frowned. 'And I've left her to have a lie down.'

Kath recalled Nancy violently throwing up in her pixie

hat. Remembering Nancy's motion sickness, she wondered why Harold had let his wife take a trip in a boat.

'She may join us later,' Harold added, 'she was hoping to scoop first prize.'

Anne ordered coffee, and as their drinks arrived, the band started to play a medley of seasonal tunes. 'I wonder if they know this song?' she asked and pointed to her chest. Her T-shirt had an image of Beyoncé with the title *All the Jingle Ladies*.

Kath sipped on a latte. She wore a pretty blouse trimmed with tinsel she'd found in the ship's shop. Jane was wearing her new kaftan, and she'd pinned a hand-written note to the front with the words *Jingle Bell Rock*.

'My goodness.' Kath stared ahead. 'Is that Bridgette?'

A goblin-like figure hurried towards them, wearing a red cloak and hood. 'Ta-dah!' Bridgette cried as she approached their table. She flung her cloak open to reveal a flesh-coloured body stocking. *I Only Get My Baubles Out Once A Year!* was written on her chest, and two globe-shaped decorations jiggled as she moved.

Harold, drinking a pint of lager, spluttered and sprayed foam all over his turkey. 'By heck, Bridgette,' he said, 'that's a winning outfit.'

Selwyn strode through the room to join them. He still wore his Fedora but had changed into smart trousers and a shirt patterned with smiling snowmen. He'd added festive red braces.

'Oh, you do look handsome,' Kath said and patted the empty seat beside her.

'Have I missed anything?' Selwyn asked.

'No, but things are about to begin.'

On the stage, Melissa Montana waved to the audience and invited everyone to join her as the band began to play 'Make My Wish Come True'. She looked pretty in high-heeled boots and a short red Santa dress, the hood and hem trimmed with soft white fur. After two more festive numbers, she announced that she would return that evening for the Christmas cabaret.

'I thought you were ill,' Dicky hissed as he stood in the wings and Melissa came off the stage.

'Whoever told you that?' Melissa smiled sweetly.

'*You* could have organised this competition,' Dicky snapped. 'I've got far too much to do today.'

'What?' Melissa raised an eyebrow. 'Deprive you of wearing this wonderful outfit?' Melissa bit her lip and giggled, then stroked Dicky's snowman sweater. She raised her hand and touched his face. 'Have you been exfoliating?' she asked. 'Your skin looks as though it's been sand-blasted.'

'Sod off!' Dicky snarled and, ripping the microphone from her hand, stepped out.

'Break a leg!' Melissa called out, 'or a carrot!'

Dicky broke into a dance as the band played an intro. He tapped and turned and, with a spin, held out his arms as he came to a stop and greeted everyone. 'Are you having a good time?' he called out.

'Not as good as you!' Harold replied.

Dicky was aware that the audience was laughing. In

fact, most of the faces were wiping their eyes and shaking their heads as they watched Dicky move across the stage. Damn Peter! he thought and cursed the entertainment director for making him wear the most ridiculous Christmas sweater he'd ever seen.

But… Things appeared to be going well, and perhaps he should play on it?

'Do you like my carrots?' Dicky called out and shook his chest.

On his sweater, two plump snowmen sat side-by-side. With coal-black eyes, they wore woolly hats and scarves. Their noses were protruding carrots, at least a foot long and cleverly sprung to bounce from Dicky's nipples as he moved.

'Look out for a pantomime horse!' Harold continued, 'he'll eat your carrots!'

'Ah, but at least I've made an effort,' Dicky said and began to parade around the stage. 'There isn't an outfit in here that can beat me.'

'Oh yes, there is!' a voice called out, and heads turned to see a newcomer hurrying through the room.

'Oh, gawd…' Harold said and put his head in his hands.

Nancy, resplendent in silky red culottes, wore a Christmas sweater. She clambered onto the stage and, grabbing Dicky's hands, turned to face the audience then placed his fingers on her breasts. Knitted perfectly into the wool were two giant traditional Christmas desserts.

'Hands off my puddings!' Nancy yelled, and the crowd,

leaping to their feet, went wild. Party poppers popped, glow sticks glowed, and trumpets hooted.

'A surprising sweater,' Dicky said and stood back to join in with the applause, 'and I think we have a winner!'

'Tosh!' Bridgette could be heard to say as she stomped out of the room. 'My baubles are much better than her puddings!'

Chapter Twenty-Three

On the balcony in Hibiscus, Boxing Day began quietly. Having left St Maarten, the *Diamond Star* was now making its way to the island of Antigua. It would be a lazy morning for Kath, Jane, and Anne, who decided on a light breakfast in their suite. They'd enjoyed a delicious meal the previous day. Kath swore she wouldn't cook a Christmas dinner again as course after course of mouth-watering food was served throughout the afternoon.

'I never thought that I could eat so much turkey.' Kath, dressed in cotton pyjamas, sipped a cup of peppermint tea and stared out to sea. 'Did we have ten or twelve courses? I lost count after a while.'

'Twelve delicious examples of Jaden Bird's wonderful creative cooking,' Jane said. 'I'm surprised he's working on a ship and not a celebrity chef on TV.'

'I think travelling the word on a cruise liner is a very

good career,' Kath replied. 'If you admire him so much, why don't you ask for a tour of the kitchens?'

Kath's comment didn't pass Jane by. As she studied the endless sea beyond the balcony, Jane yearned to look at the complex set-up that provided round-the-clock cuisine. But her days of professional cooking were long gone, and there was no reason for the chef to welcome a middle-aged, overweight retiree into a world she would never be a part of again.

She decided to change the subject and turned to Anne.

'What happened to you last night?' Jane asked. 'Did you have another night on the tables, spinning the wheel with Santa?'

'Don't call him Santa,' Anne said. 'Dicky hated that horrible heavy suit.' She flicked two aspirins out of a packet and, taking her tea, gulped them down.

'I liked his carrots.' Kath giggled. 'I'd love a sweater like that.'

'It was terrible. Dicky thinks that Peter has it in for him, and likes to make him look silly.'

'Well, he turned it round last night,' Jane said. 'The cabaret was great, and Dicky stole the show.'

Anne, wearing her La Perla nightie, had a far-off look as she leaned back in her chair. Closing her eyes, she stretched her legs and placed her toes on the handrail, 'Yes, he was rather good, wasn't he?' she said.

'Absolutely hilarious. I'm tempted to ask him for a souvenir and to sign a copy of his book for me,' Jane said.

Kath raised her eyebrows. Having read Dicky's far-fetched book, she didn't think it was that good but decided to let it pass.

'He's certainly talented, and a great compere.' Anne sighed. She laid a hand on her brow. 'I'm surprised he hasn't been approached for the Royal Variety Performance.'

Incredulous, Kath and Jane exchanged glances.

'I'm not sure he's in such a league.' Jane shrugged. 'But do tell us, where did you go with Dicky?'

After the show, the friends split up when Dicky, buoyed up by his successful performance, sought Ann out and whisked her away.

'We went for a cocktail,' Anne said and remembered how they'd made their way to the bar, where the Captain sat with Bridgette, working their way through the top shelf of malts.

But Anne's time with Dicky had been abruptly cut short.

Seating themselves, they'd ordered a drink when Dicky was approached by a woman dressed from top to toe in a designer gown and jewels. She insisted that Dicky accompany her. Anne couldn't understand why she'd called Dicky 'T.H.' and reminded him that her watch needed servicing. Dicky barely apologised to Anne as he knocked back his drink and leapt up, saying he'd catch her later. Feeling miffed, Anne decided to drown her sorrows with the Captain and Bridgette. But Bridgette was melancholy and spoke of how she missed her Hugo. The Captain, who became more lucid the more he drank, offered to marry them both.

It hadn't been Anne's best evening.

'What did you two get up to?' Anne asked.

Kath tilted her head. 'You'll be pleased to hear that madam' – Kath pointed to Jane –'came out of her comfort zone and went to the Mermaid Theatre with Selwyn.'

'Crikey.' Anne inched forward. 'Was it like a date?'

'Oh, don't be daft.' Jane felt her skin redden and a flush creep up her neck. 'We just had a drink, listened to the Marley Men for half an hour or so, and then he walked me back here.'

'But you must have had a snog?' Anne persisted.

'I did not!' Jane could feel a vein pulse in her temple. She wished she could gloss over her experience with Selwyn, but the memory was too fresh.

'I thought he looked very dashing, in his dinner suit,' Kath said, 'and that scarlet cummerbund set it off a treat.'

Jane too thought that Selwyn was easy on the eye. He scrubbed up well, and she'd been aware of heads turning as they'd entered the Mermaid Theatre together. But *why* had she drunk so much wine with each course during their meal? After coffee and liqueurs, she'd found it easy to accept Selwyn's invitation to accompany him to see the Marley Men. But during the Christmas cabaret, Jane began to sober up. She knew she'd have crept away if Selwyn hadn't been waiting when the show ended.

Jane tilted her head and felt the sun on her skin. Her emotions were all over the place, and she didn't understand her feelings. Jane couldn't remember when a man had been so kind and courteous and was sure that Selwyn must feel sorry for her. The big woman who was always ignored. But if she gave in to these strange and topsy-turvy feelings, surely she'd get hurt? When the cruise ended, in the cold light of day, Selwyn would be gone and never heard from again. As a salty spray misted her skin, Jane sighed. She was too old to have her heart broken.

'So, tell us, did you dance?' Anne was back on the case.

'Er … yes,' Jane muttered. 'For a while.'

'I've seen Selwyn on the dance floor, and he's got some groovy moves.' Anne smiled and raised her eyebrows.

Jane reached for a glass of water and took a long drink. Her dance with Selwyn had been one of her most embarrassing experiences. While Selwyn would be a worthy winner of *Strictly Come Dancing*, Jane stood ramrod straight and felt her feet turn to lead. Her body froze as the sounds of calypso filled the dance floor. With no herbal stimulant nor Spirit's bomb-proof rum to dull her inhibitions, Jane found it impossible to move.

Selwyn tried hard. He smiled, encouraged her, and even held out his hands to pull Jane into his arms and gently step from side to side. But that only worsened matters, and Jane stepped clumsily on his feet.

'Oh, heck, I'm so sorry,' she'd said, 'I think I must be very tired.'

She mumbled apologies and told Selwyn that she was heading off to bed, and he'd insisted on walking with her through the ship. When he asked if they might amble along an open deck and watch the moonlight on the sea, Jane had almost broken into a gallop in her haste to hurry to Hibiscus.

'It will s-set off m-my allergies at this time of night,' she'd stuttered. At the door to the suite, Jane swiped the card so hard she almost sliced her finger. 'G-good night, see you around,' she'd said and disappeared to bed.

'I was out for the count when Jane came back,' Kath said, reaching for her hand cream. 'I have no idea what time it was,' she added, smoothing the expensive lotion over her fingers.

'Before me,' Anne noted. 'Jane was snoring when I came in.'

'Do you mean when you fell over my bed and collapsed on the floor?' Jane corrected. 'You were away with the fairies and stank of scotch. Had I lit a match near your mouth, the ship would have gone up.'

'I may have had a little tipple.' Anne looked sheepish.

'I hope Dicky isn't leading you astray.' Kath frowned. 'The last thing you need is another Barry in your life.'

'I'm feeling hungry,' Jane announced. Standing, she placed her hands in the pockets of her Rudolph onesie and rubbed her tummy. 'Shall I order breakfast?'

'I could do with a round of toast,' Anne said. A hangover had hit her like a freight train, and her body was crying out for carbs.

'Not for me, I'll just have tea.' Kath picked up a copy of the *Diamond Star Daily*. 'As we're spending Boxing Day at sea, I'll study today's programme and we can decide what to do.'

Kath read the headlines, but Jane wasn't listening. She wondered what she would say to Selwyn. Anne was miles away too. Her gut feeling said Dicky was bad news, but how would she know if she didn't pursue it?

'There's a panto in the Neptune Lounge later,' Kath said. 'If I could find my glasses, I could tell you what it is.'

Hearing the word 'panto', Jane and Anne turned to stare at Kath.

'Have either of you seen my bag?' Kath asked.

'It's behind you.' They both grinned.

Kath fumbled about on the floor, 'Oh no, it isn't,' she said.

'Oh yes, it is!'

As Kath looked up, she saw that her friends were laughing. 'I'll reserve three seats for the panto,' she said and, shaking her head, laughed too.

Dicky was exhausted and hadn't had a wink of sleep. The previous day he'd endured a full schedule with the entertainment programme, and he'd hoped to wind down with a quiet drink and Anne's sparkling company. Maybe have a flutter in the casino. But thoughts of an early night diminished when Dicky was dragged out of the bar by his wealthy widow. An impromptu performance followed and lasted for most of the night. Thank goodness he had his little blue helpers. Without the magical pills, he would have been in an embarrassing position. Now he was the recipient of a lovely bundle of cash doled out by his bedmate, who'd urged Dicky to treat himself.

It was a shame about Anne, he thought as he dragged his tired body off the bed and into the shower. She might be cross at being stood up. But if he gave her a couple of minutes of his most effusive charm, he'd no doubt she'd be eating out of his hand. Dicky rarely lost a woman to a sulk.

He had a busy day ahead and he needed to be on the ball. At the end of last night's cabaret, Peter had nodded when Dicky left the stage to rapturous applause. It was a start. With a few more days of wooing the crowds and doing a good job, Dicky felt sure that he could talk Peter into forgoing the missed days and agreeing that he should be paid in full at the end of the cruise.

He had a final rehearsal with the *Diamond Star* entertainers in half an hour to put the finishing touches to today's pantomime. Dicky hadn't bothered to read his lines in the script of *Cinderella*; he knew the damn thing off by heart, having played Buttons often enough. He'd have no trouble ad-libbing when needed. He wished that Melissa wasn't playing Cinders. The artiste was probably dreaming up some prank to upset Dicky during the performance. He knew he needed to be on his guard. But Dicky could give as good as he got, and years on the circuit of the working men's pubs and clubs had taught him how to deal with difficulties and come out on top.

As he dressed, he ran through his schedule for the day. Rehearsals, a leisurely lunch, and a swim in the afternoon, then the panto performance this evening. But Peter would probably add an event to bugger up Dicky's leisure time. Glancing at the *Diamond Star Daily*, he saw a festive-themed quiz in the Mermaid Theatre followed by reindeer racing. *Reindeer racing?* Dicky shook his head as he sprayed cologne. Sometimes he wondered if he was working in a holiday camp and half expected the passengers to call out 'Hi-de-hi!' whenever they saw him.

'Not long to go,' he said to his reflection as he styled his hair and made a mental note to find Anne and get in her good books again. Heading back at the end of the cruise to grim and grey Doncaster, where his grumpy, disgruntled wife would be waiting, held little appeal. Dicky had decided that a vacation in Anne's comfortable home would suit him well before he took on his next gig. Then, he might even head over to perform cabaret on the Costas with the nest egg he'd accumulated safely stored away.

It was time for a change. Slipping the Tag Heuer onto his wrist, Dicky looked around his untidy cabin and then hurried out of the door.

———————

Selwyn had decided to treat himself to a luxury Boxing Day breakfast. Having risen early to swim, he'd worked up an appetite and made himself comfortable at a window table in the stunning Atrium Restaurant on the *Diamond Star*'s Marquee Deck. The restaurant was smaller than the Terrace and provided a more intimate dining experience.

As he sipped a glass of champagne, Selwyn remembered the previous Christmas. Breakfast with Flo was a bowl of porridge with golden syrup and milk. A nourishing start to most of their winter days. A meal that rarely varied. 'Oats are good for you,' Flo chanted every morning as she scooped out a gloop that would secure paper to any wall. Picking up a silver spoon, Selwyn tucked into a cocktail of Caribbean fruits. He savoured each mouthful of mango, papaya, and passionfruit and imagined Flo shaking her head as he followed this with eggs Benedict.

Such decadence. Flo would turn in her grave if she had one to lie in.

He touched the bulging plastic pouch in his pocket and thought about the tin in his cabin, which was getting lighter each day. Susan had insisted that her mother's ashes be interred at the crematorium close to their church. The good brothers and sisters of the congregation had stood alongside Pastor Gregory as he officiated over a ceremony of scripture and prayer. Thinking that Flo's remains were secured for eternity, his daughters had little idea they'd all been praying over three kilos of sugar and sand.

Selwyn smiled as he cut into a hot buttered muffin with Canadian smoked bacon and dipped it into softly poached eggs and Hollandaise sauce. He wondered how Jane would cook eggs Benedict and had no doubt that she would surpass all expectations and serve up a dish fit for a king.

'Ah, Jane...' Selwyn sighed and looked out the window at the Deck Café below. Guests were chatting and enjoying the sunshine as they dined from the buffet, and he wondered if Jane was eating there or taking breakfast in Hibiscus.

Selwyn had never met anyone quite like Jane. The

woman could be rude and abrasive, but deep down, he knew she was shy and insecure. Had she gone through life without a lover to soften her outer shell and make her more approachable to men? He had no idea why she worried so much about her size. Selwyn loved a fuller figure and, with his marriage behind him, had no interest in meeting a woman who didn't appreciate food and fine dining. From everything Kath had told him, Jane was clearly capable and had been good at her job and earned the respect of many high-profile chefs in the culinary world.

But how was he to win Jane's affection?

Selwyn mulled the question over, and as a server offered more champagne, he noticed a woman at the next table trying to attract his attention. She wore designer cruise wear and layers of jewellery that warranted an armed guard. Selwyn was tempted to humour the woman with an invitation to join him but knew she might never let go once he was in her bejewelled clutches.

There was no challenge in the chase.

On the other hand, Jane was as slippery as an eel trying to avoid his attention. Yet again, he thought of her dancing in Spirit's bar, where she'd let go entirely and danced so freely. It had been an aphrodisiac to see a woman enjoying herself so much, and he was sure that, at that moment, Jane had felt the same.

Selwyn picked up a *Diamond Star Daily* and studied the events. Nothing caught his eye until later when a pantomime promised to be entertaining. There was a festive buffet this afternoon and a more formal meal this evening.

Chef Jaden Bird invited guests to join him and decorate a gingerbread house. In any other circumstances, Selwyn would have avoided such a session. But he strongly suspected he knew who would be in the front row.

Tucking the information under his arm, he pushed back his chair. Selwyn thanked his server by placing ten dollars in his palm, then strolled out of the Atrium. He smiled at the bejewelled diner and, returning her wave, called out, 'Have a nice day!'

Chapter Twenty-Four

Boxing Day had been busy for Dicky, and now he sat at the back of the library in a dark alcove set apart from the large open room, a tumbler of whisky in his hand. His eyes were closed, and his legs twitched as he sat in the quiet corner. It was a solitary place where readers could relax, switch off, and catch up with updates from the many newspapers stacked on a nearby table or be engrossed in a page-turning book, the story too good to put down.

Dicky often came to this part of the ship when he needed a few quiet moments. There was an overhead light beside his chair, but he hadn't turned it on, preferring to sit and contemplate in the dark.

Earlier, he'd shone as Buttons in the panto.

His jokes were well received, and the audience adored him. Melissa had been unable to upstage him, but he had to concede that she made a great Cinderella. The wedding scene with Prince Charming, played by Peter, had brought the house down, with the *Diamond Star* dancers' dazzling costumes and everyone singing along. Peter congratulated the participants for their performances, and Dicky received a handshake. He was back in favour!

Dicky took a slug of his whisky. The peaty malt tasted good but did little to calm his anger. Things hadn't gone so well with Anne.

One phone call and a few flattering words, and he'd arranged to meet her.

Instead of scooping up a mountain of chips on the blackjack table in the casino, he'd been furious to find that Anne pushed him to one side and placed her own bets. For an hour, he'd stood back, wide-eyed, and watched her win a considerable sum. When they eventually moved away, he'd whispered in her ear and suggested a celebratory nightcap in his cabin. But to his utter astonishment, Anne had turned him down.

'Why would I want to be with you?' she'd asked.

Dicky spluttered that he didn't know what Anne was talking about and not to be so silly. But Anne had a determined gleam in her eye and Dicky could still hear her parting shot. 'I don't like being made a fool of and you stood me up.'

Dicky was furious. He loosened his collar and flexed his fingers. No woman had ever put him down. Still, he was grateful they hadn't been overheard, and as Anne walked off, he'd smiled at the drinkers in the bar, ordered a whisky, and made his way to the library to think.

Immersed in his thoughts, Dicky turned his head when

the door to the library opened. A woman came in, and he recognised Anne's friend. Kath didn't notice Dicky in the dark corner as she wandered over to a window seat. There was a lamp by her table, and Dicky saw Kath place her bag on a chair and remove a notebook. As he watched her settle, he wondered if it was worth a few moments of the Dicky Delaney charm. Kath was a reasonable-looking woman. Her appearance had changed during the cruise, and Dicky noted her expensive outfit and well-groomed hair. But as he remembered Anne's outburst, he decided it was safer not to dally with two close friends.

A server came into the room, spoke to Kath, and returned with a drink moments later. Not wishing to participate in conversation, Dicky sank further into his chair and decided to wait it out. Kath would have her drink and leave.

It was way past bedtime for a woman her age.

Kath stared out of the picture window. It was dark outside with only the bright, bold glow of an almost full moon, brilliant against the graphite night. There was a faint pulse from the ship's engines as it cut through the moonlit sea.

What a wonderful day it had been! Boxing Day in the eastern Caribbean Sea. Another memorable experience for Kath. Reindeer racing had been hilarious, and Kath had clapped loudly when Harold and Nancy tore off their antlers and held up the winning trophy. The panto took her back to her childhood and she was starry-eyed as she watched the dancers in their beautiful costumes. Even Dicky Delaney's corny jokes added to the magical Christmas atmosphere.

As she sat in the library, reflecting on her day, Kath stroked the embossed cover of her journal. She'd been making notes during the cruise, detailing where they had been, the islands and events she'd enjoyed on the ship. An earlier port talk about the island of Antigua had been enjoyable, and she was looking forward to disembarking in the morning to visit some places the speaker mentioned.

A server came into the room and saw Kath sitting alone. 'May I get you a drink?' he asked.

Kath had eaten earlier in the Deck Café with Jane and Anne. They'd decided on a lighter option and had enjoyed nibbling from the buffet. Now, as she studied a list of cocktails, she decided that she *would* indulge. 'Yes, please, I'd like to try a daiquiri, perhaps mango?'

As she watched the server head off, Kath realised she'd had too much to drink. There had been wine throughout their meal, and with little food in her tummy to soak it up, Kath felt quite tipsy. When her cocktail arrived, she sipped slowly as strong rum flooded her alcohol-filled veins.

Alone, Kath sighed. 'Oh, Jim,' she said out loud, 'what would you make of me now?' She continued to stare at the silvery sea. 'How did you feel when you fell? Were you angry or scared?' Kath shook her head. 'I tried to be such a good wife, always there, doing my best, running around

after you and the boys.' She tilted her glass and let the last
dregs trickle down her throat.

Suddenly, Kath slammed the glass on the table.

'Well, it served you damned right!' she swore. 'It was a
good job I saw you running off with your wretched last
will, or I wouldn't be sitting here now.'

Dicky was intrigued. Leaning forward, he cocked his head
and strained to hear Kath's conversation with herself. She
was rambling about her husband, who had taken a fall.
Dicky nearly jumped out of his skin when Kath slammed
her glass on the table.

But the words that followed left him stunned.

Had he heard Kath say she'd pushed Jim when reaching
out to grab his last will and testament? She was blathering
on, but Dicky soon had the gist. He winced as Kath
remembered the deepening pool of congealing blood and
Jim's fading pulse. He heard her laugh when she told her
heavenly husband that the ambulance crew didn't know
that his accident was her fault. A set of steep steps had
justified his fall, and no one was any the wiser.

Well, would you believe it, Dicky thought as he darted
back into the shadows. Here was an opportunity! The old
bag had a secret so big that it would ruin her golden years
should it ever be known.

The door suddenly opened, and a woman rushed in.

'There you are!' Jane called out. 'I've been looking for

you everywhere.' She moved to Kath's side and, reaching for the notebook, placed it in Kath's bag. 'Anne's dumped Dicky and had a win on the blackjack tables. She's celebrating with champagne; you must come and join us.' Jane placed her hand under Kath's shoulder and hoisted her out of her chair. 'But, by the look of things, you're three sheets to the wind already.'

Dicky watched the pair stagger out of the room. As the door closed, he stood and walked to the picture window. Staring out, he looked heavenwards. 'Well, Jim,' said Dicky, smiling. 'It looks like your trouble and strife has just done me a favour.'

Rubbing his hands together, Dicky straightened his collar and walked confidently from the library.

Chapter Twenty-Five

J ane woke early the following morning and opened her eyes to stare at the ceiling in Hibiscus. Reflecting on each day of the cruise, she remembered all the ports she'd visited with Kath and Anne and all the fun they'd had on board. There were only a few days left, and Jane intended to make the most of them.

She glanced over to Kath, who was snoring. Jane knew Kath would have a fuzzy head today after her drinking session the previous night. Anne, asleep on her back, had a beatific smile. No doubt dreaming of her casino winnings, Jane thought, and how she might spend them.

Creeping from her bed, Jane wriggled out of her Rudolph onesie and pulled on her swimsuit and kaftan. The pool would be deserted, and she could have an early dip. She closed the door of Hibiscus and made her way through the ship until she came to the lido deck, where sunlight played on the surface of the kidney-shaped pool. Leaving her towel and kaftan close by, Jane kicked off her sandals and slid in.

It was heaven. An apricot haze rose from the far horizon, highlighting the island of Antigua ahead. She swam a few strokes and turned to lie contentedly on her back, gently swishing her hands and feet. The water was her friend, and there was nothing judgemental about swimming. Immersive and supportive, it caressed her body as though lulling her into believing she was a beautiful nymph who could glide and move as free as the birds in the open sky above. Jane determined that when she got home, she would invest in structured swimwear, indulge in expensive club membership, and swim to her heart's content. She'd always been put off by the skinnies who postured by the pool, but this cruise reminded her of how much she loved the water.

Staring at puffballs of cloud floating in ripples over the blue sky, Jane thought about the cookery event, when Chef Jaden hosted an afternoon demonstration of traditional gingerbread houses. The auditorium was packed as guests waited to be entertained. Jane, the first to arrive, took a seat directly in front of the stage, and when Jaden asked if anyone would like to assist, her hand flew into the air, and she was invited to join him.

As the demonstration began, Jaden was distracted by two passengers who asked him about his background. Itching to make a start, Jane began to mix and mould and, in moments, had a tray of gingerbread ready for the oven.

'My goodness,' Jaden said as he turned back to Jane, 'how efficient, I have a new assistant!'

What followed took Jane by surprise.

Jaden, watching her work, began to ask questions, and suddenly the demonstration was turned on its head. Guests sat forward as they listened to Jane's replies. She spoke of her job, the chefs she'd worked with, and the situations she'd found herself in. Jaden was delighted to hear Jane mention many of his idols. As they explained to the audience how to decorate the gingerbread, she gained confidence and tripped out tales of Michelin star mishaps and behind-the-scenes at food festivals, where more went on beneath the celebrity chef's apron than above it.

'You should go on tour.' Jaden laughed as Jane regaled the audience with another hilarious culinary story. 'You can cook, and have many funny anecdotes. I'd pay to see you any day.'

As Jane turned onto her tummy and doggy-paddled around the pool, she wondered how on earth she'd found the confidence to be so involved with the event. It was as though stepping out of the backstage shadows had given her a shot of adrenaline. With the spotlight shining on her for a change, she'd relished the opportunity.

A crew member wiped down tables and chairs, and guests appeared dressed in swimwear. Jane decided that it was time to get out as Harold approached.

'Loved your show!' Harold called as he pulled a T-shirt over his head. 'Nancy was saying that she reckoned you should be on TV.'

Jane was about to correct Harold and remind him that it had been Jaden's show and she was only his helper, but something made her stop. She smiled as she wrapped a bath sheet around her body and picked up her belongings. 'Enjoy your swim,' she called to Harold, then headed back to Hibiscus.

Selwyn stood on deck, leaning on a handrail, staring ahead at the bay. Diwa had told him that St John's Harbour bay was also known as Heritage Quay, which hosted three piers enabling as many as five cruise ships to dock simultaneously in Antigua. He could see that the *Diamond Star* was not alone and a massive ship with an Italian emblem towered alongside. Selwyn wasn't sure he'd like to be on board with thousands of passengers and wondered how the island coped when everyone disembarked for the day. He much preferred the relative cosiness of the ship he was travelling on.

The sun was already hot, but the *Diamond Star Daily*'s weather forecast told of heavy showers in the afternoon. Selwyn had arranged a trip with Diwa's help. Now, all that he had to do was persuade Jane to accompany him.

He glanced at his gold-faced wristwatch and wondered if she would be out of bed. Selwyn knew that it was pointless to phone; Jane would turn him down, and it would be a wasted call. But face-to-face might be different. If he could catch her while Kath and Anne were around, he felt sure they'd insist she accompanied him. Only one thing for it. He'd present himself at Jane's door. If he caught her off-guard, he might have a chance, and they could enjoy a day out together.

Selwyn set off for Hibiscus, and as he made his way, he thought about Jane's performance with Chef Jaden. It was as though the woman had come to life. Comfortable in a cooking environment alongside a personality that she felt akin to, Jane had enthralled the audience without a hint of nerves or lack of confidence. Standing tall, she seemed unaware of her size. In fact, she almost embraced it, placing her hands on her hips when she laughed and giving a little wriggle when she told a story.

The applause was loud when Jaden ended the demonstration and thanked Jane for being such an interesting participant. Selwyn had been enchanted and wanted to speak to her, perhaps take her for a celebratory drink and learn more about her exploits, but she was surrounded by guests eager to chat. He decided to let her have her moment of glory. He missed her at dinner, choosing to dine in the Terrace Restaurant, where Bridgette informed Selwyn that she'd seen the three friends heading off to the Deck Café for the lighter buffet option. At the panto performance, Jane sat at the opposite end of the room.

Now, Selwyn stood outside Hibiscus. He took a deep breath and raised his hand to knock on the door.

'That will be breakfast,' Kath called from the bathroom. 'Jane, will you get it?'

Jane had changed into her reindeer onesie and a Santa hat and was relaxing on a sofa. She dropped the *Diamond Star Daily* and leapt up. 'On my way,' she said as she passed Anne's bed and grabbed hold of her friend's toes. 'Wake up, sleepy head.' She shook Anne's foot. 'Your hangover cure is here.'

'Bugger off,' Anne mumbled from beneath her quilt.

Jane flicked her braids from her shoulders and, expecting to see a uniformed server, called out, 'Hit me with everything you've got!'

The door flew open, and Jane froze.

'Oh … er…' she said as she came face to face with Selwyn. 'I didn't know you were on room service.' Jane drew her head back, and whipped her Santa hat off. 'I mean, I'm sorry … we're expecting breakfast.'

'If you'd like me to go away?'

'Bring it through!' Kath called out as she dried her face with a towel and stepped into the lounge. 'We'll eat on the balcony.' Kath looked up, and when she saw Selwyn, her face broke into a smile. 'We have company,' she said. 'How lovely, do come in and join us.'

Selwyn walked past Jane and into the suite. 'What stylish accommodation,' he said and smiled at Anne as he followed Kath to the balcony.

Anne swung her legs over the side of the bed. 'That's the best hangover cure I've ever had,' she said and reached for her hairbrush and lipstick.

With a look of horror, Jane gesticulated wildly behind

Selwyn's back, but Kath ignored her and told Selwyn to make himself comfortable.

'What do we owe the pleasure of this visit to?' Kath asked.

'I'm sorry to disturb you ladies so early in the morning,' Selwyn began, 'but I wanted to catch Jane before you made plans for the day.'

Hearing Selwyn's words, Jane began to double back into the lounge, but Anne caught hold of her onesie and pulled her onto the balcony.

'I'd like to invite you to join me on an island tour,' Selwyn said.

He stared at Jane, and she felt his eyes bore into her like lasers.

'W-we were planning—' Jane stuttered, frantically trying to find an excuse.

'Of course she'd love to accompany you,' Kath interrupted, 'that sounds like great fun. What time shall she be ready?'

Ignoring Jane completely, Kath and Selwyn arranged a time and location to meet, and Kath assured him that Jane would have swimwear and a towel should she need it.

With a polite nod, Selwyn told Jane that he was looking forward to their outing and, turning to the others, hoped Kath and Anne enjoyed their day too. Breakfast had arrived, and declining an invitation to join them, he left the suite.

'Bloody hell!' Jane cried out. 'You've really landed me in it.'

'If Jane doesn't want to go, do you think Selwyn would consider me as a replacement?' Anne asked.

'Don't even think about it,' Kath said. 'Now stop making a fuss, Jane. Eat up and then we'll decide what you'll wear – you can't go out like that.'

Jane was about to protest and dream up a million reasons for dodging her date, but she caught a waft of warm croissant and, unable to resist, sat down and tucked in. 'You're bang out of order,' she mumbled between bites of fluffy pastry. 'You do realise that I will miss Bridgette's talk, *All Muck and Magic*?'

Anne rolled her eyes. 'Mission accomplished,' she said and yawned.

'I propose that we disembark and have a day out too.' Kath looked at Anne. 'So get your skates on because the weather forecast is for a storm later in the day.'

'It will only be a shower,' Anne said, 'soon over.'

But as the friends enjoyed their breakfast and made plans for the day, none knew of the storm that was brewing.

Chapter Twenty-Six

S elwyn carried a rucksack as he stood by the gangway and waited for Jane to disembark and join him for a day he'd carefully planned. As he left the ship, he took note of the crew, who told passengers that heavy rain was expected later in the day, and they were advised to be back on board before it came.

Selwyn checked his watch. They could enjoy everything he'd planned if he kept to his schedule. He began to pace and hoped that Jane wouldn't be late, but moments later, he saw her walking towards him. She wore a colourful flowing gown and pretty sandals. Her braids were loose, and she carried a large straw hat and matching beach bag.

'You look lovely,' Selwyn said, but Jane looked flustered, unused to compliments. 'Did you pack a swimsuit?' he asked.

'I have a complete survival kit in here.' Jane pointed to her bag. 'Kath made sure I'm prepared for everything.'

'You won't need to survive.' Selwyn laughed. 'But you may find that you come out of your comfort zone during the day.'

Selwyn ignored Jane's look of panic and took her arm to walk along the pier until they came to the cruise terminal at Heritage Quay, where the port security checked their boarding passes. Before stepping onto the street, they wandered through a busy food court and a variety of duty-free shops displaying everything from internationally recognised brands to local arts and crafts.

Outside, a man held up a placard with Selwyn's name.

'Here's our driver,' Selwyn said, and together they climbed into an air-conditioned vehicle.

The driver, Curtis, handed them each a bottle of chilled water. Jane took her fan, flicked it open, and then glanced sideways as Selwyn took a drink. Condensation dripped onto the crisp cotton of his shirt, and she thought how good he looked in pristine white shorts and leather sandals. Selwyn had styled his dreadlocks into a knot on the top of his head, and Jane considered the style for herself.

'This is the northwest coast, and your first stop is Runaway Beach,' Curtis said and came to a halt beside an endless stretch of coastline.

'Goodness, the sand is almost pink,' Jane gasped as Selwyn helped her out. 'Why is it called Runaway Beach?'

The driver grinned. 'If you don't know what he has planned today, now is your chance to run away.'

'Touché.' Jane grinned.

'Shall we swim?' Selwyn asked.

Jane hadn't expected to endure the humiliation of stripping down to her swimsuit quite so early in the day, but the beauty of the beach and the inviting turquoise water were too tempting to resist. 'To hell with it,' she mumbled and kicked off her sandals, then slipped out of her kaftan, folding it over her bag.

'Ready?' Selwyn asked.

'Whatever is he doing with me?' Jane thought and bit her lip as she stared at Selwyn. He was handsome, fit, and muscular in his swimming shorts, and she remembered that he'd told Kath he regularly swam back home in Lambeth. He held out his hand, and taking a deep breath, she moved forward until his warm fingers entwined with her own.

'Last one in buys the drinks,' Selwyn called out and together they ran towards the sea.

'Oh, my word,' Jane called out as hot sand burned the soles of her feet. Her lungs felt as though they were going to explode, but as the water engulfed her, she let go of Selwyn's hand and dived under a wave. 'I won!' she called out.

Laughing with the joy of being in such beautiful surroundings, Jane began to frolic and play in the water. 'I feel like a child again,' she said as she stretched her arm and splashed Selwyn.

'That's good,' he said and swam towards her. 'Believe in yourself, and not just while you're swimming but throughout life itself.'

Jane thought about his words as they sat on the beach a

little while later to dry off in the sunshine, and Curtis produced cold beers.

If only she could believe in herself.

Studying the label on her bottle, she asked, 'Wadadli?'

'Local beer, it's good,' Curtis replied.

The beer was excellent, and Jane thought she'd never tasted anything so refreshing. The sun and salty spray of the sea must have heightened the hops' taste, and delicious froth foamed with each gulp.

Gazing around the island, Jane had a peculiar feeling. She was happy!

Not the sort of happiness she got from eating a doughnut filled with strawberry jam. This was like a bud blooming into a flower, spreading its beautiful petals to every part of her being and filling her with joy. The butterflies in her tummy began to dance.

'What are you thinking?' Selwyn asked.

Jane noticed water droplets on his smooth dark skin and longed to reach out and touch them. Realising that she couldn't possibly tell Selwyn how she felt for fear of being foolish, she replied, 'I was thinking how much I love the Caribbean.'

'Yes.' He nodded, pausing as he stared at the sea. 'The islands enter through your eyes, creating their magic before dancing into your soul.'

Jane wondered if her soul was in her tummy, which might explain the butterflies breaking into a tango.

'Ready to move on?' Selwyn asked, noting Curtis checking the time.

'Yes, of course.' Jane reached for her kaftan, then, taking Selwyn's hand, allowed him to help her. 'Where are we heading now?'

'Be patient,' Selwyn said, 'sit back and enjoy the ride.'

And, to her surprise, Jane did precisely that.

Kath and Anne walked along the pier and stood in line to have their boarding passes checked by a smiling employee of the port authority, who wished them a happy time in Antigua.

'I shall be very happy if we can visit these duty-free shops and find some lovely souvenirs,' Anne said. She took hold of Kath's arm, and they meandered slowly through a shopping village of colourful chattel houses.

'I feel a little lightheaded.' Kath reached into her bag for a bottle of water. 'I think I had too much wine last night, and I'm not used to it.'

'You must be dehydrated, drink plenty of fluids.'

'Do you know why these wooden structures are called chattel houses?' Kath asked and took a long drink.

'Nope, but I know you are about to tell me.'

'The word chattel means easily moveable, and homeowners who lived in them were sometimes forced by landowners to take up their chattel house and move elsewhere.'

'What a good idea.' Anne was thoughtful as she stood on the steps of a small boutique and studied the two-roomed property suspended on large blocks. 'It would suit me to own one of these and relocate whenever I fancied.'

They moved on, and as they approached a vendor selling wood carvings by local Antiguan artisans, a voice called out, 'Cooee!'

It was Bridgette, and she held up her hand and waved.

'Crikey, it's the Captain and his carer,' Anne said.

'Hello, Bridgette.' Kath smiled. 'Are you doing a spot of shopping?'

Bridgette spun the Captain's wheelchair around, and Anne leapt back as he yelled, 'Boo!' from behind a carved wooden mask. He wore a T-shirt that read *No Ship Should Go Down Without Her Captain*.

'Made of Caribbean mahogany, it will last for ever,' Bridgette informed them as she leaned in and tapped the smoothly carved mask.

'The mask or the Captain?' Anne asked. 'It's terrifying.' She stared at the dark seasoned wood, almost as gnarled as the Captain's skin. He held a bottle of guavaberry liquor on his knee and offered it to the women.

'Marvellous if you need the hair of the dog,' Bridgette said.

Anne turned to Kath. 'It's a sign,' she said, 'fill your boots.'

Kath, whose dizziness had worsened, didn't hesitate and, digging into her bag, produced a plastic beaker. She took the bottle and poured a shot.

'Down the hatch!' the Captain's muffled voice called out.

Following instructions, Kath closed her eyes and swallowed the drink. 'Good grief!' she said as the alcohol hit. Her eyes bulged, and she shook her head wildly. 'My body is on fire!' But, as Bridgette had predicted, the drink did the trick, and Kath felt better in no time. Digging into her bag again, she produced a guidebook. 'Do any of you fancy a trip to Nelson's Dockyard?' she asked.

'Lead on,' the Captain replied.

'Sounds just the ticket,' Bridgette said, patting the Captain's shoulder. 'Very naval and perfect for you, my dear.'

Anne felt that she'd sooner watch paint dry. But not wanting to be left on her own to wander around St John's, she helped Bridgette collapse the Captain's wheelchair and manoeuvre him into a taxi alongside Kath.

'Victory!' the Captain called out as they set off for their destination.

Kath began to read aloud. '"The dockyard started in 1725 to provide a base for British ships patrolling the West Indies. It was named in Nelson's honour."'

'Fascinating...' Anne yawned. She leaned in to study the time on the Rolex on the Captain's wrist and hoped they'd soon be there. Perhaps there would be a sunny spot where she could relax while the others caught up on naval history.

As they drove through St John's streets, Kath read from the guidebook. The passengers learnt that the cosmopolitan town was one of the most developed in the Lesser Antilles. Anne yearned to stop and window shop as she gazed at shopping malls and boutiques selling jewellery and designer clothing.

'Jane would have enjoyed this trip,' Kath said as they slowed to allow pedestrians access to a busy market. Stalls displayed fresh fruit, vegetables, and fish of every variety laid out on long marble slabs. 'But I'm sure she's having a good time with Selwyn,' she added and informed them that the area they were driving through was known as the Citadel.

After a while, they reached the island's south and, driving through the parish of St Paul, soon arrived at Nelson's Dockyard.

'It's situated in a working shipyard,' Kath commented as they got out of the taxi and began to wheel the Captain along the quayside. She studied the immaculately restored eighteenth- and nineteenth-century buildings while Anne checked the numerous bars and cafés.

'Wow, I wouldn't mind one of those,' Ann said as she turned to face the harbour and studied rows of expensive yachts.

They stopped to watch a couple driving around the bay in a speedboat, reclining on white leather seats and sipping champagne. The woman threw back her head and laughed as the man whispered in her ear. Her jewels glinted in the sunshine, and she wore a long floaty kaftan with large sunglasses.

'Dastardly Dicky…' Anne hissed and glared at Dicky. He was oblivious to the onlookers as he entertained his wealthy widow.

'Time for a livener, I think,' Bridgette said as she, too, observed Dicky showing off in the bay. Gripping the handles of the Captain's wheelchair, she set off to find refreshments.

'You've had a narrow escape with that one,' Kath said and linked arms with her friend, who brightened as they reached a bar.

'I hope the weight of her jewellery overturns the boat and they sink,' Anne said, 'but in the meantime, I'll have a pina colada.'

'Pina coladas all round,' Bridgette called out.

'Victory!' the Captain repeated.

'Husband-hunting.' Anne sighed and gazed at a group of handsome sailors on the adjacent table.

'What happened to the sunshine?' Kath asked and looked up at the darkening sky. 'Do you think the storm is on the way?'

'It will just be a shower at this time of year,' Anne replied as their drinks arrived. 'Cheers, everyone, here's to many more relaxing times during the remainder of our cruise.'

On the other side of the island, Jane was far from relaxed. Selwyn's day out continued with an off-the-beaten-path dune buggy experience, and now, taking a break, she took deep breaths to slow her heart rate. But the feeling wasn't one of anxiety or pain. Jane felt exhilarated, as though she had conquered a fear and nothing else mattered but doing it again.

Selwyn reached into his rucksack and produced a towel. 'Did you enjoy bouncing about in a buggy?' he asked.

'I think it is one of the best things I've ever done,' she said and took the towel to rub at clumps of dried earth that covered every bit of exposed flesh.

'You're an excellent driver.' Selwyn laughed. 'Even covered in mud.'

Jane thought she must look like a buffalo wallowing on a sludgy riverbank, but for once in her life, she didn't care. 'I'm a terrible driver at home, but after this, I might take to the byways in a buggy,' she said. 'It would certainly liven up life in Lancashire.'

Their drive over Antiguan terrain had begun with guidance from a local who ran the event. Selwyn insisted that Jane take the wheel, and she reluctantly agreed. But as they rode along dirt tracks and through lemongrass fields, she started to relax and discovered the open-sided vehicle was light to drive but powerful underfoot. Heading to the southwest coast, Jane put the pedal to the metal as they approached the secluded Sea Fort Beach dunes, and they flew across the sand, the buggy becoming airborne as Jane screamed with delight and Selwyn clung on tight.

Jane wiped tears from her eyes when they stopped and ran to the sea for a dip to cool down. Lunch was a curried goat roti and beer from a beach vendor, and to Selwyn's delight, his ghetto blaster played reggae music.

Now, sitting companionably in the sunshine, their shoulders touched as they joined in.

'Get up, stand up…' Bob and his Wailers sang.

'Are you beginning to like reggae music?' Selwyn asked. His head nodded as he stared out to sea.

'When I hear the words, I realise there's a message in the songs.' Jane munched on the last of her roti and took a swig of beer.

'Bob Marley sang about tyranny and anger but in enticing tones to make his point,' Selwyn replied. 'This song is about human rights and fighting to secure them.'

Jane tilted her head to listen.

'Chuck Berry was quoted as saying that "Get Up, Stand Up" was a battle cry for survival.'

'Crikey, does the song make you feel like that?'

'Yes, too many people struggle to survive in a world that takes so much for granted. I believe that everyone has the right to basic necessities, such as a proper roof over their heads and food on the table.'

'Bob Dylan was my hero when I was young.' Jane shrugged. 'I thought that his songs were visionary and far-sighted. I used to lose myself listening to his albums.'

'You talk in the past tense; did you stop listening?'

'In college, I wore long cheesecloth dresses and Jesus sandals.' Jane grinned. 'The sight of me in an Afghan coat wasn't the most popular look and I grew out of it, including the music. Earning money became a priority.'

Selwyn turned to look at Jane. 'Money can't buy life,' he said.

Jane stared into eyes that shone like polished amber, and her heart missed a beat. 'Wise words,' she mumbled.

'Not mine.' Selwyn shook his head. 'But the last sentence spoken by Bob Marley, to his son, before he passed.'

Jane was mesmerised. Sitting with this man, chatting freely, she felt like a spell had been cast. The moment felt monumental, and without thinking, her fingers reached out, almost touching Selwyn's hand. But the spell was suddenly broken when Curtis appeared and said they must be on their way.

Jane watched Selwyn gather their belongings. She must pull herself together, she thought. If she wasn't careful, their fledgling friendship would fall apart.

As Jane walked to the buggy, she wondered what was next. So far, the day had been perfect, and she was touched that he'd thoughtfully planned the outing. Every now and again, Jane had caught Selwyn looking at her and was amazed to discover that instead of shrinking away or becoming embarrassed, she liked the attention. Selwyn was wholly non-judgmental and never made her feel that her size was an issue.

On the contrary, he was complimentary and said that her swimsuit suited her and the glorious colours in the fabric of her dress made him feel light-hearted and happy. She learnt that his wife always wore dark shades and covered up with cardigans and shawls. It was the first insight Jane had into his marriage.

But Jane knew that her strange and bewildering feelings

could only be one-sided. A man like Selwyn would never consider a relationship with someone like Jane. After all, his wife had recently died, and his holiday was merely a form of escapism from his grief.

Her adrenaline pumped up again as they climbed back into the buggy and sped along a muddy riverbed, the spray from the silt splashing them both. 'That was brilliant,' she told Selwyn when they reached Curtis's vehicle and thanked the guide. 'Are we heading back to the ship now?'

'One more activity to go,' he replied.

'It looks like it's going to pour down over there.' Jane looked out to sea and pointed to the sky where dark clouds loomed in the distance.

'We will be safely undercover.' Selwyn reached out and wiped a spatter of mud from Jane's cheek, then patted her knee. 'Sit back and relax,' he said, smiling.

It was all Jane could do not to grab his hand and hold it in her own. But fearing she'd be rejected, she nodded and turned away.

Chapter Twenty-Seven

Kath and Anne returned to St John and found a restaurant near the pier where the *Diamond Star* was docked. They were eating lunch with Bridgette and the Captain, ordering drinks and tucking into sharing plates of local delicacies. Kath stared at the food in the centre of the table and, again, wished that Jane was with them. With her culinary knowledge, she would have explained each dish.

'What do you think this is?' Kath asked as she studied balls of a light-coloured mix.

'It's fungi,' Bridgette replied, 'made of cornmeal and okra paste, a staple in the Antiguan diet.'

Kath pulled a face, 'I'm not sure...'

'Try it with the saltfish,' Anne suggested and spooned fish stew onto Kath's plate.

'Conk!' the Captain called out from behind his mask and banged the table with the handle of a knife.

'Let me help you,' Bridgette said and, removing the

Captain's mask, served him a portion of conch curry. 'This is his favourite,' she told everyone. 'Conch is the meat from the beautiful conch shell that you occasionally find washed up on the beach in the Caribbean.'

'It should stay on the beach.' Anne shuddered. 'The colour is revolting.' She nibbled on ceviche, toying with the raw salted fish and the tangy taste of limes. As she ate, Anne felt disgruntled. Dicky and his companion climbed out of a taxi to sit close by.

Dicky raised his glass to acknowledge Anne.

'Be polite,' Kath whispered, 'and thankful that you didn't sleep with him.'

Anne turned away. She couldn't tell Kath that she wished she was sitting with Dicky. Even though he'd stood her up, she still fancied him. Just like Barry, bad boys would always be her downfall.

As they ate, the sun disappeared, and the sky clouded over. It was still hot, but the atmosphere had become clammy.

'I have to make my way back to the ship,' Bridgette announced, fanning her face with her hand. 'I'm giving a talk later this afternoon.'

'All muck and magic,' the Captain chipped in, aware of the topic for Bridgette's talk. He chewed the last of his curry, then glanced at his Rolex. 'Time to be off!'

Anne smiled. 'Let me help you,' she said to Bridgette as the bill was settled and everyone rose. Anne took the Captain's wheelchair and began to walk along the side of the harbour.

'Oh, here comes the rain!' Kath cried a few minutes later, reaching into her bag for a hat.

'Better get our skates on,' Bridgette said as the Captain took hold of his mask and held it over his head.

As if flicking a switch, the weather changed, and rain cascaded from the sky, ricocheting off the ground like bullets. Cruise ship passengers browsing in the shops dived for cover to shelter from the sudden storm.

'Rats,' Anne muttered as she ran behind the wheelchair. 'My hair is ruined!'

What happened next was so unexpected that later, in the lounge on the *Diamond Star*, everyone wondered what exactly had taken place.

As Anne hurried along with the Captain, a man suddenly ran out from an alley.

Reaching Anne, he pushed her violently to one side, and, despite gripping tightly and kicking out with her feet, she slipped on the wet pathway and fell to the ground. The handles of the wheelchair were wrenched from her hands, and the Captain spun around. A man of gigantic proportions was facing him, dressed all in black, with a hoodie covering his face. He thrust out his hands as the Captain beat wildly with his mask, but in seconds the Rolex from the Captain's wrist had gone.

Kath wrenched her bag from her shoulder and swung it as the man got away.

'Stop thief!' Bridgette yelled as she tried to run after the robber, but her words were lost as the rain thundered down and the man disappeared.

'Oh, my goodness!' Kath gasped as she helped Anne to her feet. 'Are you all right?'

'Traitor!' the Captain shouted and rose from his chair, teetering perilously close to the water's edge.

Bridgette steadied herself and battled to calm the Captain. Anne was bleeding from abrasions to her knees and stumbled as Kath took her arm. Shocked and dazed, they looked up as a couple ran towards them.

'Holy moly!' Kath gasped as Harold and Nancy broke into a run. They had towels pinned at the neck with plastic parrot clips, the fabric billowing like cloaks.

'It's Batman and Robin.' Anne grinned.

'Take it easy,' Harold said as he skidded to a halt on the wet ground and Nancy, hands on hips, appeared by his side. Harold scooped Anne into his arms as Nancy hoisted Kath upright.

'Thank God. The cavalry has arrived,' Bridgette said as she took charge of the Captain. 'Let's get back to the ship,' she shouted. 'No use staying here. The crew will know what to do.'

As the rain continued to beat down, the bedraggled party huddled together and made their way to the comfort of the *Diamond Star*.

Five miles north of St John, at the heliport of V.C. Bird International Airport, Jane stood on the tarmac with

Selwyn, metres from an Airbus helicopter. She stared at the giant bird-like structure and shook her head.

'Surely not?' Jane whispered.

Curtis, standing close by, spoke up. 'This is the latest technology, and we are proud to be able to offer an aerial helicopter tour of our beautiful island.' Sensing Jane's hesitation, he assured her, 'There is a climate-controlled cabin and spectacular visibility.'

'Don't be scared.' Selwyn gently took Jane's elbow. 'You'll love it.'

'Let's get you seated,' Curtis said and nodded to the pilot sitting at the controls.

Jane looked up at the sky, where darkening clouds were drifting overhead. 'We can't go up in that lot. It looks like it's about to pour down.'

'The pilot will fly around the clouds, don't worry,' Curtis replied.

Moments later, Jane found herself strapped in and seated next to Selwyn. She prayed that her muddy legs didn't mark the soft cream leather as headphones were placed over her ears. The rotor blade began to spin overhead, and Jane wanted to ask if the machine had a powerful engine – enough to take her weight? But the noise from the motor had built up, and seconds later they were rising. As the helicopter transitioned from vertical to forward, Jane's stomach lurched, and she wished that she hadn't eaten the roti.

Without thinking, she began to mutter her prayers.

'Isn't it wonderful?' Selwyn said as they dipped low

over the sea, taking in the sights in Nelson's harbour. His eyes were wide, and he pointed to the piers in St John. 'Look,' he said, 'you can see the *Diamond Star*.'

Jane opened one eye and peeped through the glass to stare at the aerial view of the cruise ships below. She heard the pilot's commentary of the island's highlights through her headphones, and slowly began to relax. To her surprise, she enjoyed gazing at the stunning beaches, sandy shorelines, and turquoise sea. How lucky she was to be doing this! If it wasn't for Selwyn, she would never have known the wonder of flying through the sky like a soaring bird.

'Enjoying yourself?' Selwyn asked, his voice raised above the sound of the engine.

'It's wonderful!'

They flew over an area named Shirley Heights, a restored military lookout and gun battery. Swooping down the west coast, Jane held her breath as a gated community called Jolly Harbour came into view, and they flew over a marina, noting exclusive homes and waterside restaurants and bars. Cade's Reef was dotted with boats on the southwestern coast, and Jane thought they looked like colourful balls bobbing about on the water. They ascended through the island's lush interior, spotting historic sugar mills nestling near large plantation houses, the connecting roads like long grey arteries pulsing through the land.

'We're heading back to St John,' the pilot spoke, 'to the heliport by the cruise ship pier, to enable you to board the *Diamond Star* there.'

Jane felt the engine's thrust as the pilot manoeuvred the helicopter and wondered if her friends would watch them touching down. She smiled as she imagined Kath digging into her bag for her binoculars.

But as they got closer to St John, the sky rapidly darkened.

'It's as though the lights have been turned out,' Jane called out to Selwyn and felt her stomach lurch again as rain thundered against the glass.

'Sorry, folks, I thought we were ahead of this,' the pilot said, his voice raised. 'Hold on tight, we may be in for a bumpy landing.'

It happened very quickly. One moment Jane was having the time of her life, and the next, she was screaming with fear as a sudden gusting wind tossed the helicopter into the air.

'Are we going to die?' she yelled as rain battered down.

'I've got you, Jane, don't be scared.'

'It's not over till the fat lady sings…' Jane was terrified.

'Shush.' Selwyn's voice was calm as he snaked his arm around her shoulders and pulled Jane into his body. Despite the turbulent bouncing around, Jane allowed herself to be held. She turned her face to nestle in Selwyn's shirt, smelling his spicy scent and feeling his warmth. His arms were solid and comforting.

'Don't worry 'bout a thing,' Selwyn began to sing softly in her ear as they were buffeted through the air, 'every little thing gonna be all right.'

And for Jane, suddenly everything *was* going to be all

right. It was as though a golden halo had enveloped them and she knew that if she were to die at that moment, she'd die happy. Letting her body relax, and despite their safety harnesses, she snuggled into Selwyn and began to sing too.

As the pilot battled with the storm, altering course to fly up and around the swirling clouds, Jane tilted her face until her lips found Selwyn's and closing her eyes, she kissed him. The kiss he returned spoke louder than the words of any song as he cupped her face with his free hand.

'Oh, my darling, I've waited so long for this,' he whispered and kissed her again.

Jane had only ever stolen meaningless kisses in the past with men who meant nothing. But now she knew that Selwyn's kiss was the one she'd been waiting for all her life.

'Looks like we've got the better of it!'

Jane and Selwyn pulled apart.

The pilot told them he'd diverted to the airport, where the weather was clear, and they could land safely. His explanation of how sudden and unexpected weather systems can play havoc went over their heads. 'Folks, I'm sorry that you had to go through that,' he continued, 'I hope it didn't stop the enjoyment of your ride.'

Too stunned to speak, Selwyn and Jane gripped each other's hands.

'It's taken a near-fatal experience to bring us together,' Jane whispered as she looked into Selwyn's eyes.

'I will make sure that there are no others to tear us apart,' he replied.

As the helicopter descended and landed safely, the sun

began to shine again. Selwyn helped Jane out and wrapped his arm around her, and she felt as though she were floating on a cloud as light as air.

It didn't matter that Jane was covered in mud and hot, sweaty, and exhausted from the day's events. She couldn't care less that her dress clung to her damp swimming costume and rode up her legs. Now she knew that strange feeling she'd experienced wasn't nerves or a tummy upset, and the butterflies bouncing around had meaning.

Love. That unfamiliar word. Something she'd never known until now. Jane was in love and wanted to shout it out to the world!

As they waited outside the terminal for Curtis, Selwyn took Jane in his arms and kissed her again.

So, this is what it feels like, Jane thought as she succumbed. She didn't care that a flight had landed, and scores of passengers were heading their way. The ordeal had brought her together with Selwyn, and now that it was over, the fat lady was most definitely singing.

Chapter Twenty-Eight

Unfortunately for Bridgette, her talk, *All Muck and Magic*, had little to do with tending to the earth to produce spectacular enchanting gardens. Instead of imparting wisdom accumulated over years of competing in award-winning floral events, she found herself far from the centre of attention in the Neptune Lounge later that afternoon.

Guests had learnt that Bridgette was amongst the party that had been robbed whilst on the island of Antigua, and, like Chinese whispers, the story had gathered pace. The atmosphere was almost party-like as passengers, drying off after the sudden storm, had no interest in gardening but wanted to hear all about the theft.

In front of an enraptured audience, Nancy grabbed Bridgette's microphone and told of the near-death experience the Captain had endured. Luckily for the old boy, Harold was the hero of the hour and had fought off multiple armed robbers, Nancy tearfully explained, but they'd been unable to prevent the theft.

Nancy had embellished the story. Refusing to give up her moment in the limelight, she led passengers to believe Anne would need knee replacements, Kath was suffering from shock, whilst the Captain had been sedated and was lying in the infirmary under the watchful eye of the ship's medics. Nancy refused to remove herself from the podium as Bridgette tapped her foot and rolled her eyes.

Was Nancy mad? Bridgette asked herself as she listened to the fictitious story that prevented her from delivering her lecture. Peter was standing on one side of the stage, and she caught his eye. Raising her hands in a questioning gesture, Bridgette drew her fingers across her throat to indicate that he silence Nancy. She was astonished to see that he merely shrugged his shoulders in a gesture of self-defeat.

'Bugger this…' Bridgette muttered. There was little point in persisting with her talk. If the audience wanted make-believe, then Nancy was the one to deliver it. Knowing that a party was taking place in the Captain's suite, Bridgette picked up her notes and, waving goodbye to Peter, stepped down from the stage.

As she wandered through the ship, Bridgette smiled. The Captain wasn't as daft as he looked. He'd laughed when they'd got him back to the *Diamond Star* where concerned crew officials wanted to alert the Antiguan police.

There was no need for police intervention, the Captain said. The Rolex that he'd worn was fake. He'd picked it up for a few euros when cruising in the Greek Islands and told the officials that he would have given it to the chap had he taken the trouble to ask for it. As for Anne's knees, there was hardly a mark, and Kath's antiseptic wipes had erased all signs of injury. Any shock that Kath experienced was soon quelled when the Captain cracked open the first bottle of Dom Perignon.

'Got room for a little one?' Bridgette called out as she entered the Captain's suite.

Anne handed Bridgette a glass of champagne and indicated that they head out to the Captain's balcony to watch the sunset.

'Did you hear that a helicopter got into difficulties during the storm?' Kath asked and chinked glasses with Bridgette.

'Nancy is giving it chapter and verse,' Bridgette replied. 'She's taken over my lecture. Anyone would think that Harold was onboard the helicopter, with first-hand knowledge.'

'I heard he was in the bar, at the time, recovering from the robbery,' Kath said.

'Nancy said the helicopter passengers were from the Italian cruise ship on the next pier.' Bridgette sipped her drink, enjoying the Captain's expensive taste.

'She makes it up as goes along.' Kath shook her head. 'But it sounds as though the pilot was very skilled and manoeuvred them out of difficulty.'

'As long as the passengers are all right, though they must have had a bumpy ride.' Bridgette took the Captain's arm and gently assisted him to a cushioned sunbed, turned to face the setting sun. She closed her eyes to enjoy the moment, and had Kath and Anne not been in the suite, she'd have stripped to the buff and lain down to share a spliff with the old boy.

'Has anyone heard from Jane?' Bridgette asked. 'I saw her setting off with Selwyn this morning.'

'I'm sure she'll be back soon,' Kath said, 'probably complaining about being stuck in his company all day. No matter how hard Selwyn tries, Jane is blind to his advances.'

'He could advance on me any day of the week.' Anne kicked off her sandals and settled beside the Captain. 'I think Selwyn is gorgeous.'

'He doesn't talk about himself,' Bridgette mused. 'Selwyn is a very private man.'

'But he recently lost his wife,' Kath added, 'and grief affects everyone differently.' She thought of her own ups and downs over the last few months.

'Quite so,' Bridgette agreed and remembered her beloved Hugo.

'I don't think Selwyn's grieving,' Anne said, 'he seems to be having the time of his life.'

Kath twirled the champagne in her glass. 'Jane told me that he had been a tube train driver and his wife a cleaner for the council.'

'Crikey.' Anne looked at Kath. 'He must have saved up to come on this cruise. It costs a fortune.' Anne knew she wouldn't be on the cruise without Kath and Jane's financial support.

'I don't think you can be judgemental about people's financial situations.' Bridgette reached out and stroked the Captain's arm fondly. 'None of us really know much about each other.'

The Captain, hand quivering, caught Bridgette's arm and returned the tender gesture. 'Another bottle, old gal?' he said.

With their glasses replenished and sitting comfortably, they stared out as the last rays of the day glowed in the darkening sky and the sun began to dip.

'Aren't we lucky,' Kath said, 'to be here, with new friends in such wonderful surroundings.'

'It's moments like this that I'll always remember,' Anne added. 'Like souvenirs.'

'Keep those moments in your memory bank,' Bridgette spoke softly, 'and remember, the best souvenirs are your memories.'

Dicky sat backstage in the entertainers' dressing room and stared at his face in the mirror. There were new lines on his forehead, and he could see dark circles under his eyes. Entertaining the ladies was exhausting, he thought, and a man his age should have early nights every now and again. His reflection told him that he was burning the candle at both ends. The wealthy widow was inexhaustible, and Dicky wondered if she was on vitamin injections. The woman had no right to have so much stamina. After a full day of sightseeing and pandering to her every wish, an energetic session had followed. It was all Dicky could do not to fall into bed and sleep for a week.

Still, there wasn't long to go, the cruise would be over soon, and Dicky, with another expensive watch on his wrist and a generous gift of more dollars to 'treat himself', was a happy bunny.

As his fingers reached out for Melissa's blemish concealer, he remembered what he'd heard in the library the previous night. If his assumptions were correct, Kath's drunken ramblings had been a confession. Her husband's 'accident' was, in fact, cold-blooded murder. Dicky smiled and dabbed his face. There was no evidence other than what he'd heard. If Kath had kept it to herself all this time and benefited from the death, Dicky knew she would never admit what she'd done. But there was no reason not to put the fear of God into her, and it would be easy to extract a good amount of money from her. She'd have no idea how he knew about her guilt, and the anxiety would send her straight to her online account to transfer a large sum.

Dicky rubbed his hands together. His plan to escape from his marriage was going well, and the nest egg in his safe was building. Soon he'd be free. Dicky fancied a spell in the Costas to indulge in warm weather and stints in cabaret clubs.

Goodbye, Doncaster. Hello, Benidorm!

If only he could get back in Anne's good books, he thought as he took Melissa's bronzer and applied it to his cheeks. Anne was unique, and he'd made a mistake standing her up.

'Get your thieving hands off my stuff!' Melissa stomped into the room and grabbed the bronzer from Dicky's raised hand. 'I don't have anything that will make you look any better.' She flung herself onto a chair. 'I could put a week's shopping in the bags under your eyes.'

'Ah, Melissa,' Dicky cooed, 'you are a miracle waiting to happen in someone else's life.'

'Bog off, Dicky. It will take a miracle to make you look human and ready to go on stage.' She shook her shoulders and began to scrape her hair into a tight knot. 'I hear the wealthiest widow on the ship has you in her claws?'

'Far from it, she likes my sparkling company and I energise her.'

'The only thing that is energising her is a daily dose of my special vitamins, and they come at a price.'

Dicky's mouth dropped open, and he leaned back in his chair. 'You're supplying her?' He shook his head. 'What else have you got in your secret drawer?'

'You're not the only one cashing in on the passengers, so don't look so shocked.' Melissa began to apply her stage makeup. 'And don't bugger up my routine tonight.' She glued on false eyelashes and glowered at Dicky. 'I want two curtain calls and the audience on their feet before you come on.'

Dicky's comedy act would follow Melissa's solo performance in the Neptune Lounge. He'd often enjoyed arriving on stage just as Melissa was soaking up the applause. Interrupting with a few clever words or a joke at her expense deflected the audience's attention to him.

'All right,' Dicky replied, 'don't get your knickers in a twist.'

'I bet Jane McDonald never had to put up with your sort of nonsense.'

'Jane and I were the best of friends.' Dicky sighed and recalled cruises in days gone by at the start of his career.

'Yeah, yeah, and I sang with Freddie Mercury...'

There was a loud knock on the door. 'Ten minutes to showtime, Miss Montana.'

'Break a leg,' Dicky quipped.

Melissa fixed her wig in place and disappeared behind a screen. 'The only thing I'll break is your neck if you try any tricks tonight,' she replied.

Dicky yawned. While Melissa slipped into her stage costume, he darted to grab her concealer. 'I hear you,' he called out and hurriedly dabbed at the bags under his eyes. When she reappeared, Dicky smiled. 'Very nice, you'll knock 'em dead.'

'What are you after?' Melissa placed her hands on her sequined hips and tilted her Dolly Parton-dressed head to study the comedian.

With his warmest smile and pleading eyes, Dicky spun around in his chair. Facing Melissa, he asked, 'Any of those vitamin pills going spare?'

Jane and Selwyn stood outside the door to Hibiscus. She leaned back to rest her weight against the wall as Selwyn moved forward to kiss her.

'Do you want to come in?' Jane asked.

'No, I won't disturb your friends, but shall we have dinner together?'

'Yes, I'd like that.'

'I'll book a table in the Atrium Restaurant. It's on the Marquee Deck.'

'That sounds very formal, I hope I have something suitable to wear.'

'You will look beautiful in whatever you choose.' Selwyn stroked Jane's cheek and smiled as a flake of dried mud came away. His fingers traced her neck, and seeing her turtle pendant, he gently touched the diamond eyes.

'Kath gave it to me for Christmas,' Jane explained.

'The enamelling is excellent; a turtle represents new beginnings.'

'Yes, I know.'

'How appropriate.'

'I'd better have a shower.' Jane reached into her bag for her key card.

'I wish I could join you.'

'Go! See you later.' She pecked his cheek, then watched Selwyn walk away, her eyes lingering longingly. *Goodness, he's handsome!* she thought.

Entering Hibiscus, Jane threw her bag on her bed and kicked off her sandals. Wandering into the bathroom, she slipped out of her dress and peeled off her swimsuit.

Staring at her naked self in the mirror, she puffed out her cheeks. 'So, this is the body that Selwyn will soon be seeing,' Jane spoke to her reflection.

She cocked her head, placed a hand on her hip, and realised she no longer cared that she was overweight. It was the most freeing feeling she'd ever experienced. Selwyn said that he loved her curves and found her body sexy. Jane felt like she was diving deep into a vat of smooth, creamy chocolate. She closed her eyes and imagined rubbing the warm sensual substance all over her body and then licking her fingers with her lips. Jane knew that Selwyn loved chocolate, and her mind conjured up fantasies that involved them both.

'Ahh….' She let out a sigh.

Jane didn't hear the door to Hibiscus open, but suddenly Kath's voice called out, 'Jane, are you in there?' The bathroom handle rattled, and Kath's head appeared. 'Good heavens, is everything all right?'

Kath's eyes were wide as she saw Jane's naked body and the pile of clothes on the floor.

'Oh, er … hello, Kath,' Jane mumbled and reached for a towel.

'Your clothes are covered in mud.' Kath bent down to scoop up Jane's discarded dress. 'Has something happened?'

Jane stepped into the shower. 'Yes, it most certainly has,' she replied, 'something very serious.'

'Oh, my dear.' Kath's face was concerned. 'We should never have let you go off on your own with Selwyn.' She clutched Jane's dress to her chest. 'Take your time in a nice hot shower.' Kath began to tidy. She placed a fluffy bathrobe close by. 'I'll make a cup of sweet tea, and you can tell us all about it. Help yourself to any of my new products. I do hope you're all right.'

Through the mist and frosted glass, Jane watched Kath go. She took Kath's Jo Malone pear and freesia body wash and stroked it over her skin.

'Don't worry, my dear friend,' she whispered. 'I'm more than all right.'

Chapter Twenty-Nine

Kath and Anne stared, open-mouthed when Jane told them that the passengers in the helicopter that got into difficulty were, in fact, herself and Selwyn. Hardly containing her excitement, Jane spoke about her day.

Anne went straight to the bar to pour herself a drink. 'You're in love?' she asked, glancing at Kath to ensure she'd heard Jane correctly. 'But you were furious this morning when Kath insisted that you accept Selwyn's invitation. I'd go so far as to say that you were practically stamping your feet and throwing a tantrum.' Anne poured prosecco. 'Yet, here you are, only hours later, all loved up and girly.' Anne smiled and punched the air. 'You didn't even like Selwyn, and now you're smouldering with passion.'

'I am overjoyed for you,' Kath said. 'Subconsciously you've felt drawn to Selwyn, but it took a day of braving new experiences to realise it.'

'Having a near-fatal experience probably sealed the deal.' Anne laughed.

'Yes, that's exactly what I told Selwyn,' Jane agreed. 'Isn't it odd how these things work out?'

'Well, I think it's wonderful.' Anne hugged Jane. 'So, what are your plans?

'We're having dinner in the Atrium Restaurant. It's very posh, and I haven't a clue what to wear.'

'Oh, how exciting!' Anne clapped her hands.

'This calls for action.' Kath crossed the room and picked up the telephone. 'Hello, reception?' she said, 'we have a special occasion in Hibiscus. I'd like you to send the stylist from the ship's boutique with a selection of evening wear for a larger lady.' Kath looked up and smiled at Jane. 'Could you also ask Philippe, from the salon, to come to our suite if he's free?'

'Excellent,' Anne said. 'Now let's get some makeup on that face.' She reached into her handbag. 'Cinderella has finally met her Prince Charming.'

Together, they helped Jane prepare for her dinner date. From several stunning gowns, Jane selected a dress that fitted perfectly over her bust, then fell to the floor in soft flowing layers. A cowl collar, trimmed with silver beading, covered the tops of her arms and showed a flattering cleavage. Philippe had worked magic, adding a pretty hair band and coiling Jane's braids into a chignon at the base of her neck.

'My goodness, so elegant,' Philippe exclaimed as he studied his handiwork, 'I hope he's worth it.'

Kath smiled. Philippe's fee for the consultation was exorbitant, but Jane had no qualms and tipped handsomely. Anne was like a teenager, applying makeup and insisting Jane borrow her silver droplet earrings. Kath was touched to see that Jane wore her turtle necklace, which was perfect against the deep navy colour of her dress.

As they watched Jane leave Hibiscus, Kath and Anne linked arms and wondered if their friend would return that night. 'We won't wait up,' they called out as Jane disappeared from view.

Jane stood by the lift and took a deep breath. Her heart was pounding as she carefully lifted the hem of her dress and stepped in.

'Which floor?' a man asked.

'The Marquee Deck, please,' Jane replied.

'Must be a special occasion.' A woman accompanying the man studied Jane's appearance. 'You look stunning.' The woman smiled.

'Yes, it is, thank you,' Jane mumbled as the lift reached the next floor, and the couple got out. The doors closed, and Jane realised that she was surrounded by mirrors. Nervously she turned to study her reflection.

What would Selwyn say when he saw her so styled, with makeup and wearing such an expensive gown? Jane bit her lip and tilted her head. Would he think that she'd overdone it?

But as she stared, she could hardly believe her eyes, and Jane had to admit that the woman was right. She *did* look stunning! Her friends had worked magic, and she felt like Cinderella going to the ball. Crossing her fingers, Jane stepped into the Atrium and followed signs for the restaurant.

'Madam,' the manager said and gave a slight bow, 'your table is this way.'

The candlelit restaurant was adorned with festive swags, lit with a thousand tiny lights. In the centre of the room, a massive Christmas tree decorated with crystal ornaments glowed as Jane was guided to a discreet booth where Selwyn was waiting.

Jane stopped and, blinking rapidly, held her breath. But her fears suddenly melted away as she stared into Selwyn's eyes.

'Wow,' Selwyn breathed and reached out to take her hand and guide her into the booth. 'You look so beautiful.'

Selwyn wore his dinner suit and the red bow tie that matched his silk cummerbund, and Jane thought that he looked like a movie star, handsome and sophisticated. As he leaned in and kissed Jane on her lips, she caught his now familiar spicy smell, felt the softness of his skin, and the butterflies in her tummy began to tango.

Their dinner was perfect.

The tasting menu that Selwyn had pre-ordered was exquisitely presented in a series of dishes that made Jane gasp as each delicacy was placed before them. But the highlight came when the pianist began to sing 'Have

Yourself a Merry Little Christmas', and Jaden appeared at their table. Standing before a trolley, he smiled and asked Jane if she liked crêpes. When she nodded enthusiastically and gripped Selwyn's hand, they watched with fascination as the chef began to flame Grand Marnier over the lightest pancakes Jane had ever seen.

'I have a gift for you,' Selwyn said as a server took their empty plates and a sommelier poured more champagne. 'I hope you like it.' Selwyn placed a gorgeously wrapped package in her hands.

'You didn't need to get me anything...' Jane began as she loosened the gold ribbon and opened a leather-bound box.

Lying on a velvet bed were a dozen tiny enamelled turtles strung together on a silver bangle. Their diamond eyes shone as Selwyn fastened it around her wrist.

'Oh!' Jane gasped. 'It's magnificent and matches my necklace.' Her fingers flew to her throat as she gently jiggled the turtles, watching them sparkle in the candlelight. 'I can't believe you've done this.'

'Happy Christmas, Jane,' Selwyn said as he nuzzled her ear, 'and may all your Christmas dreams come true.'

Hours later, Jane lay in Selwyn's arms and realised that all her dreams *had* come true. In the spacious bed in his cabin, Selwyn made love to her with a tenderness and emotion she'd never experienced. Dismissing her doubts and silencing her concerns with his lips, he was a passionate lover who made Jane feel like the most adored woman in the world. She hadn't worried about her size for a moment as he carefully slid the gown from her shoulders and kissed the soft skin on her neck. As his hands explored her curves and caressed her body, Jane gave herself entirely and, for the first time in her life, knew what it was to be loved and adored.

When Selwyn told Jane that he loved her, her reply was instant.

'I love you too,' she whispered. 'Thank you for not giving up on me.'

'I'll never give up on you, my darling, you have my heart and my soul.'

'More than reggae music?' she teased and cupped Selwyn's face.

'More than the master, Bob Marley.' He smiled and, taking Jane in his arms, made love to her again.

Chapter Thirty

Kath sat in her favourite place, the following morning, on the balcony of Hibiscus. A book lay face-down in her lap, and she cradled a coffee cup. Wearing a bright cotton jumpsuit and sparkly trainers, Kath was content. How she wished that Jim and her sons could see her. They wouldn't recognise the woman with the neat hairstyle and stylish new clothes, and with her tan developing nicely, she thought her appearance was transformed.

Another beautiful day beckoned, and she intended to relax and make the most of the ship's facilities and the gorgeous sunshine. She thought about Jane and smiled. Something quite extraordinary had happened, and it was as though the Christmas fairy had waved a wand and sprinkled magic dust over her friend. It was a wonderful thing to have happened to Jane, especially at Christmas.

Kath put down her cup and, removing her glasses, stared at the island of Antigua. She considered the Caribbean the most enchanting place she'd ever visited. Which wasn't difficult. Garstang and Bournemouth couldn't compare. No wonder Jane and Selwyn had been drawn together. An attraction sparked and fuelled by the beauty of everything around them.

Kath stood and, glancing at her watch, decided to stretch her legs and go for a walk. Taking her bag and glasses, she left Hibiscus, and as she turned a corner in the corridor, she heard a door open and saw a man backing out of a room. It was the comedian Dicky. As Kath held back, pressing herself to the wall, she heard him call out.

'Don't forget to tell your friends that they can buy my book and DVD at the reduced rate,' he said, his tone conspiratorial, 'but mum's the word, I don't want the shop manager finding out.'

Craning her neck, Kath watched Dicky wander off. He whistled to himself as he headed further along the corridor, then stopped to knock on another door. 'Dicky's delivery!' he said and disappeared inside.

'So, it's true,' Kath whispered. Nancy had mentioned that Dicky would supply reduced-price merchandise if he was paid cash. Kath shook her head. There was no end to the man's shenanigans. He must be breaking his *Diamond Star* contract with illicit sales and endearing himself to wealthy widows for personal gain. 'He's nothing more than a gigolo,' she said, feeling grateful Anne hadn't taken up with him.

Putting her thoughts aside, Kath strolled out to the promenade deck, where the sun shone, and the sky was the deepest blue. She smiled as passengers ambled by and called out, 'Another delightful day in paradise!'

The *Diamond Star*, moored in St Kitts, was quiet onboard as most passengers disembarked to head off on trips to the beautiful beaches and to see the island's delights. Anne, enjoying the solitude, lay on a sunbed on the lido deck and topped up her tan. The peace and having the pool to herself were luxuries, and she idly toyed with the ring Kath had gifted her, stroking the smooth precious stone. Anne thought about Kath and felt happy that her friend was embracing the cruise and getting over the grief of Jim's death. She smiled as she thought of Kath promenading in yet another new outfit around the deck.

Anne was delighted too that Jane had come out of her comfort zone and had, at last, hooked up with Selwyn. She remembered that they were going to visit an attraction named Demon's Bridge, a natural limestone arch formed from a reef where the Atlantic Ocean crashed into the Caribbean Sea. On her return, she expected Jane to be full of wonder.

It's amazing what love can do, Anne mused.

It wasn't that she was jealous of Jane. In fact, she couldn't be more pleased for her friend. But Jane's joy highlighted Anne's emptiness when it came to husband-hunting and, as she reached for her sunglasses, she felt a wave of loneliness. Her emotions were all over the place. From the high of a windfall in the casino to the low of being abandoned by Dicky. A couple of days ago, she'd felt green with envy when she watched him carousing around the port. It should have been her in that gorgeous speedboat, nestling in his arms. But she hadn't spoken to him, and she tried not to think of what he might be doing now.

With a sigh, she slipped into the pool. The sun was beaming down, and the water was warm and welcoming. If only Dicky were here, she thought, and yearned for his company. Anne knew that the comedian was a rascal and would lead her astray, but he had a charisma that she found irresistible.

Yet she'd pushed him away.

But what harm would a fling for a few days have done? Time was running out, and it would take her mind off the clock, counting down to their flight home, where she'd face the final act in her divorce. Anne reached the steps and, taking hold of a railing, stepped out of the pool and into the jacuzzi. Settling herself in the bubbling bowl, she thought of the packing she had to do to leave the house she'd shared with Barry. Now that Jane was in the throes of romance, would the offer of a room in her cottage still stand? The last thing Anne wanted was to be in the way of Jane's relationship with Selwyn.

Anne sighed heavily and closed her eyes. 'Please don't let Jane get hurt,' she whispered, 'and may Selwyn be the man of her dreams.'

'Talking to yourself?' A voice called out. 'Or are you inviting me in?'

Anne opened her eyes to see Dicky standing by the jacuzzi, a towel draped over his deeply tanned shoulders and a hand in the pocket of his tropical print shorts. Wearing a broad smile, he raised his sunglasses and winked. 'Room for one more?' he asked and, not waiting for a reply, threw his towel to one side and climbed in.

'Where's your widow?' Anne asked as she sat up and pouted. 'Has she sailed on to sunnier seas?'

'Aw, you know that meant nothing, it's part of my job to entertain the passengers.' Dicky inched across the jacuzzi, his arm snaking around Anne.

'Especially rich ones.'

'It was you who gave me the heave-ho,' Dicky said.

Anne felt his fingers on her skin. His touch was sensual, and her body gave an involuntary shiver despite the heat.

'Fancy a drink?' Dicky asked and raised his hand to beckon a server. 'Two double-d's, if you please.'

'Let's get one thing clear,' Anne said, 'I don't have any money.'

'Well, that makes two of us.' Dicky smiled.

'And I'm about to become divorced and homeless.'

'We have so much in common.' Dicky threw back his head and laughed.

Anne felt her mood lift. At last! A man was being honest with her. She sank into Dicky's arm with a satisfied sigh as the server placed a drink in her hand, and Dicky kissed the top of her head. The cocktail was delicious, and Anne licked her lips, 'Cheers,' she whispered, and all her cares suddenly floated away.

Chapter Thirty-One

On the morning of the thirtieth of December, the engines of the *Diamond Star* began to gently hum as the crew began preparations to leave the island of St Kitts and head southwards to Barbados. Waking early, passengers stood on balconies and decks or stared out of porthole windows as the ship pulled slowly away to enter a channel known as The Narrows. As they passed the neighbouring island of Nevis, many felt poignant knowing they were beginning the final leg of the cruise. Others thought of the previous day and the enjoyment of disembarking and discovering St Kitts' delights.

As the ship began her journey Selwyn and Jane sat upright in the bed in his cabin. Both stared ahead at the painting on Selwyn's desk.

Jane cradled a cup in her hand and sipped hot tea. 'Where will you put it?' she asked and tilted her head to study the colourful dancing woman.

'I'm not sure,' Selwyn replied. 'I thought I had a place back home, but maybe not.'

'Each time I look, she seems to be moving – it's fascinating.'

'She reminds me of you.'

'You said that when you first showed the painting to me.' Jane smiled and laid her head on Selwyn's shoulder. 'You've given me confidence I never knew.'

Her eyes closed, and very gently, Selwyn took the cup from her hands, then placed his arm around her shoulders and caressed her sun-kissed skin. It was true. As though Jane had sipped an elixir of love, her confidence had grown, and she'd become the woman he'd hoped for. The few short hours he'd spent with her had been some of the happiest of his life.

As Jane slept, he stroked her hair and thought of their day out. He'd known that she was reluctant to remove her kaftan and stand before him in her swimsuit, but she'd taken the plunge and enjoyed their swim, then sat behind the wheel of the beach buggy and took delight in the exhilarating drive. Though her confidence increased, it plummeted when the helicopter got into difficulties. But the unsettling incident had brought them together and their dinner had been magical. He determined never to let her go.

While Jane was driving, Selwyn had carefully unfolded his plastic pouch and scattered more of Flo's ashes. He'd watched a wispy trail of grey drift over the golden sand dunes that rose and fell as though breathing, before being carried in the wind over the rippled surface and out to the ocean. Flo had never liked sand on her feet and couldn't understand why anyone would want to walk barefoot on a beach. 'Leave nothing but your footprints,' Selwyn had whispered. 'Enjoy the drive, my dear.'

As they lay in each other's arms in the darkness of the night, Jane had asked Selwyn about his family. He showed her photos on his phone and told her about Gloria and Gwen. He felt sure she would like them. Susan and Raymond would be more challenging, but his granddaughter, Charlene, was adorable.

Jane expressed regret that she'd never had children but spoke fondly of her job.

'You should do more with your cooking skills,' Selwyn suggested. 'You were most entertaining on the stage with Jaden.'

'I was in my cooking comfort zone.'

'I look forward to the day you cook for me.'

Jane wanted to know what Flo was like, and Selwyn had been thoughtful before he answered. 'She was a decent woman,' he eventually replied. 'A good mother, careful with money, a person who lived for her religion and the congregation at her church.'

He failed to tell Jane that Flo was narrow-minded and mean-spirited. A person who believed that she'd go straight to hell if she didn't stand by her faith and practise it daily. There had been little warmth between them as the years passed, and the attractive girl who'd flirted and teased before marriage had slapped away any cuddles or comforts as they aged. Flo had no sense of adventure and never went far from home. Selwyn knew he should have left years ago and fulfilled his dreams of finding true love and travelling. But responsibility weighed heavy, and Flo would never have lived with the shame of divorce or been able to stand on her own two feet.

'How did she die?' Jane whispered.

'She passed in her sleep,' he replied. 'The doctor said it was her heart. It was a peaceful way to go.'

Selwyn had gone through the motions of mourning his wife, but Flo's death had opened the door to freedom, and within days, he felt reborn. The cruise was the beginning of the rest of his life, and now he hoped that Jane would share the journey with him.

Yesterday had been a wonderful day, and Jane, relaxed and at ease with herself, was excellent company. Their time at Demon's Bridge had been exhilarating, and it had felt good to share the experience with someone he now cared about. They stood arm-in-arm in awe as they watched the geysers and the blowholes, and the Atlantic waves crash into the rocks. Jane asked a guide how the bridge got its name and had tears in her eyes when she learnt that it was where enslaved Africans would commit suicide to escape the horrors of slavery. With no land between the bridge and Africa, the hope was that the raging current would carry them home to their motherland.

In the evening, the Marley Men had performed in the Mermaid Theatre, and to Selwyn's delight, Jane had taken his hands and pulled him to the dance floor. As they moved and grooved, Toots sang Selwyn's favourite songs, and he felt the music embrace him.

Humming softly as Jane laid her head on his shoulder, he wrapped his arms around her and smiled, at last a happy man.

In the Deck Café, the breakfast brunch was busy. With a full sea day ahead, the mid-morning meal was popular. After rising late, Kath and Anne sat at a corner table sipping coffee and people-watching as diners arrived and took a seat.

'Is Jane going to join us?' Anne asked. She wore a polka-dot sundress and giant sunglasses, and licked cappuccino froth from her pouting lips.

'Yes, I got a message to say she'll be along presently,' Kath replied, 'but you were very late coming to bed last night. Did you go to the casino again?' She put her cup down and began tucking into a selection of pastries.

'I had a nightcap in the bar.'

'With anyone we know?'

'Er, yes, you do know him.'

Kath tore a croissant and spooned apricot jam. She knew that the smug expression on Anne's face explained the discarded La Perla underwear in the bathroom, and it wasn't rocket science to work out where Anne had been until the early hours.

'Were you with the Captain?' Kath played along. 'Or

perhaps you enjoyed a brandy with Bridgette or drinks with Harold and Nancy?'

'Nope.'

'I give up,' Kath said. She continued to eat and waited for Anne to enlighten her.

'You won't like it...'

'Not if your nightcap ended up in a comedian's cabin below deck.' Kath shrugged. 'But you are old enough to be aware of what you are doing. I just don't want you to get hurt.'

'How did you guess?' Anne lifted her sunglasses and stared at Kath.

'Please, give me some credit.' Kath shook her head. 'I may have lived like a hermit for the past forty years and be losing my marbles, but I'm not completely without intuition.'

'It's just a bit of fun, I like him.'

Kath patted Anne's hand. 'Good, enjoy yourself, but remember Dicky is the ship's gigolo and don't let him take you for a ride. Emotionally or financially.'

Anne smiled as a server took her empty coffee cup and she ordered another. 'Oh, he won't be doing that, I think we have the measure of each other.'

At that moment, the friends were distracted. Bridgette entered with Harold and Nancy in tow, and they headed straight for their table.

'Good morning, girls,' Bridgette said and flung her bag down. 'Our penultimate day – what are your plans?'

Before they could answer, Harold pulled out a chair for

Nancy. She raised an eyebrow and studied Kath's croissants. 'Any going spare?' she asked.

'Help yourself.' Kath pushed the plate towards Nancy.

'I'll go to the buffet and get your breakfast,' Harold said and turned away.

'Is the Captain joining you?' Anne asked Bridgette.

'No, and he's not answering his phone. I'll give him a bit longer and then pop up to the penthouse. He's probably having a lie-in.'

Kath watched Bridgette flick a napkin onto her lap. 'I think it's admirable how you look out for him.'

'I'm extremely fond of him. We've had fun over the years and especially on this cruise,' Bridgette replied. 'He's very interesting when his mind is playing ball, and he's kind.' A pot of tea was on the table, and she helped herself. 'I want to make sure that he makes the most of his holiday. At our age, every day is a bonus.'

'Are you husband-hunting?' Anne grinned as she sat forward, resting her chin on her hands to stare at Bridgette.

'Good heavens no.' Bridgette laughed. 'It's not long since I buried my dear Hugo, and I don't plan on getting married again.'

'I was so pleased that the Captain had no ill effects from the robbery,' Kath said.

'Fancy him having a fake Rolex,' Anne mused.

Bridgette smiled. 'It is very sensible not to wear expensive items offshore, but I can assure you that the Captain's safe is full of the real thing.'

'Seriously?' Anne was wide-eyed.

'He's worth a fortune, but there's no family now, only a distant nephew.'

'Surely the nephew will inherit the lot?' Anne asked.

'Certainly, a good amount, but most of it will go to The Seafarers' Charity.'

'What a lovely gesture,' Kath said and was reminded of the contents of Jim's will. She shook her head as though erasing the memory.

'No sign of the lovebirds this morning?' Bridgette asked.

'If you mean Jane and Selwyn,' Kath said, 'Jane is here.' Kath held up her hand to wave as Jane entered the café.

'Morning all,' Jane said as she sat down. 'Selwyn has gone for a swim so it's just me joining you.'

'And we're very pleased to have your company,' Kath said.

As diners went back and forth from the buffet, plans for the day were discussed. Nancy held a copy of the *Diamond Star Daily* and read aloud, informing the group that, together with Harold, she was going to the ukulele class.

'I think I'll join you,' Kath said. 'I enjoyed it so much last time.'

'I'm giving my final talk later this afternoon,' Bridgette said as she bit into a slice of melon. 'It's not until tea-time but I hope you'll all be there.'

'Yes, we'd love to. You are so interesting and knowledgeable.' Kath noticed Anne rolling her eyes and kicked her under the table. 'What's the topic?' Kath asked.

'*Around the World in Eighty Gardens*,' Bridgette replied. 'As the cruise is ending, the talk helps passengers consider future cruises that stop at ports with fascinating horticultural estates.'

'And you get a decent commission when everyone races to customer services to book?' Anne grinned.

'Don't be vulgar, dear.' Bridgette dabbed her mouth with her napkin, then pushed back her chair. 'I think I'll check on the Captain, I don't want him to miss brunch.'

They watched Bridgette leave the café.

'Jaden is hosting another cookery session, and Selwyn is joining me, so that's my afternoon sorted,' Jane said.

'I've got a date by the pool.' Anne grinned.

Kath and Jane stared at Anne.

'Don't start,' Anne said, 'it's only a fling, a bit of fun.'

'Do be careful, I think there is something suspect about Dicky.' Kath pushed her plate away and folded her hands in her lap.

'Don't worry about me,' Anne replied.

Kath glanced around the table and noticed Harold absorbed in a newspaper as Nancy ate her cereal, her head cocked, and ears tuned like satellites, hanging off their every word.

'I'm going to have a walk on the promenade deck. Would anyone like to join me?' Kath asked.

'I'm in.' Jane jumped up.

'Me too.' Anne stood and linked her arms with Jane and Kath.

'Don't forget the ukulele session!' Nancy pushed back her chair.

And before Nancy could fling down her spoon and amble over to join them, the three friends made their exit.

———

Bridgette took her time as she wandered through the ship and made her way to the lift that would take her up to the penthouse. There were only two more days of the cruise, and she felt ready to return to her home. The garden, despite the season, always needed attention, and Bridgette was keen to ensure that everything was wintering well. She enjoyed the new year and always made resolutions, which she endeavoured to carry out in the following months. This year she knew she would keep in touch with the Captain and not just on cruises. She'd been surprised that she enjoyed his company so much. Despite his infirmity, they'd shared some happy times.

'Let's hope that flu doesn't strike,' Bridgette said as she tapped on the Captain's door. Remembering how quickly Hugo had deteriorated, she had little hope for the Captain should the wintery virus that attacked so many elderly folks rear its ugly head.

There was no reply to her knock, and Bridgette called out, 'Wakey, wakey, time for brunch!' She dug into her pocket and retrieved the key card that the Captain insisted she keep to allow herself into his suite. 'Come on, my dear,' Bridgette said as she opened the door and stepped in. 'It's a glorious day, let's get out and enjoy it...'

Kath, Jane, and Anne stepped onto the promenade deck, and Anne linked her arm through Jane's. 'Come on,' she implored. 'Spill the beans, tell us what the score is with you and Selwyn. Is it serious?'

'I can't explain it,' Jane began. 'I've had a funny feeling from the start of the cruise. Whenever I was near Selwyn, I couldn't understand my emotions. I was so mixed up, never for a moment thinking that he was interested in me.'

'And now?' Anne was persistent.

'It feels completely right to be with him.'

'Is it the sex?'

'Not entirely, although that is wonderful, but no one has ever made me feel so feminine and loved.' Jane looked dreamy as she cast her eyes over the tranquil sea. 'We seem to get on and like each other's company.'

'Are you sure he's not looking for a wealthy woman to ease his journey into retirement?'

'Oh, Anne, why are you so cynical?' Jane shook her head. 'I have no doubt that Selwyn has been careful with money and planned for this part of his life.'

Anne squeezed Jane's arm. 'I'm just concerned for you and don't want you to get hurt,' she said. 'What happens at the end of the cruise? You live hundreds of miles apart.'

'I have no idea, but if he wants to continue to see me, I'll find a way.'

Their conversation continued, each voicing their thoughts on where life might lead them next. Anne knew full well that Dicky was just fun whilst she was on the cruise, which would distract her from the distressing task of dealing with her divorce when she got home. Kath admitted that she was contemplating booking another holiday and had been browsing brochures.

They had been strolling for almost an hour, and as they came to the end of their final circuit of the walking track, Jane took out her fan and began to wave it.

'Crikey, Kath,' she said, 'do you have to go so fast?' Red in the face and puffing hard, Jane wiped the sweat from her brow.

'I'm only sauntering. This isn't my normal pace,' Kath replied.

'Think of the calories you're burning,' Anne said. Neat and cool in cotton shorts and a tiny white vest, she checked her watch. 'Armani is holding a water aerobics class in ten minutes. Do either of you fancy joining me?'

'I thought you were hooking up with Dicky?' Jane stopped and, closing her fan, thrust her hands into the pockets of colourful harem trousers.

'He's got rehearsals until after lunch, then we're meeting by the pool bar.'

'I'm going to put my feet up before I go to the ukulele session,' Kath said.

But Jane suddenly beamed. Selwyn was walking towards them. 'I'm going to spend time with my lover,' she announced.

'Hello, ladies.' Selwyn held his arms wide to embrace

Jane. He was dressed in swimming shorts, a T-shirt and sliders and a damp towel was draped over his shoulder.

'Did you enjoy your swim?' Kath asked.

'The water was beautiful,' he replied, staring lovingly into Jane's eyes.

Jane snuggled in close and kissed Selwyn's cheek. His skin was warm, and she trailed her fingers over his chest.

'Look out,' Anne announced. 'Here's Usain Bolt and his trainer.'

Everyone turned to see Harold jogging towards them, wearing the tiniest trunks and trainers. Puffing and panting, he stopped and placed his hands on his hips. He bent double to catch his breath Several metres behind, Nancy rode a motorised scooter. She wore a billowing kaftan and held a stopwatch in her hand.

'Hello again,' Nancy said as the scooter stopped and she addressed the group. 'I was saying to Harold that his run is getting quicker. We both like to keep fit.'

Eyes fell to the scooter, brows raised.

Harold was still catching his breath. 'Nancy rides when I run,' he explained.

'Harold is going to cool off with Armani's water aerobics. Are any of you going to join him?' Nancy asked.

But before anyone could reply, they heard footsteps hurrying towards them. It was Diwa, and her face expressed concern. 'Is Mr Alleyne here?' she asked.

'Yes, I'm here.' Selwyn stepped forward.

'Bridgette Howarth is asking for you,' Diwa said. She

lowered her voice and touched Selwyn's arm. 'She's in the penthouse suite and wonders if you would join her.'

'In the penthouse?' Selwyn questioned.

'Yes, it is rather urgent.'

'Shall we come with you?' Jane gripped Selwyn's arm.

'It may be better if Mr Alleyne goes alone,' Diwa replied.

'We'll come, but will wait outside,' Jane said.

Nancy revved her scooter and was about to follow the group disappearing towards the lifts, but Harold reached out and, turning the key, cut the engine.

'Settle yourself, Nancy,' he said. 'This isn't a party, we'll wait down here.'

Diwa led Selwyn into the Captain's suite and quietly closed the door. In the lounge, Bridgette sat on a sofa, her head bowed as she dabbed at her eyes with a tissue.

'Bridgette?' Selwyn said and padded softly across the carpet until he came to her side. Crouching down, he took hold of one of her hands. 'What is it? What has happened?' Selwyn spoke softly, but already he feared the worst. 'Is it the Captain?'

'T-thank you for coming, y-yes,' Bridgette sobbed. 'I'm afraid it is.'

Selwyn wasn't sure how to phrase his next question. He glanced at Diwa, who nodded, then turned back to Bridgette. 'I'm so sorry,' Selwyn whispered, accepting the inevitable.

'I c-came to w-wake him,' Bridgette's voice was muffled, 'but he d-didn't move, his eyes were closed, and I touched his f-face. It was so cold.'

She sobbed, and Selwyn moved to sit beside her and enfold her in his arms. 'Shush, it's okay,' he said, his voice soft, tone warm. 'It's all right, I've got you.'

The door to the Captain's bedroom opened, and Peter came out. He was followed by a medic and a nurse.

Selwyn looked up. 'What happens now?' he addressed Peter.

Peter quietly told them the Captain would be taken to the ship's morgue. As Barbados was the next port of call, the medical team would notify the Bajan authorities to make a public health declaration. Peter turned to the medic, who nodded her head.

'Do we know his next of kin?' Selwyn asked.

'Yes, there's a nephew and he will be informed straightaway,' Peter said.

'Oh, I can't bear to think of him in the morgue,' Bridgette sniffed, 'all alone, and so cold.'

The nurse came forward and, kneeling, took Bridgette's hand. 'I'll look after him,' she assured. 'It will be my honour to perform the last offices, to bathe and dress him in a shroud.'

'Thank you, my dear.' Bridgette looked up. 'You're very kind. I'm just a silly old woman who has lost yet another good person.'

'We understand,' the nurse replied.

'You'd b-better tell the others.' Bridgette sniffed and

gripped Selwyn's hand. She turned to the nurse. 'But I think the Captain would prefer a T-shirt to a shroud,' she added with a poignant smile.

Selwyn rose to his feet. 'Don't move, I'll be back in a moment.' He walked over to Peter and whispered, 'May I see him?'

Peter looked at the medic, who nodded, and Selwyn slowly entered the Captain's bedroom. The room was dimly lit, but a ray of sunshine broke through a parting in the drapes. The light shone warm and steady, illuminating the body lying on the bed. The Captain's hands were folded neatly beneath the slogan on his T-shirt, and Selwyn smiled when he read the words *Titanic 1912 Swimming Team*.

The old boy had the last laugh.

Selwyn reached out and, very gently, touched the Captain's hands. 'Goodbye, sir, it has been an honour to know you.'

But the older man's hands were cold, and his face bore little resemblance to the mischievous man they'd known in the latter days of his life. His spirit had been lifted, leaving an empty shell of skin and bones.

Selwyn heard Flo's voice in his ear. 'He's safe now,' she said, 'in the hands of the Lord, who will look after him and guide him on his final journey.'

To his surprise, Flo's words brought Selwyn comfort. 'Thank you, my dear,' he said.

Selwyn turned to leave as the curtains fluttered and the sunbeam began to fade, but a shiver suddenly ran through his body. Flo was whispering.

'Thank you for taking me to places I ought to have gone – to experience in death all the things I missed out in life.'

Selwyn smiled and, glancing out, saw waves roll rhythmically like an aquatic heartbeat. He imagined the Captain's soul slowly sinking into the depths of his beloved sea. He knew that the spiritual cruise the Captain now embarked upon would be his finest journey.

Chapter Thirty-Two

As the *Diamond Star* continued to Barbados, news of the Captain's death was spoken of in hushed whispers amongst the passengers. That afternoon, arrangements had been made to move his body, and corridors and lifts were closed to offer privacy on the route to the medical centre. Peter assured Bridgette that the Captain's belongings would be carefully packed and kept securely by the Bajan police, who would liaise with the Captain's nephew as soon as he arrived on the island.

'Well, I suppose that's that.' Bridgette sat at the Captain's favourite cocktail bar with Kath, Anne, Jane, and Selwyn. 'And I propose a toast,' she said, 'to the Captain!'

'The Captain!' Everyone raised their drink as they stared at the empty stool, where someone had placed his captain's hat.

Knocking back two fingers of the elderly gentleman's favourite malt, they sat silently for a few moments before

Bridgette spoke again. 'I expect it will take ages for him to be flown back to England,' she said. 'I hear that the paperwork can be terribly slow.'

'Especially if the local authorities decide that there needs to be a post-mortem,' Selwyn added, remembering his conversation with the medics.

'I hope he enjoyed his last cruise,' Anne said. She felt miserable and wondered if she could have done more to make the Captain's last few days happier.

'I think he had a blast,' Jane said, smiling. 'With Bridgette's sparkling company, especially the time they spent together in the comfort of his suite.'

As the group turned to stare at Bridgette, her face flushed and she slid off her stool. 'Well, I am afraid I must love and leave you all, as I have a talk in the Neptune Lounge. The show must go on, as they say.'

Onboard activities continued throughout the day, and, given the circumstances, Peter was prepared to excuse Bridgette from her talk. But she refused, stating that the Captain would have been adamant that everyone carry on. She added that his spirit would be heckling from the front row.

Kath picked up her bag and said that Bridgette was entirely right. They should continue, and she would be supporting Bridgette during her talk. Jane and Selwyn discussed whether to go to Jaden's cookery session and, agreeing with the others, decided they would. But Anne said she would stay at the bar and have one more drink, then catch up with everyone later.

But Anne's 'one more drink' soon turned into several. The Captain's death had upset her more than she realised and, thinking of her own circumstances, she felt miserable. Turning to the server, she ordered another drink. 'Lots of folk must pass away at sea,' she said, 'this ship is Neptune's waiting lounge, the last port of call before we all walk the plank of death.'

Having lost track of time, Anne was quite tipsy when she carefully negotiated her exit from the bar and began to wander through the ship, focusing on the best route back to Hibiscus. Finding herself on an open deck, she gripped the rail and paused to take a deep breath and clear her head. As she stared out at the sea, she saw the light beginning to fade, and the rainbow flames of sunset dipped beyond the horizon.

'Goodbye, captain, dearest,' Anne whispered as darkness descended. Tears fell onto her cheeks, and she wiped them with her fingers.

'Bloody hell!' A voice called out. 'There you are, I've been looking for you everywhere!'

Anne turned to see Dicky heading towards her.

'I thought we were meeting for a drink by the pool?' he asked, 'but you look as though you are several ahead of me.' He reached out to take her arm.

'Not now, Dicky,' Anne said and brushed his hand to one side. She saw him stagger and realised he was intoxicated too.

'What's up?' Dicky stood with his feet apart and stared at Anne. 'You look upset.'

'I told you, not now.' Anne began to turn away. She knew she was a mess and didn't want Dicky to see her in such a vulnerable state.

'You're surely not sad about the old fart who died?' Dicky eyes were wide, and he swayed as he leaned in to study her face. 'For goodness' sake, they drop like flies on these cruises.'

Furious by Dicky's indifference, Anne suddenly raised her arm and struck out. Her palm slapped Dicky's face. 'Don't call him that!' she shouted. 'Don't you have any respect?'

Dicky was too shocked to reply as he touched his fingers to his stinging cheek.

'I'll meet you when I'm ready to meet you,' Anne said and, without looking back, turned, and moved away.

Dicky was speechless as he watched Anne walk off. He couldn't remember a woman slapping him, even though he'd deserved it many times. He could accept a pillow or flying ornament but not a physical whack like the one Anne had delivered. His cheek smarted, and he hoped he wouldn't need Melissa's concealer again. Who the hell did Anne think she was? He felt his blood boil and cracked his knuckles as he turned to lurch along the deck. Another one bites the dust!

He'd been drinking at the bar by the pool all afternoon as he waited for Anne, furious that the wealthy widow had given him the elbow earlier in the day to flirt with the restaurant manager, Nathaniel. Dicky had been counting on Anne to let him stay with her when they returned to the UK as he readied himself for further opportunities, but now that looked unlikely. To make matters worse, he had no idea what had provoked her into such a rage.

'Bloody women…' Dicky muttered to himself.

'You should show more respect.'

'Eh?' Dicky looked up.

Kath was standing before him. 'We've just lost a very dear person and you called him an old fart,' she said. Gripping her bag Kath stood solidly. 'Don't you ever think about anyone but yourself?'

Her heart was thumping, and she bit her lip. She hadn't anticipated a meeting with Dicky when she'd left Bridgette's talk and come searching for Anne, fearing that her friend might be upset. Kath hated confrontation and had never stood up to Jim in case a blow might occur. But Dicky had no right to speak to Anne like that, especially when her friend was clearly distressed.

'What did you say?' Dicky asked and took a step forward. A vein pulsed on his brow and sweat was visible on his skin.

'You heard me.' Kath felt a flash of sudden anger, as though years of pent-up emotion had bubbled up and boiled over. 'You abuse women and mistreat them,' she burst out. 'I've seen you flaunting yourself and your merchandise in and out of cabins. Does your contract allow you to sell directly to the passengers?' Kath stood tall and held her chin high as she stared at Dicky. But when she saw his eyes bulge and he took a step towards her, she knew she'd overstepped the mark.

'Who the hell are you to preach to me?' Dicky's voice was low and menacing. 'This from the woman who killed her husband!'

Shocked, Kath yelped and stumbled back. She felt winded as though she'd been punched, and as her hand gripped her throat, her bag fell to the floor. 'W-what did you say?' she asked, her whole body trembling.

'I know what you did,' Dicky spat, 'so don't preach to me.' He waved a finger in her face. 'And if you don't want to find yourself being arrested at the end of this cruise you can cough up cash to silence me.'

Kath began to sway. Her mind scrambled, and she couldn't think straight. Had Dicky just told her that he knew her secret? How could he possibly know that Jim's fall wasn't an accident?

Kath gripped the rail and tried to clear her head. Dicky's face had turned into Jim's. His lips curled into the same sneer Jim had given her that morning so many months ago, and she couldn't shake it away. Dicky was ranting, but his voice was distant as the memory of Jim opening the front door of their house became vivid.

'I'm off to the solicitor's,' he'd called out, 'it's time I updated my will to make sure that Hugh and Harry inherit the lot.' He'd waved an envelope in her face. 'You can't be trusted with finances but no doubt the boys will make some provision for you.'

'Provision', Kath knew, was a nursing home. She'd heard her sons discuss the subject many times when they thought she was badgering away in the kitchen, preparing yet another meal. As soon as the soil covered Jim's coffin, she'd be packed off to spend her days propped up in a chair with other nameless souls whose pointless lives ebbed away in the dreary confines of a shared old folks' home where time was a thief who stole what little you had left.

When Jim turned to leave, something in Kath had snapped. As he opened the door, she rushed forward and, grabbing the envelope, shoved her brutish husband hard with all her might. Startled, Jim tried to cling onto Kath, but she leapt back, and he lost his balance. The steps were steep, and Jim misplaced his footing. Kath watched the dead weight of his body fall, his eyes wide with fear, as he catapulted fatally to the ground.

Within seconds the envelope was buried in Kath's pocket.

Within minutes, Jim was dead.

Time stood still as Kath gripped the rail, stupefied by the haunting memory. Jim had provoked Kath for months by telling her he was changing his will. She couldn't have allowed him to travel to the solicitor that day.

Suddenly, she realised that Dicky was leering up in front of her. She saw his lips move and his teeth flash. He spoke with menace and told her how much money he wanted. Close now, Kath smelt Dicky's stale boozy breath and felt the heat from his body. Then, without warning, Dicky raised his fists to gesticulate and rant.

Kath cowered, fearing a blow. Instinctively she thrust out her arms, and when her hands connected with Dicky's chest, she pushed as hard as she could.

'What the hell…' Dicky swore as he stumbled on Kath's bulky bag. His feet lost their grip, and still unsteady, he skidded backwards on the deck's surface. Before she could reach out and stop him, Dicky had lost his balance and careered over the railing.

Kath was motionless, too stunned to move. One moment Dicky was yelling at her, and the next, he was gone.

'Oh, my goodness!' she blurted out. 'What on earth have I done?'

Glancing around, Kath saw no one other than herself on the deck. Before she had time to linger and consider her actions, she reached down to grab her crumpled bag and raced back to Hibiscus.

Chapter Thirty-Three

'Don't be so ridiculous!' Jane said as she gripped Kath's flapping arms and held her tight. 'You can't possibly have killed Dicky!'

Kath stood in the centre of the suite, her eyes closed and body trembling as she repeated that she'd pushed Dicky into the sea.

'You couldn't have done. Anne stood alongside, her face puzzled. 'I was with him not a quarter of an hour ago.' She looked at her drink and decided it was time to stop; her brain was befuddled, and she couldn't make sense of Kath's ramblings.

'You don't understand,' Kath insisted. 'Dicky knows what I've done!'

Jane, who'd returned to Hibiscus to get changed, shook her head. 'I don't have the foggiest notion of anything you are saying, but I suggest that you have a seat, take a deep breath, and tell us all about it.' She took Kath's shoulders and eased her onto a sofa. 'That's a good girl,' she said as she sat beside Kath and motioned for Anne to sit too. 'You're with friends and whatever has happened can be sorted.' She held out a glass of water for Kath to sip.

'B-but it can't,' Kath stammered, 'I'm a murderer...' She pushed the water away.

Jane shrugged and looked to Anne, who shook her head and frowned.

'Start at the beginning and tell us exactly what has happened and what you think you might have done.' Jane spoke softly and stroked Kath's arm.

Fifteen minutes later, Jane found herself sitting bolt upright, and Anne was sober.

'Holy shit…' Anne whispered, 'are you sure Dicky went over the rail?'

'Of course I'm sure,' Kath replied. 'He was very tipsy and when I pushed him, he stumbled over my bag and disappeared in a flash.'

'O.M.G.' Anne's mouth fell open as she stared at Kath and blinked slowly.

'Whoa…' Jane stood up. 'Firstly, we need to retrace your steps and see if there is any sign of Dicky, and if not, we may need to notify someone in authority that there might be a man overboard.'

'But what about Jim?' Kath sobbed. 'Now you know the truth.'

'Oh codswallop!' Jane shook her head. 'For heaven's sake,

please stop all thoughts of Jim's death being your fault. The man had a very unfortunate accident and simply misplaced his footing. It could have happened to anyone. The steps to your house are terribly steep, as your postman told the police. We all know how forgetful you are. You're confused, due to shock.'

But Jane had doubts, and as Kath's tale of her husband's will unfolded, she knew it was likely to be true. She remembered many occasions when Kath made excuses for a cut or bruise, saying she'd been clumsy in the kitchen or garden. Who could blame her for striking out at her bullying husband when he threatened to ruin what was left of her life? If Kath had managed to destroy Jim's updated will, Jane could hardly blame her. She felt guilty that she hadn't been a better friend over the years and realised that Kath was being abused.

But now was not the time to ponder on problems from the past, and Jane knew that swift action was necessary. More than ever, Kath needed her friends, and Jane was not about to let her down.

'Come on.' Jane pulled Kath to her feet. 'Show us exactly where you were when Dicky went over.' She turned to Anne. 'And you can pull yourself together and help us, instead of sitting there stunned and useless.' Jane gave Anne's foot a nudge to jolt her into action. 'You were trained for emergency situations,' she added.

'Abusive passengers and a possible hijacking,' Anne mumbled as she reached down to slip her sandals on. 'Not manslaughter and drownings.'

Minutes later, the trio stood on the deck where Kath had last seen Dicky.

'Are you sure this is the spot?' Jane asked. She placed her hands on her sturdy hips as she looked around.

'Yes, it's the deck leading from the side of the Neptune Lounge where I'd been to listen to Bridgette's talk,' Kath replied.

'And it's adjacent to the bar where I spent the afternoon,' Anne said.

Jane gripped the rail and, leaning precariously, looked over. She closed her eyes and sighed with relief when she saw that it would have been impossible for Dicky to fall overboard. The lower deck jutted out into an area popular with sunbathers.

'Come on,' she said to the others. 'He can't possibly have fallen into the sea. It's too dark to see what's down there, but there's a fair chance he might have broken his back when he plunged over the rail.'

'Oh, God, what have I done,' Kath wailed as she hurried along behind Jane and Anne.

They took the stairs at speed to the deck below. Jane, unused to exercise, suddenly had wings on her feet as she sped several metres ahead of her friends. 'Here we are,' she called out, 'I think this must be the spot.'

Kath covered her eyes. 'Is there much blood?' she wailed.

Anne rushed forward. 'Do I need to carry out C.P.R.?'

But the trio were mystified. There was no sign of Dicky, dead or alive. There was nothing on the deck but a long bench, closed off by a rail, where several sunbed mattresses had been stacked directly below the deck above.

'Shush! Listen…' Jane held up her hand and cocked her head to one side.

'What is it?' Anne whispered.

'It sounds like a cat purring.' Kath frowned and closed her eyes to focus on the sound.

'Bloody hell!' Jane suddenly shouted. 'It's no stowaway pussy,' she said and began to clamber over the rail and onto the bench. 'It's a comatose comedian, flat out and snoring like a trooper!'

'Oh, my darling Dicky!' Anne squealed and, in seconds, hoisted her skirt and joined Jane. She gripped the mattresses to ease herself up. 'He's here!' she exclaimed and threw her arms around the sleeping body.

'W-what's happening?' A very dozy Dicky began to stir. His eyes were wide as he realised Anne was straddling him, flashing her lacy knickers, and stroking his face.

'We thought you were dead,' she cooed and kissed his ears.

'Oh, darlin',' Dicky mumbled. 'I thought you'd given me the heave-ho again, but where am I?' Ostrich-like, he raised his head and looked around. When his eyes connected with Jane's ferocious gaze, he winced.

'You're with three extremely close friends,' Jane said, her voice low and threatening, 'and one of them is very forgetful.'

Dicky could feel Jane's hot breath on his skin as his

encounter with Kath began to come back, and everything suddenly fell into place.

'Should our forgetful friend ever find out that you are telling stories about them, she can be assured that you and your sewer mouth will have me to deal with.' Jane raised herself up and gripped Dicky's arm hard. 'Do I make myself clear?'

Dicky, pinned to the mattress that had broken his fall, couldn't move. Anne was caressing his arm on one side, but a steel-like grip numbed his circulation on the other. This mountainous female was the most terrifying woman he had ever encountered. With no desire to be further maimed, he nodded his tousled head.

'Good, I'm glad that we are clear on that matter. As long as you keep your word, I'll also have temporary amnesia and not report your illicit sales and cabin visits.'

Jane released her grip and climbed down. 'Normal service resumed,' she said to Kath and took her arm.

'D-do you mean Dicky won't get me into trouble?' Kath spluttered.

'Not unless he wants to find himself airborne and sinking into the sea.' Jane grinned and nodded towards the pile of mattresses, where Anne stroked Dicky's brow. 'Let's leave the lovebirds alone, shall we?'

Reaching out and snaking her arm around Kath's shoulder, Jane led her friend away.

In Hibiscus, Jane made Kath a cup of tea and added plenty of sugar. Kath was still upset, and her hand trembled as she took the tea.

'Drink this,' Jane said, 'it's good for shock.'

'Th-thank you.' Kath avoided Jane's eyes and began to drink.

Jane placed her hand on Kath's arm to ensure they were both comfortable. 'You've had an upset today,' Jane began. 'What happened with Dicky must have been a horrible reminder of Jim's death.' Jane's voice was soft, and she felt Kath shudder.

'I am so terrified that the truth will come out about Jim,' Kath muttered.

'Well, we need to clear that up once and for all,' Jane said. 'You have to get it out of your head that you pushed Jim. With the greatest respect, we all know how forgetful you are, and I think you're confused on that point.'

'B-but...' Kath stammered.

'Let me finish.' Jane was insistent and held up her hand. She paused to consider how to phrase her next sentence. 'We don't need to go over all the unpleasantness with Jim, but I must tell you that I feel that I failed as your friend. I didn't realise that you were being so badly treated.'

'No ... no, you don't have to apologise,' Kath interrupted, 'it wasn't your fault.'

'Please, don't.' Jane raised her hand again. 'You are the victim here, the one who put up with an atrocious situation because you were scared and bullied. I should have noticed.' Jane shook her head. 'But what's done is done and thankfully you are in a position now to enjoy your remaining years.'

Kath looked up at Jane. Everything felt so confusing that she was beginning to think that Jim really had tripped, and she'd caught the envelope as he fell.

'But…' Jane paused. 'I must ask, and please know that what you say will never leave this room.' She fixed Kath with an open gaze. 'It's the matter of Jim's last will. Did anyone ever question what happened to it?'

Kath tilted her head as though remembering. 'We made a will, in our early years together, leaving everything to each other should anything happen to either. It was witnessed by our neighbours, who both died many years ago.'

'Did you have a solicitor witness it too?'

'Yes, Mr Clarke, of Clarke & Co. Family Solicitors of Garstang, had a copy and that was used in probate.'

'And do you know what happened to the will Jim was taking to the solicitor on the day that he had the accident?'

Kath turned and looked innocently at Jane. 'It was destroyed, with a lot of Jim's papers. He was fanatical about keeping old bills and receipts and I burned the lot.' She shook her head. 'I smashed up the computer Jim had in his office, in case there was anything on it that he didn't want the boys to see.'

Jane's eyes widened. A computer that Jim had used to write his new will before taking it to the solicitor to be witnessed – destroyed. Gone for ever. Any information floating in Jim's cloud was lost in cyberspace.

'Excellent!' Jane beamed. 'That clears that mystery up.' She patted the cushions on the sofa and busied herself about the room. 'I think that this has been a long day for you and it might be a good idea if you have a lovely soak in the bath and get a good night's sleep.'

'Well, if you think so, but do you think Dicky is all right?'

'Don't worry your pretty little head over him. Anne will be administering plenty of tender loving care.'

'What are you going to do?'

'Me?' Jane stopped and smiled at Kath. 'As soon as I know that you are settled, I will slip away for a late supper with Selwyn.'

She scooped Kath into her arms and gave her a hug.

'Oh, Jane, you are so kind.' Kath sank her head on Jane's shoulder.

'Nonsense, now look lively, while I run a bath for you.'

As Jane busied herself in the bathroom, she thought of everything she'd learnt that evening. She remembered Kath's responses and wondered if she was as innocent as she seemed. But it wasn't for Jane to throw a spanner in the works; after all, many things became problematic as one got older. She and Anne had often witnessed Kath's forgetful memory playing tricks.

Jane swished bubbles in the bath and dried her hands. No need for Anne to know more. Anyway, with events unfolding on the sundeck, Kath's problems would be the furthest thing from Anne's mind.

'What a day!' Jane sighed as she placed a fluffy towel

within Kath's reach. The Captain's death had been shocking enough but with Kath's revelations, who would have expected things to turn out the way they had? Still, all's well that ends well, she thought and dimmed the lighting. Satisfied with the setting, she called out, 'Your bath's ready!'

Chapter Thirty-Four

The final day of the cruise began as the *Diamond Star* sailed into Barbados, and passengers woke to the sound of the ship docking in Bridgetown. In the ship's foyer, Dicky stood by the curved reception desk and drummed his fingers on the counter.

Diwa sat before him, her fingers tapping on a keyboard as she stared at a screen. 'I shouldn't give you access,' she frowned, 'but here's the account.' Diwa printed off a statement and handed it to Dicky.

Dicky sighed. The amount was far more than he'd anticipated. He dug into his pocket, pulled out a money clip, and then peeled off dollars. 'I'm adding an extra five hundred,' he said, remembering the day out that Anne had paid for.

'But that will put the account in credit?' Diwa looked puzzled.

'That's right.'

'Then we will credit the passenger's card when she checks out.' Diwa took the money and, satisfied that she had the correct amount, handed Dicky a receipt.

As Dicky pocketed the receipt and moved away from the desk, a guest tapped him on the shoulder.

'We've loved your shows,' Harold said, 'thanks for being so entertaining.'

Dicky smiled and, taking Harold's hand, shook it firmly. 'It's my pleasure. I'm honoured to be able to entertain you.'

'In fact,' Harold continued, 'I said to Nancy, we should ask Dicky for a couple more copies of his book, they will be great gifts for the neighbours.'

'That's very kind.'

'Can you call by our room a bit later?' Harold asked.

'I'm sorry, mate.' Dicky shook his head. 'You'll have to get them in the shop, where I've signed several copies.'

Harold was about to protest, but Dicky extracted his hand and, with a smile, turned away. He glanced at his watch and, noting the time, realised that it would be very early in Doncaster. Still, he had a phone call to make, and it was no use putting it off. Whatever the time, the end result would be the same.

Acknowledging greetings from smiling passengers, Dicky made his way to his cabin.

In Selwyn's room, Jane was awake as she heard the engines subside and looked out to see the sun rise over the island.

'Selwyn,' she whispered. 'Wake up. I am sure that the Captain will be leaving the ship soon and I'd like to be there to see him off.'

'Of course.' Selwyn shook his sleepy head and patted Jane's rear as she climbed out of bed.

In Hibiscus, Kath was also awake.

'Anne,' she whispered. 'Do you think the authorities will meet the ship early to come for the Captain?'

'Yep.' Anne stirred and flung the covers off her bed. 'They're bound to.' She sat up and with a yawn, stretched her arms, tired from lack of sleep.

'Let's go, shall we?' Kath asked. 'I'd hate to think that no one was there as he's taken off the ship.'

Bridgette, too, was awake and dressed, ready for the Captain's departure from the *Diamond Star*. 'I hope they look after you,' she said silently to her dear departed friend as she made her way through the ship.

It was New Year's Eve and the crew were busy decorating the ship with banners and balloons in preparation for the celebrations. Several stopped, curious to see the activity taking place on the decks where passengers were gathering.

Bridgette stepped onto the main deck and gasped at the sight of so many people. Selwyn and Jane, alongside Kath and Anne, stood with Harold and Nancy. The railings were lined with passengers. Bridgette stared as many of the crew were also present to pay their respects.

A long black hearse pulled up alongside the gangway as the authorities arrived. Everyone stood silent as the Captain's coffin was wheeled off the ship and lifted into the vehicle.

'The Captain!' the crowd called out, their voices echoing along the quayside.

In the absence of flowers, many had picked leaves from the Sago palm trees dotted around the ship, and they threw the foliage onto the water. Bridgette winced and tried not to think of the damage to the plants.

Kath smiled when she saw Dicky appear. He gave her a sideways glance as he slipped his arm around Anne's waist. 'God bless the old gentleman,' Kath overheard Dicky say, as he respectfully bowed his head.

Bridgette wished something more appropriate could be done to see the Captain off. She wanted to sing a hymn or let off fireworks but knew that he would have been touched that so many had watched his departure from his final cruise.

But suddenly, a voice rang out. Clear and melodic, a woman began to sing.

Should auld acquaintance be forgot
And never brought to mind.

It was Melissa Montana. She stood by a railing and stared at the hearse slowly moving away from the ship. Melissa raised her hand and began to wave. Everyone joined in, raising their hands, too, and Bridgette felt hot tears trickle down her cheeks as she whispered,

'For auld lang syne, my dear, for auld lang syne.
We'll take a cup of kindness yet, the sake of auld lang
syne.'

Chapter Thirty-Five

Following the sad start to the day, New Year's Eve soon kicked in, and the last few hours of the cruise became a whirlwind of activities for the passengers. Dicky, who was about to begin rehearsals for the evening's show, caught Anne's hand as they moved away from the railings.

'Can I speak to you?' he asked.

'Yes, of course, is everything all right?'

He led her into the library and they sat in the quiet corner that he favoured. 'I've had a bit of an epiphany since I fell over the deck,' he began.

Anne smiled. 'Did you think that your number was up?'

'Well, actually, yes, I did.'

'Goodness.' Anne reached out and took Dicky's hand. 'How are you feeling?'

'I'm feeling that if I don't say what I am about to say, I will regret it all my life.'

'Go on.'

'I've been an idiot over the years, made stupid mistakes and treated people very badly.' Dicky hung his head.

'You don't have to explain—' Anne's comment was cut short as Dicky gripped her hand.

'But I do, I've thought about it a lot because I want to put things right.' He stared deep into her eyes. 'Do you think you might consider spending time with me after the cruise?'

'Dicky, I don't know.' Anne shook her head. 'What we've had was just a bit of fun.'

'You know I'm married, but I've spoken to my wife, and she feels the same. We've agreed that it's best that we part company and get a divorce.'

'Are you sure?'

'Yes, she's going to keep the house, it's only fair, and I want to start again.'

Anne's head was spinning. Had she really heard Dicky own up to the mistakes he'd made? They'd had a good time on the cruise but she didn't want to fall into another bad relationship. She studied his face as he waited for her response, his fingers gently stroking her hand. Dicky's eyes were anxious, willing her to reply.

Anne sighed.

Barry had always lied to her. He'd never told the truth or faced up to his faults, and even now he was still treating her dishonourably, disputing every penny they had left. But here was Dicky, wearing his heart on his sleeve and asking if they could make a go of things.

'I don't expect you to contribute to anything,' Dicky added. 'I'll pick up all the bills and work to pay our way.'

'Can you give me a little bit of time to think this through?' Anne asked and loosened her hand from his grip.

'Of course,' Dicky said.

He looked at his watch and sighed. He was running late for rehearsals. As Dicky watched Anne walk away, he felt a lump in his throat and his shoulders slumped. Time had run out and the comedian wasn't laughing. This time the joke was on him.

As many passengers spent their final few hours on an island tour of Barbados, others headed off on catamaran trips or snorkelling adventures.

For the group who'd met at dinner on the first night, a beach day was agreed upon, and Kath, Anne, Jane, and Selwyn climbed into a people carrier with Bridgette. Keen to join the group, Harold and Nancy came along too. The Boatyard Resort in Carlisle Bay promised entertainment, and they could see inflatables on the water and happy hour at the bar as they turned into the parking area and gazed across the sandy beach.

'I'm first on the water-slide,' Jane said as they disembarked and settled in cabanas within feet of the turquoise sea. 'Where's Dicky?' she asked as Anne slipped out of her sundress.

'He's rehearsing for the show tonight,' Anne said as she sat on a soft mattress.

'You spent most of the night with him.' Jane began to untie her sarong. 'Are you all right?'

Anne sighed. 'He wants to spend some time with me when we get back.'

Kath and Jane exchanged anxious glances.

'He wants to see if we could make a go of things.' Anne shook her head. 'But it's never going to work. I'll be up to my ears in packing boxes with Barry badgering me from the Costas to sort everything out as completion day looms.'

'So, what will Dicky do?' Jane asked.

'Probably head off to Benidorm. He wants to do cabaret there.'

Jane turned, distracted by Selwyn tugging her hand, and together they set off for the sea.

'Are you sure you should be thinking about Dicky?' Kath stretched out beside Anne, lowering her hat over her face.

'Probably not, but he's fun, and I like him, and God knows, I could do with some fun.' Anne noticed her friend fumbling about, searching for her sunglasses. They peeked out of her bag, and Anne placed them beside Kath.

'Does he have a wife at home?'

'He did have, but he's left her, *and* he's got no money.'

'Somehow, I'm not surprised but I'm delighted that he's being honest with you,' Kath said and patted Anne's hand.

'But what about you?' Anne asked. 'What does life in Garstang hold for you in the coming months?'

'I'm not sure.' Kath was thoughtful. 'Hugh and Harry will be shocked when they see my new appearance. I don't think they'll like it.'

'To hell with them, it's your time now.'

Anne secretly thought Kath should do what she could while her memory still allowed. The confused story she'd told them about Jim's death was obviously dementia. Anne worried that the onset might be sooner than they realised.

But their worries were forgotten when Harold and Nancy came into view, wearing matching beachwear of tropical shorts, shirts and Panamas and carrying a tray loaded with cocktails.

'Happy hour,' Harold sang as he handed them out. 'These are called Set the New Year On Fire!'

'We're up for that,' Anne said and handed one to Kath.

Bridgette appeared wearing her poppy-printed skirted swimsuit, disappointed that Barbados banned nude sunbathing. 'It's so silly,' she said, 'there should be a separate section of the beach for naturists.' Seeing the drinks, she reached out. 'I need one of these,' she muttered.

'Relax, it's happy hour, you've got two,' Nancy thrust another into Bridgette's hand.

The group sat happily in the sunshine, watching Jane and Selwyn frolic in the water, riding giant flamingos, and shooting down slides.

'Just look at her.' Kath smiled.

'Whoever would have thought it?' Anne grinned. 'She's transformed herself.'

'This is the life,' Harold added. 'It beats Britain on a wintery day.'

'Not for long.' Nancy killed the moment. 'This time tomorrow we'll all be heading back.'

In a synchronised line, hands reached out, drinks were downed, and Harold went for refills.

Jane and Selwyn came out of the water and walked hand in hand to join the group.

'I read somewhere that once you've been to Barbados, the island gets into your bones, and you never forget it,' Kath mused. 'The locals have an expression that means you will always return.

'Please enlighten us.' Bridgette stared at Kath.

'They say, "My bellybutton is buried in Barbados,"' Kath informed everyone.

'I think my bellybutton is buried on the *Diamond Star*,' Anne nodded.

'And I can't find my bellybutton!' Jane added and prodded her tummy.

Harold returned and everyone chinked beakers. 'Happy New Year!' they called out.

The evening cabaret had a party-like atmosphere as the passengers, dressed in movie-themed fancy dress, enjoyed a spectacular show by the *Diamond Star* entertainers. Dicky, as host, was at his most comical as he introduced acts. Playing Danny to Melissa's Sandy, he wore jeans, a white T-shirt, a leather jacket, and his hair greased into a quiff. They sang a medley from the musical *Grease*, as Melissa gyrated in a Bardot body suit and red high heels, her blonde hair bouncing. The audience was on their feet as Danny and Sandy told each other that they were 'The One That I Want!'

The finale saw the band join with all the artistes as they sang their farewell song. The Marley Men linked arms with the dancers, and Melissa and Dicky invited everyone to raise their arms and sway.

'We'll meet again, don't know where don't know when...'

There were tears in the eyes of many as they all sang along.

'Now don't be sad,' Dicky called out, 'it's almost midnight and don't forget that the party continues after the countdown.'

'Are you ready?' Melissa encouraged the audience.

'Ten, nine, eight...'

Together with Dicky, to a drumbeat, they counted down the seconds.

'Three, two, one... HAPPY NEW YEAR!'

Everyone was on their feet, turning to their partners and friends to embrace.

Anne hugged Kath, and they turned to reach for Jane. But their friend was wrapped around Selwyn and unlikely to come up for air anytime soon.

'Happy New Year!' Harold and Nancy cried out.

The pair were unrecognisable as Morticia and Gomez

from *The Addams Family*. Nancy tripped on the hem of her long black gown, dislodging her jet-black wig and smearing ruby-red lipstick.

'Steady on, lass,' Harold, wearing a pinstriped suit, spluttered on an unlit cigar as he caught her.

With Nancy back on her feet, Harold turned to stare at Armani, who'd appeared on rollerblades wearing a visor and with a glow stick in her hand.

'By heck, it's Barbie!' He grinned and stared at Armani's low-cut leotard worn over baby-pink biker shorts.

'Down, Gomez!' Morticia roared.

Nets on the ceiling parted to send balloons and golden confetti cascading onto the partygoers, and, under a spinning disco ball, the dance floor filled as the band began to play.

In round spectacles, with a Gryffindor scarf knotted at his neck, Peter held up a wand, pointing to Kath and Anne. 'Have you enjoyed your cruise?' he asked.

'Brilliant, Harry!' they both replied.

Kath was unmistakable as Mary Poppins and held onto her bulging bag. 'Tell me again, who are you supposed to be?' she asked Anne.

'Lora Croft.' Anne rolled her eyes. 'From *Tomb Raider*.'

'I've no idea who she is but I like your hair in a ponytail and those combat boots look comfortable.'

Anne shook her head. She'd watched the film with Kath twice on Netflix.

Bridgette joined them as Cruella de Vil. 'Having fun?'

she asked, raising sharp eyebrows, and pouting bold red lips.

'Goodness, how on earth did you squeeze into that?' Kath asked and stared at the tight leather pantsuit clinging to every inch of Bridgette's body.

'No underwear and plenty of talc.' Bridgette shook her two-toned black and white wig. 'I think the Captain would have liked it.'

Jane was dressed for a Caribbean carnival, and, in terms of costume, she stole the show. Over a colourful swimsuit cut deep into the cheeks of her bottom she wore a giant headdress with vibrant feathers that fanned out like a peacock displaying its tail. Covered in body glitter and eyes dazzling with makeup, Jane was first on the floor with Selwyn. The pair made an eye-catching sight.

'I can hardly believe my eyes,' Kath said as she watched Jane twerk whilst Selwyn, as Maverick from *Top Gun*, moved and grooved in a green flying suit, dog tags flying, aviator glasses firmly in place.

'Me too.' Anne grinned. 'Whatever happened to the plain and timid Jane who set off on this cruise?'

'She fell in love.' Kath smiled. 'I believe that anything can happen on a cruise.'

'To think it was me who came on this holiday to husband-hunt!' Anne pondered as she watched Jane jiggle around.

But Kath had gripped Anne's shoulders as Danny Zucco danced towards them, flicking his quiff, a determined gleam in his eye.

Anne stared at Dicky and her smile began to spread. She remembered going to customer services to settle her onboard account, only to be told that it was paid in full and five hundred dollars credited to her card. Dicky had come up trumps.

'You're the one that I want!' Dicky sang and held out his hands.

'As one of the Captain's T-shirts might say' – Kath laughed and thrust Anne into Dicky's arms – *It's Time to Seas the Day!'*

Chapter Thirty-Six

Three months later

On a long stretch of golden beach beneath the white cliffs of Dover, a group stood together and stared out to sea. Gathered from different locations, they'd come together to say goodbye to the Captain, whose nephew had been happy to let the friends scatter his uncle's ashes.

'It seems fitting to scatter him in the sea he often sailed from,' Bridgette said as she clutched a ship-shaped urn.

One by one, they took a handful of ashes and threw them into the English Channel.

Bridgette called out to the sky that in time, she would join the Captain and Hugo, but first, she had more cruises to sail on and talks to give.

Anne and Dicky stood hand in hand. Soon they would be heading off to Benidorm, where Dicky had a six-month gig in a club. He'd eased all the anxieties of her divorce as he worked hard to help Anne pack up the house, and they'd enjoyed staying at Jane's cosy cottage while the paperwork was completed. Anne had abandoned her husband-hunting. She had her casino winnings in a deposit account and confided to her friends that she was going to have fun with Dicky and see how things worked out.

'We're taking a leap of faith!' Anne called out to the wind as she tossed ashes into the sea.

'Just like the Captain!' Dicky said and hurled a handful too.

His grin was wide, and as he hugged Anne, he silently vowed to do everything he could to make her happy. With his cruise contract money in place, they were able to make a fresh start. Peter had paid the whole amount and told Clive that Dicky had exceeded all expectations and would be welcomed back anytime.

For Kath, the day felt like a new beginning. Instead of returning home, she was heading to the cruise terminal in Dover to join a *Diamond Star* World Cruise. She would be gone for almost a year. Her sons had been furious when Kath rented out the house and told them she had no idea when she would return, but Kath was oblivious to their anger. 'I'm just a silly forgetful old woman,' she'd muttered to Hugh as he ranted in a phone call.

Then she'd hung up and blocked her sons' numbers.

The wind suddenly changed, and the Captain's ashes blew back and covered Kath's damp coat. She grinned as they set like cement. 'It looks like you'll coming with me, dear captain,' Kath giggled. 'We'll both carry on cruising.'

When it was Selwyn's turn, he added the last of the contents from his Typhoo Tea tin and said his final goodbye to Flo. Perhaps she was already enjoying paradise together with the Captain. In death, she'd experienced what she'd never known in life as Selwyn distributed her ashes around the Caribbean. He hoped that she'd enjoyed her post-death experiences and that wherever her spirit had come to rest, she was happy.

Selwyn himself could not have been happier.

He'd left the ship with Jane on the morning of New Year's Day and never looked back. They'd heard Peter shouting as they'd walked away, his voice full of concern as he told them they had to be accounted for and would miss their flight. But a missed flight was immaterial as they'd climbed into a taxi to head for an expensive west coast hotel and begin plans for their marriage, on a beach in Barbados.

Jane held the Captain's ashes in her hand and felt the soft gritty substance as she stood on the sea's edge, her classy new boots touching the icy water. She smiled as her diamond-studded wedding ring glinted in the morning sunshine. As she flung the Captain's ashes, Jane wanted to pinch herself, for she still wondered if her new life was a dream.

A dream she could never have imagined at the start of the cruise.

Now married and madly in love, Jane was about to begin a career as a TV chef on a morning show. Her afternoons with Jaden had paid off. Unbeknown to Jane, an executive from Optimax TV had watched her on the ship and invited her for a screen test in London. They had adored her easy-going natural style, and the executive assured Jane that she would be a massive hit. He said that *Jazz It Up With Jane* would capture the nation's heart and viewers would love her.

Jane thought of the young team from the production company who'd outed her many months ago and smiled.

But her biggest surprise had been Selwyn.

She'd worried about moving in with him in Lambeth. What would his daughters think of their father replacing their mother in the marital home, so soon after her demise?

Selwyn had merely smiled and, sitting Jane down on the soft sand of a Caribbean beach at sunset, he took her hand and told her he had a secret.

During their marriage, Selwyn said, while Flo gave money to the church each month, he'd also put a little to one side. In time he'd accumulated enough for a deposit on a terraced house in Notting Hill. The modest rent he charged underprivileged folk who needed a roof over their heads while they established themselves easily covered the mortgage. Soon, with property value increasing, Selwyn bought another terraced house on the same road. As Jane listened, he explained that property at the end of the 70s and in the early 80s was affordable.

'My goodness, the houses must be worth a fortune now.' Jane was astonished.

'Both houses, recently sold, had an eye-watering value, as have the other six I have in the portfolio.'

'S-so what are you saying?' Jane was staggered.

'Flo never wanted riches, so I never gave them to her,' he said. 'She was content with what she had. I've waited to find the right person. My family will benefit and of course, the church, but you and I can find our own place where we will start our new life together.'

And that is how Jane found herself viewing apartments overlooking the River Thames with the man of her dreams and planning their future together. She thought back to the meeting in the pub all those months ago when Anne had told her about Sylvia Adams-Anstruther's husband hunting at sea. 'Who would have thought it? Jane said as she felt Selwyn's warm hand snake around her body.

Far into the distance, a weak British sun began to peek between the line of grey sea and a cloudy sky as a cruise liner moved slowly on the horizon. Jane wondered where the ship was heading and what adventures the passengers would experience on their journey.

'To the cruise,' Jane whispered

'The cruise,' her husband replied.

Acknowledgments

I never wanted to go on a cruise and couldn't understand the attraction of being stuck on a ship with the same people every day, rarely venturing further than the ports listed on the itinerary. But my sister Cathy changed all that. She loved cruising and even got married at sea. One day she asked, 'How can you criticise something you haven't tried? If you were a guest speaker, you could try cruising for free.' So, I took her advice and interviewed with an agent who placed speakers on cruise ships. Several months later, I set sail, and the love affair began. Cath, thank you for your spiritual guidance; you were with me throughout the writing of this novel. We always were able to 'Seas the day' together, and I hope you are enjoying many happy sail-aways in your heavenly home.

I must thank the fabulous team at One More Chapter, especially Charlotte Ledger, who had the vision for The Cruise and enabled me to virtually revisit a place I know well – the Caribbean. Charlotte, thank you for believing in my writing.

Finally, as ever, I thank Eric, my rock. ILYTTMAB.

A weekend at the spa will leave four old friends with a whole lot more than they'd bargained for…

The glossy brochure promised a serene experience of total tranquillity and rejuvenation, but what best friends Bridgette, Emily, Serena and Marjory get is a weekend that upends their lives!

There for a girls' weekend to celebrate Bridgette's impending seventieth birthday, the spa soon has these spicy sexagenarians realising that there are unexpected benefits to age and experience, and that over the hill certainly doesn't mean out of the game…in any respect…

ONE MORE CHAPTER

YOUR NUMBER ONE STOP
FOR PAGETURNING BOOKS

The author and One More Chapter would like to thank everyone
who contributed to the publication of this story...

Analytics
Emma Harvey
Maria Osa

Contracts
Georgina Hoffman
Florence Shepherd

Design
Lucy Bennett
Fiona Greenway
Holly Macdonald
Liane Payne
Dean Russell

Digital Sales
Laura Daley
Michael Davies
Georgina Ugen

Editorial
Arsalan Isa
Charlotte Ledger
Jennie Rothwell
Tony Russell
Caroline Scott-
Bowden
Kimberley Young

International Sales
Hannah Avery
Alice Gomer

Marketing & Publicity
Chloe Cummings
Emma Petfield

Operations
Melissa Okusanya
Hannah Stamp

Production
Emily Chan
Denis Manson
Francesca Tuzzeo

Rights
Lana Beckwith
Rachel McCarron
Agnes Rigou
Hany Sheikh
Mohamed
Zoe Shine
Aisling Smyth

**The HarperCollins
Distribution Team**

**The HarperCollins
Finance & Royalties
Team**

**The HarperCollins
Legal Team**

**The HarperCollins
Technology Team**

Trade Marketing
Ben Hurd

UK Sales
Yazmeen Akhtar
Laura Carpenter
Isabel Coburn
Jay Cochrane
Alice Gomer
Gemma Rayner
Erin White
Harriet Williams
Leah Woods

**And every other
essential link in the
chain from delivery
drivers to booksellers
to librarians and
beyond!**